Survival

Survival

RITA POTTER

SAPPHIRE BOOKS PUBLISHING
SALINAS, CA.

Editor - Kaycee Hawn
Book Design - LJ Reynolds
Cover Design - Fineline Cover Design

Sapphire Books Publishing, LLC

P.O. Box 8142
Salinas, CA 93912
www.sapphirebooks.com

Printed in the United States of America
First Edition – November 2021

This and other Sapphire Books titles can be found at
www.sapphirebooks.com

Dedication

For Terra: I love you with all my heart.

Acknowledgements

Three books in one year, and I have to keep coming up with nice things to say about the people in my life. Honestly, there are so many people that have helped me along my journey, it is hard to keep it brief.

First, thanks always to Chris at Sapphire who took a chance on this old "rookie". I appreciate your patience and guidance as I try to figure out this crazy business.

To my editor, Kaycee, I hope over time you won't have to work your "red pen" as much as I continue to improve.

To all my family, biological, inherited, work, and chosen. Without you, none of this would be possible.

To everyone from the GCLS Writing Academy, you will forever be my writing family.

To my mentor, Jae, who has done more to improve my craft than anyone. I can't write without your voice inside my head.

To Terra, you are the reason I can do what I do. Thanks for being on this journey with me and allowing me all my crazy schemes. And for those people who actually read acknowledgements, I still haven't asked her to marry me, even though we celebrated the seventh anniversary of our wedding.

And, of course, Chumley the cat, who would be very

offended if he were not included. There would be hell to pay.

And lastly, to my readers. With so many choices out there, I appreciate your willingness to spend your valuable time reading my books.

Dillon Mitchell's Group

Name	Role	Occupation
Dillon Mitchell	Owner	Construction Company
CJ McCormick	college bestie	Computer Expert
Karen Foster	CJ's wife	Event Planner
Maria Alvarez	Dillon's friend	Attorney
Tasha Nicks	Maria's girlfriend	Mechanic
Katie Grogan	Dillon's dead wife, Jane's, best friend	Caterer
Leslie Freeman	Dillon's friend	Marketing
Denise Freeman	Leslie's Wife – died when event occurred	
Skylar Lange	Dillon's girlfriend	Bartender, Nursing Student

Tiffany Daniels Group

Tiffany Daniels	Ultra-wealthy,	worked in father's company
Anne Templeton	girlfriend	Fashion Design
Cynthia Kramer	college friend	Doctor
Diana Hughes	college friend	Engineer
Willa Andrews	groupie	Independent Film Producer
KC Jasper	groupie	Publicist

Renee Lipinski Group

Renee Lipinski	Owns restaurants in LA	
Sid Tate	Renee's friend	Marketing
Tina Sexton	Renee's friend	Realtor
Dee Devonte	Renee's friend	Heavy Equipment Operator

Jake Stein Group

Jake Stein
Lily Stein   Jake's wife Nurse
Tad Stein   Lily and Jake's teenage son
Kelly Stein   Lily and Jake's grade school
                     daughter
Nancy Thorton   Hairdresser
Nikki Thorton   Nancy's daughter
Tonya Thorton   Nancy's daughter

Chapter One

Hello…hello my friends. We need you to answer our call. We know what happened. We want to share the answer with you. Is anyone out there? We ask that anyone that hears the sound of my voice, please respond."

The message reverberated in Dillon Mitchell's head, even though CJ muted the sound several minutes before. The male voice had a deep timber, with a slight hint of an accent that Dillon couldn't place. *Why did the voice sound so familiar? Even the words?*

Dillon turned to her best friend, CJ McCormick, who must've been pondering the same question. CJ's eyes were closed, and a deep furrow creased her brow. Her blond hair fell loosely to her shoulders and her flawless skin glowed in the dim light of her computer.

Karen Foster, CJ's wife, stood behind her with her arms wrapped around CJ's shoulders. CJ clutched Karen's arms. Dillon suspected it would be a long time before CJ let Karen out of her sight. Karen had been missing, and up until an hour ago, Dillon believed Karen was dead.

While CJ turned heads whenever she entered a room, no one would register Karen's arrival. She epitomized the girl next door, but as soon as Karen spoke, her charisma shone through, and her magnetic appeal drew people to her.

The volume in the room grew as nearly thirty people, mostly women, pushed in around CJ's computer, imploring her to answer the man. They were in the far corner of a cavernous atrium in the Whitaker Estate mansion, where CJ had set up her makeshift computer center. Three massive skylights, which bathed the entire area in sunlight during the day, provided little illumination. Tonight, the sky was overcast with no hint of the moon or stars, so they had to rely solely on the scattered lamps throughout the expanse. The dim lighting created eerie banks of shadows that only made the man's voice creepier.

It had been nearly forty-eight hours since the world, as they knew it, ended. Two days ago, they were celebrating Tiffany Daniels' thirty-fifth birthday, their biggest concern being whether they should order wine or beer. Now they were riveted to the disembodied voice that issued forth from the computer speakers.

They'd been partying in the ultra-modern nightclub, which had originally been Whitaker's underground bunker. Thomas Whitaker, an eccentric billionaire and avid, one might say fanatic, survivalist, spared no expense in building his elaborate encampment. The entire estate was designed in preparation for the end of times. As luck would have it, he never lived to see this moment.

When they'd emerged from the bunker, they'd discovered everyone on the surface dead. They'd left the mansion and searched nearby Lake Piru and Santa Clarita, finding the same. For the past two days, they'd tried in vain to contact someone, anyone, before the power grid failed. The man's repetitive call was the first sign that someone else might be out there.

CJ held up her hand and shook her head, her

eyes still closed in concentration.

"What the fuck," Tiffany said, pushing through the crowd. "Dillon, tell CJ to stop being an idiot. Somebody's out there. Answer him, for fuck's sake."

After only forty-eight hours, Dillon was tired of Tiffany's spoiled rich girl act. Dillon, and many of her friends, had spent the last two days with little sleep working to help the group come to terms with the Crisis, while Tiffany and her entourage spent most of their time drinking and continuing to party as if nothing happened.

Before Dillon could respond, Anne, Tiffany's girlfriend, slid between them. "Come on, honey, let CJ do her thing." Anne gently put her hand on Tiffany's arm.

Tiffany defiantly peered over the head of the much shorter Anne. "I've had enough of their bullshit. Who put them in charge?" Tiffany raised her finger and pointed it in Dillon's face.

Dillon's muscles tensed and she stood up as straight as possible, trying to get the most of her five-foot, seven-inch height, but Tiffany still towered over her. Before Dillon could respond, Dr. Cynthia Kramer moved beside Dillon and touched her arm.

Matching Tiffany's height, Cynthia looked her squarely in the eye and said, "Tiffany, you need to relax."

Tiffany started to protest, but Cynthia held up her hand. "I've already been injured because of this petty fighting, and I really don't want anymore."

Dillon peered around Cynthia's shoulder. A pained look crossed Tiffany's face before her eyes fell to the ground. "Fine! But we need to do something." She walked over to a nearby couch and flopped down next to her friend Diana, who was still passed out from earlier. She crossed her arms over her chest and glared at Dillon.

In two short days, Cynthia had become someone Dillon relied on. She'd shown herself to be conscientious, caring, and willing to take responsibility not only for herself, but for the group. Cynthia's biggest flaw was being an old college friend of Tiffany's, but it proved helpful in moments like this.

"What are you thinking, CJ?" Cynthia asked, turning away from the sulking Tiffany.

"That voice," CJ said. "It's right on the tip of my tongue. I swear I've heard it before. Maybe if we could get everyone to be quiet, I might be able to figure it out."

The decibel in the room had increased now that the excitement with Tiffany appeared to be over.

"Play it again," Dillon said. "Maybe something will come to you."

"We won't be able to hear it over this noise." CJ scowled at the boisterous women all talking at once.

"Let me see what I can do." Dillon put two fingers to her mouth and let out a loud whistle. It took several minutes to get everyone's attention and for a hush to settle over the room.

CJ clicked the mouse, and at once, the deep rhythmic voice streamed from the speakers. "Hello… hello my friends. We need you to answer our call. We know what happened. We want to share the answer with you. Is anyone out there? We ask that anyone that hears the sound of my voice, please respond."

CJ let it play on a loop several times before shutting it off.

"No wait," Cynthia said. "Turn it back on."

CJ obeyed. The words reverberated off the walls, again. Dillon swore the accent had become more pronounced, but that would be impossible. Something about the sing-song nature of the cadence caused the effect.

"I feel like I'm a kid back at church," someone called out.

"That's it," Cynthia said. "The guy sounds like a preacher."

An excited buzz filled the room.

CJ cranked the volume louder, and the booming voice filled the space around them.

"Hello...hello my friends. We need you to answer our call. We know what happened..." The voice abruptly stopped.

"I've almost got it," CJ said, closing her eyes. "What's that weird guy's name? He started a cult in Colorado. He built his church in the side of a mountain."

"Yes, yes...that's him," Cynthia said excitedly.

"Braxton Babcock," a voice called out.

"Yes!" CJ said. "Great, just who we want to make contact with. He's a whack job."

"Who cares?" Tiffany said. "If someone's out there, we should answer."

"No, we need to think this through. There's something seriously wrong with that man," Cynthia said.

"Of course you side with Dillon," Tiffany said. She emphatically shook Diana, trying to rouse her. "Diana, get your ass up. I need reinforcements."

"What?" Diana said groggily, swiping at the drool that ran down her chin. Her eyes were glassy, and she blinked several times as she looked around the room. "What the fuck's going—" Before she could finish, she slumped back against the couch.

"Dammit, Diana." Tiffany shook her, but it only elicited a groan from the inebriated woman.

Dillon's lip curled in disgust. *Good, maybe Tiffany will shut up.*

Tiffany shoved Diana one last time before getting to her feet. She pointed to a small group who stood a few feet from the couch and seemed to hang on Tiffany's every word. "What about you guys, don't you think CJ should answer?"

The room erupted in argument, as each side tried to shout the other down. Dillon kept quiet, watching the melee. She smiled when her friend Maria jumped into the fray. Not one to tolerate bullshit, Maria's voice rose as she argued with Tiffany.

Dillon had met Maria Alvarez years before, when Maria's law firm defended Dillon's construction company against a bogus lawsuit. Maria not only won the case but found a lifelong friend in Dillon.

"I think Maria's going to blow a gasket," Cynthia said. "Don't you think you should say something?"

Dillon smirked. "But she's so fun to watch. Look at the veins popping out in her neck. Pretty impressive."

Cynthia laughed. "I've got Tiffany if you can calm down Maria."

Cynthia and Dillon inserted themselves into the skirmish. After several minutes, both sides retreated, and the yelling stopped.

"We obviously have differing opinions on whether we should answer Braxton Babcock's message," Dillon said.

"Could you possibly state more of the obvious?"

Tiffany glowered.

Dillon ignored the taunt. "In order to decide, we need to hear both points of view. But we can't do that when everyone is yelling over the top of each other."

"I think we should let Maria explain her opposition," Cynthia said, drawing a groan from Tiffany. "Tiff, you can offer your rebuttal after we hear Maria out. But it's pretty hard to rebut something you haven't heard."

Tiffany scowled but remained silent.

"First off," Maria began. "The guy hates lesbians. Have you heard some of the crazy shit he talks about?" Several women nodded in agreement. "He's been running his own conversion therapy program for years, while keeping the human rights groups at bay by hiding behind religious freedom. The fucker's on record saying if conversion therapy doesn't work then we should be put out of our misery."

"Where did you hear that shit?" Tiffany asked. Despite her look of skepticism, her opposition appeared to be waning.

"Firsthand. I was on the board of one of the groups fighting him," Maria answered. "I'm telling you; the guy is a piece of work."

"My aunt used to love him," another woman piped up. "Until she had health problems and ordered his holy water."

"What, didn't it work?" Maria asked sarcastically.

"We don't know," the woman answered. "She paid $125 for a tiny bottle of it, but it arrived in the mail broken. When she called Braxton Babcock's help line, they told her she would have to pay for another bottle. When she protested, they said it was God's will. The asshat's net worth is in the hundreds of millions, but he had to have another $125 from my aunt. Most likely, he fills the bottles with tap water. My dad teased her mercilessly about pissing off God, but she survived without it."

Dillon stifled a giggle. "While that's a compelling story, I think we should focus on his hatred of lesbians, since there's a roomful of us here."

"I don't think we want a guy like this knowing where we are," Maria said.

"I've got it," CJ said, nearly forgotten during the disagreement, since she was bent over her keyboard, frantically pounding.

"What?" Dillon asked.

"I should be able to mask our location, so Babcock won't be able to trace it."

"Are you serious?" Tiffany said. "I didn't take you for a conspiracy theorist. Do you really think the guy is thinking that way in the middle of an apocalypse?"

CJ ignored Tiffany and continued typing. Dillon looked over her shoulder, as if it would do any good; the coding on the screen looked like hieroglyphics.

"CJ, do you really think it's necessary?" Cynthia asked.

"Better safe than sorry. We have no idea who or what is responsible for what's happened." CJ looked up at Cynthia. "I've almost got it. It will appear that our message is coming from the east coast, not the west."

"Why do we even want to know what the asshole has to say?" Maria asked.

"If he has the answer to what's happening, I don't care who he is," Tiffany shot back. "He could be Adolf Hitler or Donald Trump for all I care."

"Seriously?" Maria said, her voice rising again.

"Ladies." Cynthia stepped forward and held up her hand before Maria could say more. "Let's talk about the pros and cons of hearing him out."

Dillon looked down and shook her head. Agreeing with Tiffany was a bitter pill to swallow, so she'd better speak now before she changed her mind. "Since CJ's figured out how to keep our location secret, I'm not sure there are any cons."

Tiffany triumphantly raised her hands in the air. "Finally, Dillon is showing some sense. What do you have to say to that, Maria?"

"The argument is sound." Maria's dark eyes burned into Dillon, and she looked as if she'd just drank expired milk. "There's no harm in seeing what the idiot has to say."

Dillon mouthed the word 'sorry' at Maria. She breathed a sigh of relief when Maria winked back.

With Maria giving in, the rest of the opposition soon followed suit.

"Let's do this, CJ." Dillon put her hand on CJ's shoulder.

The women crowded around where CJ sat at her computer, and Dillon cringed. CJ preferred to be left alone when she worked on her equipment.

"Hey y'all," Karen said in her Texas drawl. "Why don't we take a couple steps back and let the maestro work?" Everyone reluctantly moved back. Karen studied CJ before adding, "Come on, let's back up a couple more steps. There's nothing to see. We just need to be using our ears."

Once CJ seemed sufficiently satisfied with the space she'd been given, she tapped a few keys and said, "I'm answering your call. Who am I speaking to?"

Silence.

CJ tapped a few more keys and repeated, "I'm answering your call. Who am I speaking to?"

More silence.

CJ frowned and reached for her mouse.

"Praise Jesus, you are a miracle." The unfamiliar voice came through the speakers. It wasn't the deep powerful voice of Braxton Babcock but rather a high pitched nasally voice.

"Is that a guy or a woman?" someone in the group whispered.

"Who am I speaking with?" CJ answered.

"You are in the presence of Jesus," the voice answered.

"Wow, you're Jesus?" CJ said, before anyone could stop her.

"Dammit, CJ, don't antagonize him, her, whoever it is," Dillon said. "We need to figure out what they know."

CJ gave Dillon an innocent look and shrugged.

"No," the voice said with a slight giggle. "I am his spokesman."

"Don't do it," Dillon said, shooting CJ a look.

"Fine. At least we know he's a he." CJ turned back to the computer. "You said you have the answer. We've been searching for some answers ourselves. We'd appreciate hearing what you've discovered. Would you be willing to share with us?"

"Of course, my sister," the man said. "God is very angry, and he has spoken."

"You mean God caused all of this?" CJ said, putting a note of surprise in her voice.

"What the fuck, CJ. Would you knock it off?" Dillon said.

Survival   21

"Relax, he's too stupid to figure out I'm mocking him."

"Yes, we have made God angry. Terribly angry because of the wickedness we've let seep into the world. He is looking for us to repent."

"But do you know what happened? How did you survive? How did we?"

"God moves in mysterious ways. He is demanding we begin anew. This time in purity. He has allowed the righteous among us to survive."

A few of the women giggled. "CJ, tell him that God must really love lesbians," Maria said, laughing.

"Don't you dare." Dillon turned to Maria. "And don't you encourage her."

"This isn't getting us anywhere," CJ said. "I'm not sure how much longer I want to listen to his schtick."

"You need to confirm where he is and find out how many people are with him," Dillon said. "I know how you feel about their ministry. How we all feel, but we need to know more about them."

"Why? We certainly aren't going to go rushing to join them. Somehow, I doubt if we'd be welcome," CJ answered.

"Dillon's right, baby." Karen squeezed CJ's shoulders. "See if you can get him to tell us who he is and where he's broadcasting from. Lay on some of the charm I know you have."

"You're the one with the Southern charm. Why don't you talk to him?"

"No sense confusin' him with another person. You've got this." Karen winked and gave CJ an encouraging smile.

Dillon was grateful for Karen's intervention. CJ

would continue to antagonize Dillon, but she always listened to Karen.

"I'm so glad that he spared us," CJ said, flashing a cheesy smile at Dillon. "Can you tell me who you are and where you're broadcasting from?"

"First, my child, you must tell me who you are and where you're at," the man answered.

"Not quite as dumb as we'd thought," CJ said, before opening the channel to respond. "My name is Maryann, and I am in the beautiful state of North Carolina."

"Maryann?" Dillon shot CJ a sideways glance.

"CJ might sound too butch. Don't want to make him suspicious."

They waited, but there was no response. "Shit, do you think he figured out you were lying?" Tiffany asked.

"How could he?" CJ slid the mouse around on the desk, causing the cursor to jump around the screen. She leaned in and stared at the small window in the corner of the monitor. "Maybe he's trying to track our location."

"Are you sure you scrambled it or diverted it or whatever the hell you did?" Maria asked.

"Maybe you should shut down the computer before he finds us," a panicked voice said from the crowd.

"Would you all just relax?" CJ said. "I know what I'm doing."

"What if he sends drones after us?" another voice said, causing the crosstalk to begin.

The group quieted when the voice returned. "Sister Maryann, it is nice to make your acquaintance. Who are you with, Sister Maryann?"

"It's just me and my husband, and our two kids," CJ lied.

"Your husband? Then why isn't he the one speaking with me? I'd like to talk with him."

"You've got to be kidding me," Maria sputtered. "The sexist pig doesn't want to talk to a woman."

"Jake, it looks like you're up," Dillon said, her eyes searching the group for Jake.

Jake Stein and his family had joined the group when Dillon had nearly run him over with her truck on their return trip from Lake Piru. They had escaped death probably because they were deep in a cave when the extinction event occurred.

Jake strolled to the front of the crowd with his signature smile. "Honey, I'm home," he said to CJ.

CJ laughed and showed him which buttons to push to respond.

"Hello, I'm CJ's–" he started to say before CJ cut his mike.

"Sheesh, Jake. Don't you know your own wife's name? Maryann, remember?" CJ said.

"Oh shit, sorry." Jake gave her a sheepish smile. "Let me try that again."

"Uh, sorry," Jake said into the computer. "Maryann knows how to work these damned computers better than I do. The name's CJ Simpson. And who might I be speaking with?"

"Well, hello, Brother CJ," the man answered. "My name is Brother Marcus."

Dillon shivered; somehow hearing him say CJ's name sent a chill up her spine.

"Hello, Brother Marcus," Jake responded. "My lovely wife told you that we're in the beautiful state of North Carolina, and where might you be?"

"Have you ever heard of the Braxton Babcock Ministries?"

"Oh my God, Pastor Babcock is almost as famous in North Carolina as our very own Reverend Graham," Jake said.

"Wow, laying it on thick, aren't you?" CJ said, shaking her head.

"Let the man of the house handle it, little lady." Jake rolled his eyes and laughed.

Jake continued talking to Brother Marcus for nearly fifteen minutes, discovering that Braxton Babcock was alive and well, along with seventy-three of his followers. The disaster struck during a spiritual retreat in their mountain sanctuary, and they were convinced God had saved them to spread his word to the people. For the past twenty-four hours, they'd been broadcasting their message. Thus far they'd contacted a family outside of Tallahassee, Florida and one in Maine. Both families confirmed they'd found nobody alive. Brother Marcus repeatedly asked Jake to bring his family and join their ministry, but Jake remained elusive without offending Brother Marcus.

Brother Marcus warned that soon the Internet and other means of communication would likely begin to fail. He offered his suggestion of locating a satellite phone and insisted that Jake take the Ministry's phone number and keep in touch.

When they disconnected, Jake said, "He seemed like a nice enough fellow."

The room erupted and Jake looked around, his eyes wide. "What did I say?" he asked Dillon.

"Dude, haven't you ever heard of conversion therapy?" Dillon scowled at Jake.

Lily stepped up beside her husband and took his

hand. "I think you owe these ladies an apology, Jake."
Jake looked panicked, as several women continued to yell in his direction. "I'm sorry…" he stammered. "I didn't mean to offend anyone. Please help me understand what I said wrong."

"I told you we shouldn't let the breeders stay with us." Tiffany dismissively waved her arm in Jake's direction. "They don't belong."

Dillon took a deep breath and looked into Jake's worried eyes. "Conversion therapy is one of the worst things you can ever mention to a gay person."

"I've heard it talked about on the television before, but I have to admit I really didn't pay much attention to what they were saying." Jake looked directly into Dillon's eyes. "But I want to understand."

"Sure, now he wants to know since his privileged ass is in the minority. Well fuck that shit," Tiffany said.

Dillon ignored her and turned to Jake. "Conversion therapy is pretty ugly. It's a way to condition the gay out of people, sometimes by whatever means possible." Jake looked at her puzzled, so she continued filling him in on the horrors of conversion therapy.

As Dillon spoke, Jake first turned bright red, until all the color drained from his face. "Oh my God, I didn't know. Honestly, Dillon, I am so sorry."

Chapter Two

J ake insisted on apologizing to the group, and Dillon suspected most saw the sincerity in his words, except for Tiffany's group, who whispered amongst themselves the entire time he spoke.

Shortly afterward, the party began to break up. It had been a long two days, and everyone looked exhausted, except for CJ and Karen, who snuggled in the corner giggling like schoolgirls. Dillon couldn't help but smile. *As if they weren't sickening enough.* Soon she'd need to bring them back to reality, but she'd give them a few more minutes to enjoy their reunion.

The infighting that had already developed the past two days worried her. She knew enough about human nature that if they didn't get it under control, the entire group could split, which would be devastating during such perilous times. As much as she wanted to crawl into bed and sleep for two days, she knew time was of the essence.

Dillon turned to Skylar Lange and reached out her hand. Skylar had remained quiet, almost withdrawn, while they'd listened to Brother Marcus speak. Even though Dillon had only met Skylar two days before, she longed for her touch.

The tension in Dillon's shoulders eased when Skylar took her hand. Dillon had been drawn to

Skylar, much to her friends' astonishment. With all the successful women in attendance at the party, the bartender caught Dillon's eye. They'd been sharing their first dance when all hell broke loose.

The Crisis seemed to accelerate time, every hour seemed like a week, and Dillon felt a level of intimacy with Skylar that she doubted would have developed so quickly in normal times. The corner of Dillon's mouth turned up. *U-Hauls and lesbians.*

Dillon squeezed Skylar's hand. "I feel like we're in a powder keg that's about to blow."

Skylar shivered. "All the tension in here is making my skin crawl."

"Come on." Dillon led her away. The atrium was enormous and had multiple sitting areas sprinkled throughout. They came to an area that sported two over-sized couches with a glass coffee table in the middle, but they didn't sit. Even though they'd moved nearly twenty-five yards away from the others gathered in the atrium, they could hear the raised voices clearly.

"All of this yelling is getting old really fast. Maybe we'd be better off on our own," Skylar said.

Dillon put her arm over Skylar's shoulders. "And that's exactly why we need a plan. As much as I'd like to get away from Tiffany, there's still strength in numbers. Babcock said his group has more than seventy people. I prefer not to be any more outnumbered than we already are."

"Can't I just dream for a minute?" Skylar leaned into Dillon and wrapped an arm around her waist.

"Surviving is going to be hard enough, but if the group gets any smaller, we're probably doomed. We need a plan sooner rather than later."

"Buzzkill." Skylar sighed. "What do you have in mind?"

"We need to talk tonight. I really want Cynthia there, but if I go anywhere near her, Tiffany will scream bloody murder. Do you think you can get her alone?"

"Sure, not a problem. Should we invite anyone else?"

Dillon's eyes narrowed and she studied the crowd. "As much as I'd like to, I think it's too risky."

"Risky?"

Dillon nodded. "People might get pissed if they find out they weren't invited but others were. It could mess up everything we're trying to do. So, it can only be our suite mates and Cynthia."

"You know I like Cynthia, but why take the risk with her?"

"Because she's the only one that might be able to control Tiffany."

"Gotcha." Skylar squeezed Dillon tightly before letting go.

"I'll meet you in the lobby, so we can go back to the room together."

"Sure." Skylar smiled. "See you in a few."

Dillon admired Skylar as she made her way across the room. Dillon had already grown accustomed to the way Skylar moved. Her shoulders were slightly wider to support her ample breasts, which tapered into a smaller waist. The purple highlights in her brown hair caught the light. Skylar flashed a smile, complete with dimples, at one of the women, and Dillon's heart raced. For Dillon, it was Skylar's big gray eyes that attracted her most. So many emotions were veiled there, and Dillon sensed there were many more layers to peel away. Skylar made Dillon believe the adage that the eyes were the gateway to the soul.

Shit. She needed to stop staring. She waited until Skylar joined the group before she began walking. It didn't take long for her to locate her suitemates, all seven.

Dillon's jaw clenched when she thought of the ugly confrontation last night. Establishing room assignments hadn't gone well. Due to the uncertainty of the situation, it made sense to stick together in one wing of the mansion, which meant thirty people crammed into five suites. Tiffany's refusal to give up the Redwood Suite, which was the largest, created tension. While Tiffany enjoyed the spacious three-bedroom area with only two others, Dillon shared her two-bedroom suite with seven others, including Skylar.

She shook her head, hoping to rid herself of her thoughts. No sense in dwelling on it. Being angry did nobody any good.

♫♫♫♫

Skylar tried to hide her smile as Dillon talked about the events of the evening. The closer they got to their suite, the more Dillon rambled. Apparently, they dealt with their discomfort in opposite ways. Where Dillon talked faster and chattered about nothing, Skylar withdrew and became quiet.

Skylar still had a bad taste in her mouth from yesterday evening. Everyone at the party was with a group of friends, except her. She'd felt like the kid in gym class that nobody picked for their team. *That's what happens when you're the hired help.*

Hopefully, with the work that needed to be done, Katie would leave her alone. Skylar was never one to back down from anyone, but she certainly didn't need an enemy, especially living in the same suite. Katie didn't even try to hide her animosity, nor the reason for it. She'd been in pursuit of Dillon for years and resented the budding relationship between Skylar and Dillon.

Dillon stopped before turning down the corridor to their suite. "Are you okay?"

Skylar gave her a cautious smile. "I can't say I'm looking forward to this, but I'm okay."

"She'll come around."

"I hope so. We don't need this when the world is collapsing around us."

"Definitely." Dillon looked into Skylar's eyes. "Are you ready to go in?"

"Let's do it." Skylar took Dillon's hand.

Dillon swung open the door, and Skylar paused, wondering when she'd get used to the sight that greeted them. The Sequoia Suite was enormous. The living area alone was probably over a thousand square feet, which was double the size of her apartment. Skylar loved the decor and the warm feeling of the suite. The entire common area looked like a cabin in the woods. All the furnishings were made of rustic distressed wood.

Skylar quickly scanned the room. *Good, Katie wasn't here yet.*

Maria arranged logs in the fireplace, which made it even more cozy. She looked up from her task and smiled. Her dark brown eyes were intense and penetrated anyone she set her focus on. "Hey kids, about time you two got home."

"Stop being so melodramatic," Dillon said. "You only left ten minutes before us."

"Lots can happen in ten minutes." Maria smiled and raised her eyebrows several times.

"There are so many things I could say to that, but I know you'd turn it against me somehow, so I'm not saying anything." Dillon turned to Skylar. "I know better than to match wits with a lawyer. Especially that one."

Maria laughed. "Hey, Babe. We need a couple more drinks here."

"Pick your poison," Tasha Nicks said with a smile. She had several bottles out on the kitchen island that doubled as a bar.

Tasha could only be described as striking. Her skin tone was a rich brown, which complimented her dazzling smile. Her close-cropped hair made her high cheekbones more prominent. Her dark mysterious eyes only added to her allure.

"Why don't you have a seat? I'll pick up our drinks from Tasha," Dillon said. "What would you like?"

"Something strong. How about a rum and coke?"

"Did ya catch that?" Dillon called out.

"I'm on it." Tasha replied.

"I'll just have a beer." Dillon said, walking toward the kitchen.

"Come join us." Karen patted the seat next to her on the couch, where she and CJ snuggled. Skylar couldn't imagine how they must have felt wondering if the other was alive. Looking at them now, she had no doubt they would savor every minute they were together.

As soon as Skylar sat, Karen touched her knee.

"We're so glad you're here with us. With Dillon."

"Thanks." Skylar felt her face redden. Dillon's friends were well-meaning, but she sometimes felt on display.

Karen must have sensed her discomfort. "How are you holding up with all this craziness?"

Before Skylar could answer, Katie burst into the room, followed by Leslie Freeman. Katie's eyes went to Skylar and she frowned.

So much for things being better. Skylar's body tensed, and she braced herself for what might come.

Katie glowered a few more seconds, before her eyes shifted to Dillon. A smile lit her face, and she sauntered over to the bar where Dillon stood talking to Tasha.

Leslie didn't say anything and made a beeline toward the bedroom.

Skylar's heart went out to Leslie. While everyone faced the possibility that their loved ones were possibly gone, Leslie knew for sure her wife, Denise, was dead. Leslie's bloodcurdling scream still haunted Skylar. How horrible it must have been for Leslie. If Denise hadn't left the party with a migraine, she'd still be alive. Skylar shivered. How would Leslie overcome the horror of not only discovering Denise, but encountering many more bodies when she ran back to the party for help?

The moment Leslie entered the club screaming, their old way of life ended.

"I'm going to go check on her," Karen said to CJ. "I'm afraid I haven't been a very good friend."

"Cut yourself some slack. You've only been back a couple hours," CJ said.

"Yeah, and somebody hasn't left me alone."

Karen playfully bumped her shoulder into CJ and smiled.

"Who?" CJ smirked.

As Karen rose from the couch, Dillon arrived with Skylar's drink. "Perfect timing. You can take my seat."

Before Dillon could sit, there was a knock on the door. "I've got it," Dillon said to the room.

She barely opened the door when Cynthia slid inside. Cynthia pushed the door shut and her gaze darted around the room.

"Are you okay?" Dillon asked.

"Sorry. Tiffany almost caught me. Luckily, I heard her and Diana coming and hid in the other hallway." With the Redwood Suite and the Sequoia Suite being right next to one another, Cynthia would have to be careful.

"Shit. But no worries, this place is well built. No sound will get through these walls." Dillon turned and called to Tasha. "We need another drink over here."

❧❧❧❧

Karen and Leslie hadn't returned, but the group decided to get started, anyway. Dillon didn't want to chance Cynthia being missed. If they were going to keep the group together, they couldn't antagonize Tiffany.

Dillon pulled out a chair for Skylar and admired the craftsmanship. They looked like a child's craft project, with no two chairs being alike. Dillon appreciated this type of furniture; it was an art form. The enormous rustic dining table was made of actual logs that still showed evidence of the branches that once grew out of them. The tabletop also had no clean lines, with each side taking on the natural shape of the wood.

Once everyone was seated with their drinks in front of them, Dillon began. "I know we're all exhausted, but I'm afraid this group is going to implode if we don't come up with a plan. In the last two days, we've seen tensions rising." She scanned the faces around the table, and Katie looked down at her own hands when Dillon met her gaze. "Everyone is scared and freaked out. Rightfully so, but we can't afford infighting."

"No doubt," Maria said. "I love zombie movies, but the people are way scarier than the zombies. They turn on each other so quickly."

"Exactly," Cynthia said. "We're already seeing signs of it. People are in pain and grieving. And once the shock wears off, we're gonna have trouble."

"But I think most people are looking for someone to follow," CJ said.

"All I know is the yelling and screaming is driving me nuts," Maria said. "I'm gonna lose it on somebody if we have to make every decision that way."

"It's exhausting," Skylar added. Everyone around the table nodded in agreement, even Katie.

"I feel like we're coming out of the haze we've been under the last couple days," Dillon said. "With no sleep and so much uncertainty, I don't think we've even begun to wrap our brains around what this means. We might be in one of the best possible places to survive, but there are no guarantees. Things are going to get hard. Real hard. We haven't seen anything yet."

"Aren't you a ray of sunshine," Katie said. The

strain showed on the normally perky Katie. Her naturally perfect blonde hair needed a brush, and her porcelain skin looked even more pale tonight. But it was her light blue eyes that told the tale; at times they seemed lifeless as the reality set in.

Dillon took a deep breath and looked Katie in the eye. "I'm sorry, Katie. I know none of this talk is pleasant, but I think it's dangerous to pretend things aren't as bad as they seem." There was no hope in keeping the entire group working together, if their small group couldn't manage to do it.

"Fuck," Tasha said. "Do you know what's gonna happen when people start to come out of the shock we've all experienced? The shit's gonna hit the fan."

Cynthia nodded. "Which is why we need to have a plan in place before grief starts clouding everyone's judgment."

"God, are you people robots?" Katie said, her eyes filling with tears. "Are you listening to yourselves? More than likely, everyone we know that's not here is probably dead, so how can you talk like this? Apparently, grieving doesn't fit into your stupid plans."

Dillon looked around the table, hoping someone else would speak. They all remained silent. She hadn't wanted to talk about her wife Jane's death, but knew she must. Being Jane's best friend, Katie might understand. "We're all grieving. Katie, you know that I understand grief and loss as well as anyone. I've been living it since Jane died and doing it badly. If everyone behaves like I have the last couple of years, we're all in trouble."

Katie's eyes softened. "Oh no, that's not what I meant. I know you understand loss. It's just too much."

Dillon kept her gaze solely on Katie. "It is. I've felt despair, even with all my friends around me. I can't even begin to wrap my mind around how grief at this level will feel."

"It isn't going to be easy," Cynthia said, rejoining the conversation. "But I've seen incredible stories of resilience. The human spirit is not one to take lightly."

"Well said, Doc," CJ said. "So, what do we do now?"

It didn't take long for the group to agree they needed to create a governing body, who would have the authority to make decisions for the entire group. Trying to have meaningful discussions with a roomful of people was impractical and created animosity.

"I can't believe I'm saying this, but we need Tiffany on board with the plan," Dillon said. "She still holds sway with some of the women. We can't afford for her to sabotage everything we're trying to do."

"I'll deliver Tiffany," Cynthia said, without hesitation.

Chapter Three

After the meeting wrapped up, tiredness descended like heavy fog. Cynthia excused herself, not wanting Tiffany to get suspicious of her absence. With everyone pitching in, cleanup went quickly, and after a round of good nights, the group headed to their bedrooms.

Dillon led the way, fighting to keep her eyes open. She couldn't wait to fall into bed and sleep for the next eight hours. *Maybe ten.*

Dillon froze just inside the doorway, and CJ, who followed behind, rammed into her back.

"What the hell are you doing?" CJ grabbed Dillon and steadied herself.

"I...um...I'll go sleep on the couch in the common room." Dillon pushed past CJ.

"What's your problem?"

How stupid. In her excitement over Karen's arrival and sheer exhaustion, she hadn't thought about their sleeping arrangements. After last night, she figured she would sleep in CJ's bed, but now that Karen was back, that wasn't an option.

The previous night had gone terribly wrong. In their grief, or fear or maybe just needing to feel human, Dillon and Skylar had slept together. Not just slept together; they'd had animalistic sex. They both apparently had needed a release, and the act had taken no more than five minutes.

Dillon had woken up the next morning to an empty bed; Skylar was gone. The night had left Dillon feeling empty – ashamed. Dillon couldn't believe she'd let pure lust, or whatever it was, overtake her. She'd never been one for casual sex or one-night stands, so a quick romp in the sack was nothing she'd experienced. She liked Skylar and was no doubt attracted to her, but she feared Skylar would feel used.

Dillon's fears had been confirmed at breakfast the next morning. As a bartender, Skylar used her sexuality as a show, but it was all an illusion. She wore tight shirts that highlighted her cleavage and moved with a practiced sexuality, but by staying in constant motion, she never let any of the patrons get too close.

Her act with Dillon, in front of everyone, had been different. Skylar had performed a slow grind against Dillon, while the rowdy crowd had cheered her on. Dillon had run from the room when Skylar had poured champagne over her breasts and had pushed Dillon's face into her cleavage.

While everyone else probably believed they had been a witness to the budding relationship, Dillon had felt the anger in Skylar's actions. There was an undeniable connection between them, and Dillon had feared their brief loss of control had threatened to destroy it, almost before anything began.

The incident at breakfast had culminated in a confrontation in their suite. Skylar had been distant and edgy and had become more enraged when Dillon had confessed that she regretted sleeping with her. The tense scene flooded Dillon's thoughts.

"So, you regret sleeping with me?" Skylar said.

"Yes. At least the way it happened."

"And you don't want to sleep with me now?"

"No," Dillon said.

"So, you don't find me attractive, now that you fucked me?"

"I find you extremely attractive. Every time I look into your eyes, I'm lost."

"So, you didn't enjoy yourself last night," Skylar said, raising her voice.

"If you're asking if I came, you know I did. But if you're asking if I liked how I felt when I woke up this morning, then the answer is no."

"And how did you feel, huh, Dillon?"

"Empty. Ashamed that I'd treated you that way. Sad because it wasn't how I hoped it would be."

"So, you thought about how it would be?"

"I hadn't gone that far in my mind. I was still thinking about our first kiss."

"Un-fucking-believable."

"I don't know what I keep saying wrong."

"That's because you're an idiot." Skylar's voice cracked and tears ran down her face.

"I never meant to hurt you."

"If someone told me that the woman I slept with the night before would tell me she regretted it and didn't want to do it again, I would never have believed her if she told me I'd be happy about it."

"I'm not sure I completely followed that."

Skylar ran the back of her hand across her eyes, trying to stop the tears that were flowing harder. When she couldn't stop them, she looked at Dillon. Her eyes were still full of pain, but Dillon saw something else. The anger was gone and so was the guardedness.

"Please tell me what you mean," Dillon said.

"I should be angry or at least hurt, but I'm happy."

"But you're crying."

"Haven't you heard of people crying when they're happy?"

"So, you're happy?" Dillon asked cautiously.

"Would you stop talking and come over here and give me my first kiss again?"

A loud voice pulled Dillon out of her thoughts.

"Dillon, are you listening to me?" CJ asked.

"What?" The images from earlier faded from Dillon's mind.

"I asked what your problem is. Everyone's exhausted. Why would you want to sleep on the couch?"

Dillon stared blankly at CJ, not wanting to answer.

Skylar came to her rescue, putting her arm around Dillon. "Don't worry, I won't bite," she said with a wink.

"I might," Karen said, patting CJ's buttocks. "I've missed you."

Dillon laughed. "Oh, hell no! There will be none of that in this room."

"There's a big jacuzzi tub in the bathroom." CJ raised her eyebrows a couple times for emphasis.

Dillon covered her face with her hand. "Would you stop already?"

Karen flopped onto the bed. "It's your lucky day. As sexy as I find CJ, I'm exhausted."

CJ sat down beside her and put an arm over her shoulder. "I think we all are, but after everything you saw in LA, I can't even imagine how you must be feeling."

Dillon took Skylar's hand and they sat on the

other bed. "How are you doing? It's been so crazy since you arrived, I never thought to ask."

Karen had been on a redeye flight from Chicago when the incident occurred. Of the planes that should have been landing at LAX, only Karen's and two others had survived. Earlier, Karen described the surreal scene in Los Angeles, many areas on fire because of the downed aircraft that crashed into various locations throughout the city.

Karen put her hand on CJ's knee and laid her head on her shoulder. "It was the worst two days of my life. I never stopped believing I'd find you guys alive, but as we found more and more dead people, it got harder. I'm not sure I'd have made it without Nancy."

Karen had met Nancy and her two daughters on the flight from Chicago. When they'd landed, they'd stayed together without any serious discussion of separating. Nancy had flown to LA to see her convalescing father, who they'd found dead at the hospital; with nowhere else to go, they'd made the trek to the Whitaker Estate. What should have only taken them a couple hours took them much longer, as they were forced to find their way through roads littered with death.

"I still can't imagine what LA must be like." CJ shook her head, almost as if she were trying to shake the images out. "The last I knew, there's over four million people in LA. Are they all dead?"

"I'd say most of 'em." Karen said. "I never want to see anything like that again."

Dillon cleared her throat. "I'm afraid we might have to."

Karen's head lifted off CJ's shoulder and she

turned to look at Dillon. "Why the hell would we want to do that?"

"Supplies. To get a handle on what we're dealing with."

Karen groaned and fell back onto the bed. "I don't want to think about it. Can't we just get some sleep tonight?"

Skylar patted Dillon's hand. "I think she's right. I don't think any of us have anything left in the tank tonight."

"Yeah," CJ said. "We need to get some sleep, so we can be ready for tomorrow."

"But—" Dillon started to say, but was stopped by Skylar.

"No, Dillon. I know you want to solve all the problems of the world, but we aren't going to be able to do it in one day. You'll burn yourself out trying."

Dillon sighed and rubbed her burning eyes. She knew Skylar was right. Her mind was cloudy and her thoughts were becoming more jumbled. "You win."

Chapter Four

Once the breakfast dishes were cleared, Dillon leaned back in her chair. Since the Crisis, they'd been eating their daytime meals in the conservatory located at the far end of the atrium. The area was packed with exotic plants and colorful flowers, which gave the room a tropical feeling. A large fountain graced one end of the room, filling the area with the soothing sound of running water. Definitely something they needed for their frayed nerves.

Tiffany's voice invaded Dillon's thoughts, and she was brought out of her reverie. Dillon suppressed a smile when Tiffany's words began to register. *Well played, Cynthia.* Tiffany and Cynthia were standing at the front of the room, addressing the group. Without being aware of it, Tiffany outlined the plan they'd agreed to last night.

Dillon looked at Cynthia and warmth spread across her chest. Three days ago, Cynthia was a stranger; in fact, Dillon had taken an immediate dislike to her. In Dillon's eyes, she'd been guilty by default when Tiffany had harassed Skylar at the bar. At the time, Cynthia had the decency to seem embarrassed by Tiffany's antics and had offered an awkward apology.

It wasn't until the Crisis hit and Cynthia showed her true colors that Dillon's opinion began to change.

Cynthia was doing everything in her power to keep the group together and help people who were mostly strangers to her. In this short time, Dillon already considered her a friend.

"We have much work to do, but with everyone's cooperation, I feel we will overcome. As everyone knows, trying to make decisions with a group of over thirty people is difficult. That's why I've laid out a plan for selecting a Commission. But time is of the essence, so we need to act as soon as possible," Tiffany said. "I'd like to open the discussion to the floor."

"So why six members instead of seven?" someone called out. "With an odd number of people, you never have to worry about a tie vote."

"Well..." Tiffany looked around the room like a deer in headlights.

"That's a great question," Cynthia said, bailing Tiffany out. "When Tiff talked to me about this, she was concerned about relying on a simple majority. In times like these, we need to make sure decisions have broad support."

"What the hell does that mean? You sound like a lawyer," another woman called.

"Sorry, I certainly don't want to be accused of that." Cynthia smiled and looked toward Dillon's table. "No offense, Maria."

Maria dramatically threw up her hands, but her smile gave her away. "What? I don't understand why we always get such a bad rap."

The group laughed and the tension in the room went down a notch, but Dillon could still sense the underlying current of unease.

Cynthia continued. "Let me explain. Any decision will require four of the six people to agree, which is two thirds. In political terms, it means it'll require a supermajority. While this may make it harder to reach an agreement, it will also mean that all decisions will be well thought out and best for everyone."

The recommendation was accepted with little debate but developing a slate of nominees proved more controversial.

"Why can't each suite have one representative?" Diana asked.

"There's only five suites," a voice from the crowd said.

"Then elect one wild card and the problem is solved,' Diana said. "Let each suite decide who they want to represent them."

"Easy for you to say, with your posh uncrowded living arrangements." Maria's jaw clenched, but she kept her voice even. "One person out of your four would be there, but what about the rest of us piled into our rooms like cattle?"

Dillon's eyes shifted between Maria and Diana, and then moved to the front of the room. She resisted speaking, not wanting to tip the precarious peace that saw Tiffany cooperating. Instead, she shot Cynthia an encouraging smile.

"Tiffany, remember when we talked about this idea," Cynthia said. "We didn't think it would be fair to break it down by suite."

"Yeah, Diana, I told Cyn earlier that we needed to make sure everyone was represented and not put unnecessary constraints on who can serve," Tiffany said in an official tone.

Dillon smirked. *Cynthia had coached Tiffany well.* The best part was Tiffany seemed none the wiser.

"Okay, whatever you think." Diana returned

her focus back to her orange juice that likely had a large splash of vodka in it.

"I think we should put in some restrictions," Renee said, standing when she spoke. "Like for instance, only one person from a romantic partnership. With only six members, it could give a couple way too much power."

The group agreed.

"I propose we require there be at least one heterosexual member," CJ offered.

"Hell no," someone yelled. "I don't recall our government caring if we had a voice at the table."

"Exactly my point. We want to treat people better than we've been treated."

The room erupted, with shouts coming from all directions. Cynthia and Tiffany tried to calm the room but were having no luck. The anger and passion in the room was palpable.

After several minutes of chaos, a loud voice called out. "May I please have permission to address the group?" Jake said. The women quieted, but several glared at him as he stood.

"Looks like you have the floor," Cynthia said, cutting off the rest of the whispered conversations.

"First, I would like to thank CJ for her thoughtful recommendation." Jake smiled and nodded in her direction. "But I would like to speak against an automatic seat at the table for a straight person. This issue is obviously creating a divide in the group, a divide we can't afford at this time. I can only speak for myself, but in the brief time I've been here, I've met some incredible women. I have no doubt there will be plenty of nominees that I know will represent me and my family fairly."

Jake sat down and several women applauded his comments. "Well, can I assume Jake speaks for you also?" CJ said, looking toward Lily and Nancy. They both nodded. "Okay, I take my recommendation off the table."

They debated the merits of other constraints but settled on only the one. Both members of a romantic partnership could not serve together.

"Why don't we take fifteen, so everyone can decide who they'd like to nominate?" Cynthia said.

The volume in the room suddenly grew loud, so Dillon leaned forward and put her elbows on the table. She glanced around at her friends. "What's our strategy going to be?"

"It's all about the law of averages," CJ said.

Maria rolled her eyes. "What are you talking about?"

"She's speaking geek again," Dillon teased.

"Seriously!" CJ glared first at Maria then Dillon. "If we allow too many nominees from our suite, we run the risk of taking votes from each other, so we need to decide as a group who will accept a nomination and who won't."

"She's got a point," Tasha said. Maria whipped around and looked at Tasha in horror. Tasha smiled and said, "I guess I speak geek too."

Maria groaned and dropped her head into her hand. "I'm speechless."

"Then why do we still hear you talking?" CJ teased.

With little debate or dissension, they decided that Dillon, Karen, and Maria would be their nominees. "Very efficient," CJ said, looking at her watch. "That only took four minutes and thirteen seconds."

"And she threw a fit when we said she's a geek," Dillon said, shaking her head. "Unbelievable."

When they came back together with the entire group, the nominees were decided upon in less than five minutes. Apparently, several of the groups had a similar strategy to theirs.

In the end, there were thirteen nominees for the six seats. It was agreed that each candidate would be given five minutes to speak about their leadership experience and what they felt should be the top three priorities for the community. At the end of their presentation, they would be asked to endorse two other candidates. This turned out to be the most controversial, and the tension in the room rose as each candidate revealed their choices.

Dillon was grateful when several candidates endorsed her. Tiffany bristled when Cynthia endorsed both Dillon and Tiffany. Dillon suspected it was Cynthia's way of soothing Tiffany's ego, but it didn't appear to have worked.

Dillon was strategic in her endorsements, choosing to give her nod to Jake and Cynthia since they knew the fewest people. It would be a given that she supported her suitemates Karen and Maria, so there was no sense verbalizing what everyone would already know. She'd encouraged Karen and Maria to do the same.

While the speeches were being delivered, CJ and Anne excused themselves to create a simple computer program to allow for anonymous voting. It surprised Dillon how readily the group entrusted the pair to run the election. She hoped it was a sign that the factions would come together to support whoever was chosen.

A short time later, CJ and Anne returned with

their equipment and set up the voting station next to the fountain. They'd pulled a high-top table from the bar to set the computer on. For privacy, they encircled the table with a couple Japanese screens they'd taken from one of the atrium seating areas. They were running through their final testing when the last speaker finished.

Anne stepped from the booth and said, "It looks like we are about ready to start, but we wanted to give you a quick overview of how this will work. If everyone could step over here, we should be able to do this relatively quickly."

"We will call you one at a time to the voting center." She turned to point at their makeshift voting booth, and as if on cue, CJ appeared at the opening. "And as you can see, it allows for voting privacy. Is everything ready, CJ?"

"Everything is a go," CJ answered. "It's a simple program. You need to put a check mark next to six candidates. If you choose too few or too many, you won't be able to submit your ballot until it's corrected. When you hit submit, it will display the six individuals you have chosen and ask for your confirmation. You *must* click yes before your vote is completed."

"How will we know our vote went through?" someone called out.

Anne laughed. "CJ has programmed it so you will have no doubt that your vote has been properly submitted."

"When will we know the results?" Maria asked.

"We should have the results immediately after the last person votes," Anne said. "Then in alphabetical order we'll announce the six who have been elected."

"I think you should announce them based on

the highest to lowest vote total," Tiffany said.

"As your election officials, we feel it would only cause division, which is something we cannot afford, nor do we want." Anne gave Tiffany a disarming smile before she continued. "I think that's all the instructions you'll need. Let's vote!"

When it was Dillon's turn, she walked into the tiny space and looked at the screen. The names were listed in alphabetical order, and as promised, the voting was simple. She quickly placed a check mark next to her six candidates and clicked the submit button. The six names popped up in the middle of the screen in large letters and asked if the names were correct. As soon as she clicked the yes button, the computer screen gave the impression of shaking before a virtual crack split the screen. Dillon stifled a laugh when the cracked virtual pieces flew from the screen to reveal Spock dancing in the middle of the screen, holding a banner that said, YOU ROCKED THE VOTE.

Another reason to love CJ. Dillon exited the booth with a smile. She looked at CJ and shook her head. CJ beamed.

Once the last vote was cast, CJ and Anne disappeared into the voting booth. In less than five minutes, they emerged, with unreadable looks on their faces. CJ held a folded sheet of paper, but Dillon doubted she would need to consult it to reveal the names. Neither CJ nor Anne made direct eye contact with anyone; instead, they looked over the heads of the crowd as they spoke.

"We have our results," Anne said. "CJ will call out the names in alphabetical order. When CJ calls your name, please come stand in front of the fountain, so we can meet our new Commission."

"Tiffany Daniels," CJ called out to cheers and catcalls. Tiffany rose from her chair, bowed, and jogged to the front of the room, her hands held over her head in a Rocky pose. Several at Dillon's table protested at the egotistical display. Maria Alvarez was the loudest, knowing she'd not been selected. Dillon searched CJ's face, trying to decide whether the election had gone badly, but CJ kept a poker face.

Once Tiffany stopped showboating, CJ glanced down at her paper and said, "Karen Foster."

"This thing is rigged," someone called out.

The rest of the group laughed.

"Must be Russian interference," someone else joked.

Karen laughed as she made her way to the front of the room, and in an exaggerated Texas drawl said, "And to think, we pulled it off without mail-in ballots."

"I promise, the next name called will not be one of our partners," Anne said, joining the banter. "Who do you have for us next, CJ?"

CJ glanced at her paper again before speaking. "Cynthia Kramer."

Dillon breathed a sigh of relief. Things were looking up with the last two choices. Cynthia ambled to the front of the room. Her awkwardness was endearing, but also seemed out of place. It surprised her to see someone with so much natural beauty seemingly uncomfortable in her own skin. Dillon caught her eye, smiled, and gave her a thumbs up. Cynthia smiled for the first time as she took her place next to Karen.

The side conversations rippled through the crowd, as more people realized they'd not been selected.

"Renee Lipinski," CJ announced. *Another good choice.* Dillon bumped fists with Renee as she passed. Renee carried her added weight well and bounded to the front. Her short, spiked, brown hair and horn-rimmed glasses gave her a spunky look. Behind her glasses, her blue, nearly aqua colored, eyes stood out.

There were only two seats left. Dillon glanced around the room, trying to remember whose names were still in play.

"Dillon Mitchell." CJ kept her demeanor neutral, as she delivered the news.

Upon rising to her feet, Dillon bent down and gave Skylar a quick kiss before she made her way to the fountain. She stopped in front of Tiffany and held out her hand. Tiffany stiffly shook it but did not return Dillon's smile. Dillon moved on and hugged Karen and Renee before she arrived in front of Cynthia.

Cynthia's eyes danced when Dillon approached. They clasped hands and pulled into one another, bumping chests. After only two days, this had become their signature hug. Dillon let go and took her place in the line.

"And last, but certainly not least, Jake Stein."

Dillon clapped as a stunned Jake stood and walked to the front. Unable to contain her enthusiasm, she met Jake a few steps from the fountain and wrapped him in a bear hug. She whispered in his ear, "I guess it's a good thing I didn't run your ass over."

He laughed and a huge smile broke out on his handsome face.

"There you have it," Anne said, pointing at the six individuals standing in a row. "Our first elected Commission. I think this calls for some photos."

Several women pulled out their cell phones. Dillon shivered. *Would future generations look at these as the first government of a newly formed society?* She pushed the thought out of her head. She wanted to hold onto the belief that this wasn't as widespread as it seemed, and they would find a whole world of people outside of their confines.

"When should we call our first meeting?" Dillon asked once the photo shoot ended.

"It needs to be soon," Cynthia answered. "There's a lot we need to talk about."

"Definitely," Renee said. "My crew has a big meal planned for tonight, so I need to get things organized before we meet."

"It's a little before noon, what about one thirty?" Karen asked.

Everyone nodded in agreement.

"Where do we want our official home to be?" Renee said.

Cynthia waved her hand. "I explored earlier and there's a beautiful library on the other side of the mansion. It has a meeting room off the main floor that I think would be perfect."

"Sounds great. I love a good library," Dillon said.

"Then I can't wait for you to see this one."

The Commission discussion ended, as the rest of the group approached to offer congratulations. While they mingled, Dillon quietly alerted Jake, CJ, and Cynthia that she had an idea and would like to meet in the atrium to discuss it. Once she'd shaken several hands, received many hugs, and accepted congratulations, she nodded to the others. Taking Skylar's hand, she moved toward the doors. The others extracted themselves from the crowd and followed. They were nearly to the door when a loud voice stopped them.

"Cyn, where the hell are you going?" Tiffany shouted.

Dillon had already cleared the doors and stood in the atrium when she looked back. Tiffany strode across the room with a frown on her face, looking as if she were on a mission. Cynthia stopped a few steps from the door, a defeated look descending. She gave Dillon a slight smile before answering Tiffany. "I was just going to use the facilities."

"Great, I'll go with you." Tiffany wrapped her arm around Cynthia. "We've got a lot to discuss before the meeting."

"Sounds good, Tiff," Cynthia said without enthusiasm.

Shit. Dillon turned away. They'd have to do it without Cynthia.

Chapter Five

Dillon's stomach lurched when they brought their ATVs to a stop outside the museum. Two days ago, under much different circumstances, she'd entered this building. She didn't realize that their lives were about to change forever, and life as they knew it would be over.

Dillon only agreed to attend the party with CJ because of her fascination with the Whitaker Estate, not to celebrate Tiffany's birthday. She'd always found Tiffany to be shallow and superficial, and hitting on Dillon's wife, *twice*, only solidified her feelings.

This was the first time since Jane's death that Dillon had agreed to go away for the weekend. CJ had been elated, but still had teased Dillon mercilessly about her giddiness over visiting a museum. It was the only thing she'd talked about for weeks, driving CJ crazy. Her glee had risen when she'd discovered she was the only person signed up for the guided tour. The highlight had been the replica of Whitaker's Bunker, before it had been converted into a nightclub. It was this that brought them to the museum now.

Jake jangling a wad of keys interrupted Dillon's thoughts. She couldn't afford to think about the past, with so much to be done.

"You look pale. Are you sure you're up for this?" CJ asked Dillon quietly, so only Dillon and Skylar heard.

Dillon smiled. "I have to be. There are things in here we can use."

"It's crazy that it was only two days ago that we were here," CJ said. "It feels like a lifetime ago."

Dillon swallowed hard but could find no words, so she gave CJ a weak smile.

"It's okay, Dillon," Skylar said, taking her hand. Dillon wasn't sure why the museum caused her so many emotions, but she was glad to have Skylar's hand in hers.

Jake methodically inserted one key after another, looking for the one that would open the door. Dillon felt her anxiety rising with each key that failed to spring the lock. Maggie had been so kind to her on their tour, so the thought of smashing in the door of the museum seemed like an affront to Maggie.

After trying over a dozen keys, Jake finally landed the right one. He pushed open the door with his foot and held it so everyone could enter. A musty smell assaulted Dillon when she walked in. It was the stale smell of a building that had been closed up for too long. Her imagination must be running rampant since it was opened only two days ago, but she couldn't shake the smell.

"We don't have much time," Dillon said, hoping to refocus. "It would be bad form to show up to the first Commission meeting late."

"What's our game plan?" Karen asked.

"We should start in the gift shop," CJ said. "I remember seeing some great survivalist books. I think there were even some do it yourself growing kits."

At the gift shop, they separated, each taking a section of the store to explore. Dillon grinned as she deposited an armful of items on the growing pile near the cash register. *Old habits die hard.* It wasn't as if they were planning on paying for the goods, but everyone had automatically brought their take to the checkout.

"I found a bunch of backpacks that we can load all the stuff into," Lily called from across the store.

"Lily, why don't you and I get everything loaded up, while Dillon takes everyone else to the replica of the shelter?" CJ said.

"You'll do anything to get out of the tour, won't you?" Dillon said.

CJ laughed. "We'll catch up with you, once we're done, but it's important that Karen and Jake get a good look since they'll be in the meeting this afternoon."

Karen, Jake, and Skylar followed Dillon out of the store. She led them toward the back of the building, which housed the replica of the bunker. Dillon threw open the door Maggie had led her through to begin the tour. The smell of decay hit them, and they covered their noses.

Dillon coughed and pulled her shirt up over her nose. "What the fuck." She stared down at the two guards that were slumped over their desks. "Tiffany's crew was supposed to check all the buildings for bodies."

"Apparently they didn't." Jake instinctively checked the pulses of the men who were obviously dead.

"Maybe we should scour the building before we check out the bunker," Skylar said. "Cynthia will want to process the bodies and put them with the others."

They found no other bodies until they came to the curator's wing. The area was done in all dark heavy wood and had the feeling of an old-time library. Heavy blinds that let in little light covered the windows. Dillon suspected this was to keep the older display pieces from being damaged by the sunlight. They entered a modestly decorated office, which was equally as dark. The furniture was utilitarian; nothing seemed to be there strictly for decoration. The floor to ceiling bookshelves were chock-full of books. The desk held several meticulously arranged piles of file folders with three pens lined up equidistance apart next to a pad of paper. The curator was nothing if not tidy.

Skylar opened a large wooden door. "Hey, it looks like the curator had an apartment. By the smell, I think we better check it out."

They entered through the kitchen, which was as tidy as the office. Skylar led the way into the living room and abruptly stopped. "I think we found the curator."

Dillon stopped short when she saw the woman slumped in the recliner with a book on her lap. She blinked back tears and brushed past Jake and Karen as she made her escape.

"What's wrong?" Karen called to the retreating Dillon.

Dillon didn't stop to answer. She needed air. She made her way across the museum and burst through the door back into the sunlight. She put her hands on her knees and breathed in deeply when she felt a hand on her back.

"Are you okay?" Skylar lightly rubbed her back.

"Maggie's dead."

"Who's Maggie?"

By the time Skylar and Dillon returned to the

museum, the other two couples were gathered just inside the entrance to the bunker replica. CJ and Lily had finished loading the carts and were ready to join the tour.

"I see you found an unpleasant surprise," CJ said, pointing at the bodies.

"Fucking Tiffany." Dillon yanked her cell phone out of the clip attached to her belt. "I'll handle this. You guys go ahead in, and I'll catch up."

"I'll stay here with Dillon," Skylar said to the others.

Dillon angrily swiped her finger across the phone and aggressively tapped it several times before she held it to her ear. "What the hell was Tiffany doing when she searched for bodies?"

"Hi Dillon, nice to hear from you," Cynthia said with an edge to her voice.

"Is Tiffany with you?"

"Yes."

"Well, we're in the museum and found three more dead."

"Hold on." Dillon could hear voices but couldn't make out the words. She heard Cynthia say, "Jesus, Tiffany," before she apparently clamped her hand tighter over the phone.

"Apparently they didn't check any of the buildings," Cynthia said, once she returned to the call.

"Great, and can I ask why the hell not?"

"She said they didn't know where the keys were."

"Really? Funny, but we found them with no problem, from the same building they got their golf carts. Apparently, they were too busy checking out the wine cellar."

There was silence on the other end of the line, so

Dillon continued. "Are you still there?"

"Yes."

"Why aren't you saying anything?"

"What is it you want me to say, or for that matter, do?" Irritation was evident in Cynthia's tone.

"What the hell? This is completely unacceptable. Now we're going to have to do another round of body bagging. Won't that be a lot of fun? Maybe we can have Tiffany come along and throw wine all over me while she's at it."

"Well, maybe yelling at me some more will help." Cynthia's voice rose.

Skylar glared at Dillon. *Great, now they're both pissed off.*

"I'm sorry, Cynthia. I need to stop taking the shit she does out on you."

"Ya think?" Cynthia said, her tone dripping with sarcasm.

"I'm truly sorry. Seeing Maggie, that sweet little old lady, dead just got to me. But that's still no excuse." She needed to stop letting her disdain for Tiffany interfere with the way she treated Cynthia. If she weren't careful, she would chase Cynthia away, which was the last thing she wanted to do.

"I guess Tiffany just brings out the best in you," Cynthia said with a lighter tone in her voice.

"That's no excuse. We're all under stress, including you, and I shouldn't be adding to it."

"Thank you, but it's okay."

"No, it's not okay, Cynthia. If I act like this again, you have permission to rip me a new one."

"I'm a doctor. I'd prefer to cut you a new one. Ripping is so messy."

Dillon laughed. "Deal. Shit, has Tiffany been listening to this whole conversation?"

"No, I walked away, and I think she knew better than to follow. You guys finish up, and we'll talk about the bodies at the meeting."

"Sounds good. You know I really am sorry."

"Stop, I've already accepted your apology."

"Okay, see you soon," Dillon said before disconnecting.

"I hope Cynthia let you have it," Skylar said.

"Not as much as I deserved," Dillon said sheepishly.

"Well then, I will. You need to knock that shit off and stop taking things out on her. She has Tiffany doing it, so she certainly doesn't need it from you too."

"I know."

"She's a sweetheart. She's nothing like Tiffany, and you have to stop acting like she is."

"I know."

"If you're not careful, you're going to drive her away."

"I know."

"Are you going to say anything else other than I know?"

"If I do, will you stop yelling at me?" Dillon turned her puppy dog eyes on Skylar.

"Stop looking at me like that." Skylar pointed and attempted a glare. "I'm done. Let's catch up with the others."

They found the rest of the group in the large weapons room. Skylar's eyes grew large as she took in the hundreds of weapons encased in the glass lining the walls. Dillon knew little about guns, but they looked like ones she'd seen in action movies. Maggie had told her that every five years, the arsenal was upgraded to the newest models to ensure they always had the most technologically advanced weaponry. The room gave her the creeps.

"What are you guys doing?" Dillon asked.

"You said there were a lot of weapons, but I didn't expect this much firepower." Jake's gaze darted around the room. "This is fucking impressive."

"Did you break the glass?" Dillon asked, finally noticing the broken glass littering the floor.

"Yeah. Would you look at all this shit?" Jake held up a large machine gun.

"Whoa!" Dillon took a step back. "Should you be swinging that thing around like that?"

"Relax, it's not loaded." He handed the gun to Lily and reached into the case for another. "I think we need to take all of these."

"What the hell for?" CJ asked.

"Protection." Jake opened the chamber of the gun and checked inside.

"From what?" Karen said. "Jesus, nobody needs this many guns laying around."

"I think he's right," Skylar said, joining the conversation. She picked up a shotgun and flipped it open.

"What are you doing?" Dillon tried to disguise the revulsion she felt.

Skylar studied the barrel. "Making sure it's not loaded."

"Why do I think you've handled one of those before?"

"There ain't a girl in the hills of Tennessee that doesn't know how to use one of these." Skylar flicked her wrist and closed the barrel.

"I thought you were from San Francisco."

"That's where I was before Los Angeles."

"So, you grew up in Tennessee?"

"We have more important things to talk about than my childhood." Skylar's voice held a chill and her back stiffened. "We need to finish up or you guys are going to be late." She turned and pulled another weapon off the wall.

"Really? After all the senscless shootings in this country, you want us to arm up?" Dillon searched her friends' faces. "What's the point?"

Karen squeezed Dillon's arm. "As much as I hate the thought, I think they're right. We might need to defend ourselves."

Dillon held up her hands. "Apparently, I'm out-numbered. Let's load up a few to take to the meeting and let the Commission decide what to do."

Each selected a couple guns to take with them, Dillon chose two handguns, not wanting to touch any of the bigger weapons. They stashed the guns in the carts along with everything they'd found in the gift shop. Dillon started to get on the ATV but stopped. "Jake, did you lock the building?"

"Shit, I left the keys on the counter in the museum shop." He started to dismount.

"I've got it." Dillon jogged back to the museum. When she emerged, she tried to hide the smirk on her face as she crammed a t-shirt into her pants pocket.

"What are you up to?" CJ asked.

"Nothing." Dillon climbed onto the ATV and fired up the engine. She revved the motor, cutting off further conversation.

They pulled to the front of the mansion with about twenty minutes to spare. Dillon let her ATV come to an idle and raised her voice to be heard over the engines. "Do you think we should go around back to the service entrance?"

"Why don't you guys head to your meeting?" CJ said. "We can unload."

"Oh God." Lily laughed. "I've never driven one of these things. Should be fun."

Jake looked at her skeptically. "Are you sure?"

"Typical man, never letting his woman drive," Dillon said. "I guess you're gonna pay for it now."

Jake laughed at Dillon's ribbing. "I'm afraid we're all going to be doing things we never thought we would." He dismounted and smiled at Lily. "It's all yours, Babe."

She beamed at him as he gave her quick instructions on how to operate the machine. Dillon got off her ATV and said to Skylar, "I'm figuring a girl from the hills of Tennessee already knows how to ride one of these."

"You figured right." Skylar winked. "Ready, ladies?"

Lily let out a whoop and hit the accelerator. She half laughed and half screamed as she shot forward. CJ and Skylar followed.

Laughing, Dillon turned to Jake. "I think she's going to have way too much fun."

Jake started to respond, but another scream followed by laughter interrupted them. Lily swerved to miss the flower bed she was heading toward. "I'm not sure the landscaping will ever be the same."

❧❧❧❧❧

Cynthia emerged from the mansion and waved to them before starting down the long flight of stairs.

Dillon took the steps two at a time to meet her. "Do you have a second?"

"Sure."

Dillon called down the stairs to Karen and Jake. "I want to have a word with Cynthia, so I'll see you guys at the meeting."

When they entered the mansion, several women milled around, so Dillon motioned Cynthia down a side hall. They rounded the corner and no one else was around, so Dillon reached in her pocket. She pulled out a piece of navy-blue cloth and held it out to Cynthia. "Truce."

Cynthia took the mangled ball and shook it out. A broad smile played on her face, and she laughed as she looked at the t-shirt. "How could I stay mad when you come bearing such nice gifts?"

"That's what I hoped you'd say." Dillon smiled. "You know I feel terrible about being a jerk to you, don't ya?"

"We better head to the library, or we'll be late," Cynthia said, deflecting Dillon's question. She turned and started down the hall.

Dillon didn't follow. Cynthia's brush off stung. *Serves me right.* She'd repeatedly taken out Tiffany's behavior on Cynthia. No wonder she didn't want to talk now.

"I'll catch you there." Dillon turned and started down the hall in the opposite direction, hoping she would be able to find another route to the library.

"Wait, Dillon," Cynthia called.

Dillon stopped and turned slowly. Cynthia walked toward her, but Dillon struggled to read the look on her face.

Cynthia stopped in front of Dillon and shifted

her weight from one foot to the other. She made eye contact before shifting her gaze to the floor. "I'm not comfortable with this kind of conversation."

Shit. Was this "the friendship isn't working out" talk? Dillon inhaled and let it out slowly. "What kind of conversation?"

"Sharing feelings. Being emotionally vulnerable. I thought if we walked and talked, it would be easier."

"So, you want to talk?" Relief flooded over Dillon.

"Oh God, you thought I was blowing you off?"

"Kinda felt that way when you changed the subject and walked off."

Cynthia smiled. "Let me try this again. Why don't we talk about this while we walk to the library? Better?"

"Much. Lead the way."

"For the record, you were heading in the wrong direction."

"I would've gotten there...eventually." Dillon bumped Cynthia with her hip as they walked. "So, where were we?"

"You were telling me you felt terrible about being a jerk." Cynthia hip checked Dillon back.

"Nothing like diving back in." Dillon's expression suddenly turned serious. "I wouldn't blame you if you were mad. Every time Tiffany pisses me off, I seem to act like an idiot to you. I need to stop letting her get under my skin. It's not fair to you."

"Is that what you're worried about?"

"Yeah." Dillon studied Cynthia, as they walked. "Why do you look so surprised?"

They turned down the long empty corridor leading to the library. "You've got everyone here with you, all your closest friends."

"So? I'm afraid I'm not following."

Cynthia's brow furrowed, but she didn't reply right away. In the silence, their footsteps echoed off the walls.

How ugly. The corridor looked like it belonged in a hospital. The bright, sterile look didn't fit the rest of the Estate. Earlier, when Dillon explored the mansion, she'd bypassed this hallway because it was so unwelcoming, which is why she'd not seen the library.

"You're not going to make this conversation easy, are you?" Cynthia finally said.

"Honestly, I'm not trying to be difficult. I don't understand what you're trying to tell me."

"You don't really need me." Cynthia picked up her pace, forcing Dillon to take longer strides to keep up.

"I *need* you to slow down." Dillon faked being out of breath and broke into a jog. She hoped it would make Cynthia relax.

Cynthia smiled, but there was still tension in her face. She glanced at Dillon and blurted out, "I need you a lot more than you need me. I don't have a hell of a lot here, other than a couple old college friends that I seem to have outgrown. Anne's the only one I enjoy being around anymore."

"No," Dillon said, finally understanding. "Don't you remember our conversation behind the hotel?"

"You mean the one we had after you puked in the bushes?"

"That's the one, thanks for reminding me." Dillon smiled. "I told you that you were the first friend I made at summer camp, and bonds like that go deep."

"You've got a point." Cynthia smiled. "Why am

I feeling so insecure? I'm a successful professional, for fuck's sake, not a fourteen-year-old kid."

"You're human. The world is a scary place right now. We all need an anchor." They'd reached the end of the corridor and Cynthia turned to the left. There was a short hallway before they reached the nondescript metal doors. Above the door was a sign that said, Whitaker Library. Dillon stopped, wanting to finish the conversation before they entered. "If it helps, I'm feeling it too. Why do you think I was so afraid you'll get tired of my tirades about Tiffany?"

"But you have so many other people."

"But they're not you."

"What's so special about me? Especially since I'm friends with Tiffany."

Dillon felt Cynthia's pain, and wanted to hug her. She sensed it wasn't easy for Cynthia to talk so openly. It was times like these that tended to change people. "You're good people. That's what my dad would say. And as for being friends with Tiffany…" Dillon paused and shook her head. "That still has me puzzled, but maybe one day I'll understand."

"Honestly, there used to be a good person under all that bravado. Her arrogance was just a front, but I can't find the person I used to know anymore. I still believe she's in there, somewhere."

"I'll have to take your word for it. But I'm not interested in Tiffany. I want to know about you."

"I just want to stop feeling so all alone." Cynthia looked down at the floor, no longer able to make eye contact with Dillon.

Dillon put a reassuring hand on Cynthia's arm and lightly squeezed. "You're not alone."

Cynthia raised her eyes and Dillon saw the in-

tense pain there. "I don't want you thinking I'm a dis-
loyal jerk."

"Whoa, where did that come from?"

"I've known you for two days and Tiffany for
fifteen years."

"Okay?" Dillon said questioningly.

"I don't want you to think you can't trust me."

"I'm sorry if I've given you that impression."

"You haven't. It's just that I feel guilty and dis-
loyal to Tiffany for bonding with you so soon. I need
you to know, that's not who I normally am." Cynthia's
words were increasingly coming out faster. "I don't
want you to worry that I haven't got your back, because I do. A week or two from now, I don't want
you thinking that I'll switch gears again and leave this
friendship in the dust for a newer shinier model. Once
I make a commitment, I keep it."

"Slow down. I wasn't thinking any of those things.
I trust you."

"How, when I turn away from my friends of
fifteen years? What kind of person does that?"

"First off, you haven't turned your back on Tiffany." Dillon put her hand on Cynthia's arm. "You're
still trying, despite her asshole behaviors. Even when I
get frustrated with her, you're still trying to work with
her, so stop selling yourself short."

Cynthia looked up. "And second?"

"Second, you are good people and only other
good people can tell."

"Is that so?" A smirk formed at the corner of
Cynthia's mouth.

"Yep, it is. Do you think you could stop beating
yourself up now?"

"But I do it so well."

"Obviously." Dillon smiled. "Seriously, though, I don't want you feeling alone anymore. We're friends and that's not going to change."

"Promise?"

"I promise." Dillon grabbed Cynthia's hand and they bumped chests.

"I just have one more question," Cynthia said, with a twinkle in her eye.

"Shoot."

"Do you think I should wear this to the meeting?" Cynthia held up the t-shirt Dillon had given her.

"Absolutely."

"If it offends anyone, I'm blaming you." Cynthia pulled the shirt on over the one she wore and smoothed out the wrinkles.

Chapter Six

"A re you ready for this?" Cynthia said with her hand on the door.

Dillon looked around the corridor. "You raved about this library, but I'm having trouble believing it's anything special, considering the path that led us here."

"Famous last words." Cynthia threw open the doors.

"Holy fuck." Dillon's eyes widened as she took in the spectacle.

The large open floor was done in black and white square tiles. They were highly polished, and Dillon suspected she could see her reflection in them if she looked close enough. Cynthia laughed as Dillon's head swung from side to side, trying to take it all in. The bookshelves were a dark mahogany, lined with more books than she'd ever seen in one place. She'd seen places like this in pictures but never in real life.

"I didn't know they actually did that anymore." Dillon pointed at the hundreds of thousands of books that spanned three stories. There were winding staircases leading up to each level. The staircases emptied out onto a narrow balcony that encircled the bookshelves. There were small tables sprinkled on each level for patrons to look at a book they'd pulled from the shelves.

"Did you notice the ladders?" Cynthia pointed toward the stacks. On each bookshelf there were sliding ladders that could be used to get to the books that were out of reach from the floor.

"No way. I'm not sure how I'd feel about being on a ladder on the third level." Dillon pointed up at the ceiling that must have been at least sixty feet above where they stood.

"You're a builder. Shouldn't you be used to it?" Cynthia teased. "But you certainly won't get this doctor up there."

"That son-of-a-bitch had a sense of humor." Dillon laughed. "I think he intentionally created the drabbest hallway ever, in order to dull the senses before they were assaulted by this."

"Come over here. I want to show you my favorite area."

"You mean there's more?"

Cynthia led Dillon through an opening in the bookshelves, and once again her senses were awakened. A large mural of Raphael's School of Athens fresco filled one wall. The room was bright, with floor to ceiling windows covering the length of the south wall. A door led to a small outdoor patio.

"This is where I intend to do all my reading." Cynthia fell onto one of the comfortable looking couches in the center of the room. Dillon sat on the other and put her feet on the glass table between the couches. "This is the life, huh?"

"Do we have to go to the meeting? Can't we just stay here?" Dillon rested her head against one of the cushions and closed her eyes.

"Speaking of." Cynthia looked at her watch. "We only have a couple minutes."

They didn't speak as they made their way back across the library. Dillon was too busy gaping at the things she'd missed earlier. The bookshelves all had various carvings of different historical periods. She'd have to come back later to check them out. Cynthia led her past a large meeting room. There was a massive solid wood boardroom table that would seat fifty people. Definitely overkill for their tiny group.

"The smaller meeting room will be better," Cynthia said, as if reading her mind.

As they approached, Dillon heard voices from inside. When they entered, everyone else was already seated around a solid oak table in the center of the room. There was a chair on each end of the table, six chairs on one side and only five on the other. Dillon quickly did the math and smiled. *Was this another one of Whitaker's jokes?* Thirteen seats at the table. *The Last Supper?*

"Oh God, where did you get that?" Jake laughed and pointed at Cynthia.

"You like it?" Cynthia stood with her arms out, modeling the front of her t-shirt before she slowly turned in a circle.

On the back was a picture of the inside of Whitaker's original bunker, and on the front, in bright yellow letters, it said:

I SURVIVED THE APOCALYPSE
AND ALL I GOT WAS THIS
LOUSY T-SHIRT

"That's hysterical." Karen laughed. "Dark, but hysterical."

"I think we need to make it the official Commission uniform," Tiffany said, putting her arm around Cynthia.

"Dillon, do you think you could hook everyone up with one?" Cynthia asked.

"How sweet, a gift from Dillon." Tiffany's smile disappeared, and she dropped her arm from Cynthia's shoulders. "Shouldn't we get to work since you guys have already made us late?"

The light-hearted mood in the room evaporated and a palpable tension replaced it. Dillon watched Cynthia's face drop and wanted to throttle Tiffany but knew their work would be simpler if everyone got along. As much as she wanted to protect Cynthia, she had to let her fight her own battles.

Jake and Karen busied themselves looking through the bags they'd brought back from their trip to the museum. They pulled out several books and tossed them onto the table. Karen held up a book and said, "I think these will give us a good starting point. I don't know about the rest of you, but I haven't given much thought to what to do in a situation like this."

"Apparently someone has." Renee picked up a book and leafed through the pages. "I used to see books like this and think, who the hell reads this shit?"

"Lucky for us, someone did." Jake picked up a thick book from the table and opened it.

They each grabbed several books and went to work. The only sound was the turning of pages and pens scratching over paper. After nearly forty-five minutes, Cynthia said, "Anyone else getting overwhelmed?"

"Slightly." Karen sighed and put her book onto the table.

"I think we need to divide and conquer," Dillon

said.

"Meaning?" Karen asked.

"Maybe we can all choose a specialty. Then we can research our topic and take the lead in that area."

"I like it," Jake said. "Now the trick is for us to figure out what areas we need to focus on. There's a lot of things in here I hadn't even thought of." Jake tossed the book he'd been reading onto the table and ran his hand over his eyes.

"Should we brainstorm?" Cynthia flipped the page of the tablet she'd been writing on. "Anyone mind if I man the list?"

"Go for it," Renee answered.

After some debate they narrowed their concerns to eight areas: food, shelter, power and water, medical, transportation, communication, defense, and basic supplies. Renee, who owned several award-winning restaurants, was the obvious choice to take on food, while Cynthia was given medical. Dillon, with her background in construction, volunteered for the shelter assignment, which evolved into building and grounds. Karen and Tiffany both spoke up for communications. To keep the peace, they compromised. They would defer anything to do with communications to CJ and Anne. They would develop their own strategy and simply report to the committee. Tiffany snatched up energy and water since Diana was an electrical engineer. Karen agreed to take on transportation and supplies since they went hand in hand. They laughed at the stereotypical decision to put Jake in charge of defense, but it wasn't much of a stretch since none of the others had ever handled a gun.

"Now that we have our areas of expertise, I think

as a group we should agree on a general direction each of us is going to take," Dillon said.

"Why waste our time on that? We don't need anyone looking over our shoulder," Tiffany said.

Because the last time we put you in charge of something you screwed it up. Dillon kept her thought to herself.

"I think Dillon is right," Cynthia said.

"Of course you do." Tiffany flicked her wrist and tossed the book she held onto the table. The book skittered across the surface and would have fallen to the floor had Jake not swatted it back.

"Come on, Tiffany." Cynthia's tone came out light, but the vein throbbing on her forehead gave her away. "We need to be a team, not a bunch of individuals. I, for one, would like everyone's opinion on what I'm doing, so I don't miss anything."

"Whatever, seems like a waste of time to me." Tiffany pushed her chair back and hoisted her feet onto the table. She crossed her arms over her chest and glared at Dillon.

Dillon could see Tiffany out of the corner of her eye but refused to give her the satisfaction of looking in her direction. *What a waste.* Tiffany was gorgeous, with long dark hair and piercing ice blue eyes. But Dillon didn't find her remotely attractive; her surly personality saw to that.

"Renee, would you like to start us off?" Dillon said. "I'm sure you have the most developed ideas."

"I'm not sure about that," Renee said, but her smile gave her away. She picked up her notebook and quickly scanned the page. "I've come up with short and long-term concerns. I'm guessing within a couple months we'll run out of supplies, but we won't know that until a full inventory is done." Renee looked around the room. All eyes were on her, except for Tiffany, who leaned back in her chair, staring at the ceiling. "Supplies cross into Karen's area, so the two of us will need to work together closely." Karen nodded and smiled. "Long term, we'll need to grow and raise our own food, so I'll need Dillon and her Building and Grounds crew for that."

"Tell me what kind of ground you need and how much, and I'll locate a perfect spot for your fields."

"I hadn't thought of how much crossover there would be," Karen said. "Just let me know what you need, and I'll do my best."

"Probably more crossover than you think," Cynthia chimed in. "I'll need medical supplies, and I'm sure Dillon will need supplies too. We probably all will."

"That'll teach you to agree to tackle supplies, just because you love to shop," Dillon said.

"Shut up." Karen good-naturedly slapped Dillon on the wrist.

"That wasn't so hard. Who's next?" Cynthia asked.

"I'll go," Tiffany said, dropping her feet from the table. "We've got power, so all is good."

They waited for her to say more, but when she didn't Renee asked, "How long do you think the power will last?"

"How the hell should I know?"

Here we go. Dillon braced herself. It was short-sighted of them to put Tiffany in charge of something as important as power, compounded by having the drunk Diana working with her.

Dillon fought to rid her face of any negative

expression before she spoke. "I've had quite a bit of experience with generators, since most businesses want them nowadays, so I'm willing to help any way I can."

Anger flashed across Tiffany's face; her casual approach obviously hadn't worked. "Diana's a fucking engineer. I'm sure she knows more than you."

"Okay." Dillon raised her hands in surrender and pushed down her anger. Cynthia would have her hands full babysitting Tiffany and Diana. Hopefully, Diana would stay away from alcohol long enough to fulfill her duties, but Dillon had her doubts. "There's a whole display area concerning power and generators at the museum, in case you wanted to take a look."

Tiffany looked bored and doodled on the piece of paper in front of her. Cynthia looked at Tiffany, seemingly waiting to see if she would respond. When she didn't, Cynthia shook her head. "Jake, what about defense?"

"First, we need to bring all of the weapons back from the museum." Jake looked at Karen.

"The supply team will get right on it." Karen groaned. Everyone laughed, except for Tiffany, who had laid her head on the table.

"Second, everyone needs to be trained on how to use a gun."

He was greeted with loud protests. He listened politely, letting them finish airing their grievances before he spoke. "I hear your concerns, but we are living in a world we are yet to understand. I saw how some of you reacted when we found the guns. If we ever come under attack, we'll need to be able to defend ourselves and the people we love." He looked to Dillon, as he delivered the last line.

"As much as I hate to admit it, I agree." Dillon ran her hand through her hair on the top of her head and down her skull before resting her hand at the base of her neck. She might not be willing to shoot someone to defend herself, but there was no doubt she would for the people she loved. She pointed at Jake and tried to look angry. "Don't think I don't know you're manipulating with your skills of persuasion."

Jake smirked and winked at Dillon but said nothing.

After a short debate, the rest of the women were convinced, except for Tiffany, who seemed to no longer be listening to the conversation.

"Sticking with the topic of defense. I want to make another suggestion," Dillon said. "I thought a lookout tower about twenty feet higher than the mansion would be nice. I think at that height we could see all the way to the road and Lake Piru. That would alert us to anyone coming our direction, so we could get into the shelter if need be."

Renee began to speak, but Tiffany lifted her head from the table. Renee stopped mid-sentence and looked at Tiffany.

Dillon's gaze shifted to Tiffany, as well. *Maybe she was finally going to participate.*

"Sounds like a waste of time letting Dillon build something like that. Isn't there better things she could be doing? We're in the middle of nowhere."

Renee let out a loud breath. "I think a tower is a great idea."

"Who the hell is gonna find us here?" Tiffany said.

"Braxton Babcock," Karen said. "That guy and his people freak me out."

"For fuck's sake. You're going to let some religious nut scare you?" Tiffany rolled her eyes and began picking at her fingernail.

"He wanted to wipe us off the face of the earth before the world ended," Renee said. "Ya think he wouldn't do it now that there's no laws?"

The others nodded, except for Tiffany, who seemed more interested in her fingernails than continuing her involvement with the conversation. "Whatever."

"Dillon, it looks like you're gonna build a tower," Cynthia said.

"I'll need supplies, which means you're up again, Karen," Dillon said.

"Get me a list of what you need, and I'll find the nearest Home Depot."

"Anything else, Dillon?" Cynthia asked.

"Yes, I thought the living quarters we're in now are fine for a while, but long term we need to do something else. The crowding is going to start causing tensions." Dillon searched the faces of the others, looking for a reaction. "I'd like to build individual rooms outside the atrium, which would put us closer to the bunker, in case we needed to get there quickly. Plus, I think we could create solar power out there."

"I'm with you," Renee said. "I love the girls, but I'm not sure I can live with all of them for a long time."

"Does anyone have anything else?" Cynthia asked.

"I need a drink," Tiffany said, finally speaking. "Are we about done here?"

Cynthia ignored Tiffany. "I think the last order of business is determining who is going to speak at the dinner tonight."

"I nominate Dillon," Karen said.

"I second it," Renee added.

"Whoa, wait a second." Dillon waved her hand.

"For once, I'm with Dillon," Tiffany said. "Why the hell should she get to do it?"

"All in favor of Dillon, say aye," Cynthia said.

Everyone but Dillon and Tiffany said aye.

"Looks like the ayes have it." Cynthia winked at Dillon.

Tiffany stood and walked out.

Chapter Seven

Skylar lifted her face to the sun. The day was beautiful, with only a few wispy clouds breaking up the solid blue canvas. The sun warmed her face, while Dillon's touch heated her hand. They'd been walking in silence, along a path that snaked its way through the woods. They came to a grassy clearing that was rimmed with a variety of spring flowers. Skylar tried to take in the overwhelming splashes of color, but her eyes kept returning to the crisp white daisies that stood out among their colorful counterparts.

"Do you want to sit here for a while?" Dillon asked, breaking the silence.

Skylar squeezed Dillon's hand and moved toward one of the benches nestled amongst the flowers. When they neared the sitting area, the chirping increased. Skylar spotted a tree located about fifty feet from the bench, which seemed to be home to many of the birds.

Skylar abruptly stopped and tugged on Dillon's hand to stop her as well.

"What's the matter?"

"Why are they still alive?"

"The trees?"

"No, the birds."

"Holy shit. Good question."

They stood in awe, watching the birds swoop

in and out of the tree. Suddenly, Skylar's eyes shifted to the ground, and she peered into the dense forest. "There's a squirrel, and remember we saw those bunnies playing earlier."

"How did we not see that until now?"

"Maybe because we've been in shock for the past two days."

"True. So, it's only humans that died?"

"It appears that way." Skylar knelt and ran her hand over the grass.

"What are you doing?"

Skylar stood and held her hand out. There was a tiny spider crawling along her palm that skittered up her arm. "The bugs are alive too."

"The mystery deepens." Dillon stared at the spider with a slight smile on her face, but it was soon replaced by pain. "But why just us?"

"I don't know, but I bet Cynthia has a theory. Maybe we should find her." Skylar bent and gently guided the spider back onto a blade of grass.

"I think it can wait. Finding out an answer won't change anything." Dillon took Skylar's hand. "If it's okay with you, I'm not ready to go yet. I'd like to enjoy you and the outdoors for a while longer."

"I'd like that." Skylar smiled and squeezed Dillon's hand. "I like this place. It's peaceful. Can we just sit on the bench for a while and pretend that everything is normal for a little while?" Dillon started to speak, but Skylar interrupted. "Listen. Do you hear running water?"

Dillon closed her eyes. When she opened them, she pointed to the right. "I think there might be a creek over that direction. Should we go check it out?"

"Do you mind if we just sit here and enjoy the

birds and flowers for a little bit first?"

"Not at all."

❧❧❧❧❧

Could they just stay here forever? It was the first time in two days that Dillon felt at peace. Sitting on the bench, soaking up the sun, and listening to the birds almost made her forget the world was changed. She looked at the well-manicured grass in the clearing and frowned. A realization punched her in the gut. Without the groundskeepers, the estate would quickly start to look run down and overgrown.

"How many groundskeepers do you think the Estate employed?" They'd been sitting in silence for the past ten minutes, so Dillon knew her question came out of nowhere.

"Huh?" Skylar opened her eyes.

"I was just wondering how many workers it took to keep up such a large property."

The peaceful look on Skylar's face was replaced by a look of confusion. "Seriously? We're in this beautiful clearing and you're thinking about groundskeepers?"

That was stupid. She didn't want Skylar to think about the things that had invaded her mind. Reality would smack them in the face soon enough, so she wanted Skylar to have a little more time to feel at peace. "Oh, nothing," Dillon stammered. "Just trying to figure out how much it cost to run this place."

Dillon looked into Skylar's gray eyes and saw the realization dawning. "Oh God. This isn't going to continue looking so beautiful much longer without someone keeping it up."

"I'm sorry. I need to keep my mouth shut." Dillon ran her hands through her hair. "Just forget I said anything."

"No, you're right. Without somebody tending to it, this place won't look like this much longer, will it?"

Dillon's eyes circled the area and settled on the large section of wildflowers. *Maybe they don't need much care.* She wanted to offer Skylar reassurance, but instead she said, "Probably not."

Skylar's eyes glistened in the bright sunlight. "Have you ever seen that TV show? The one where they talked about what would happen if all the people disappeared?"

"I remember hearing about it, but never watched it."

"I only made it through the first two episodes. I couldn't take it. Now I wish I would've finished watching. Maybe I'd know what to expect."

Dillon put her hand on Skylar's knee. "I'm not sure there's any way to know what to expect."

"Do you think we're in shock? We jumped right in and started doing stuff. Electing Representatives. Cleaning up bodies..." Skylar's voice trailed off.

"It's what humans do, I guess. Try and make some sense of our world. Trick ourselves into believing we have some sort of control."

Skylar put her hand on top of Dillon's. "We thought the last two days have been bad, but what happens next when reality sets in?"

Dillon turned and searched Skylar's face before responding. "I'm not sure. I'd be lying if I said I thought it would be easy, but I also know that people are surprisingly resilient."

"Meaning?"

"Meaning, we do what we have to do to survive

because the alternative isn't a good one."

❧❧❧❧

Dillion and Skylar stepped onto the paved walkway. When they emerged from the wooded area, the sun was lower in the sky than Dillon expected. She'd thought the waning light was because of the heavy tree covering, but it had gotten later than she realized. She looked to the right and then the left. "I'm afraid I'm not a woods woman. I have no idea where we are. I thought we'd come out by the hotel."

Skylar smiled. "That would be a pretty good trick, since we walked almost a mile along the creek." Skylar pointed to the left. "I believe the hotel is probably about a mile back that way."

"Do I lose my butch points?"

Skylar laughed. "Naw, you can keep them. After all, you did bravely catch that frog."

"I still can't believe you wouldn't let me keep him."

"He had a wife and kids. You didn't want to take him from his family, did you?"

"How do you know he was a he?"

"I just know these things." Skylar took Dillon's hand. "Are you ready to go back?"

"Do we have to?"

"Afraid so." Skylar glanced at the sky. "Dinner's at seven. We've been out here longer than we intended."

"Shit, are we late?"

Skylar shook her head. "It's probably around six-thirty. We should make it back in time if we start walking instead of standing around talking."

Skylar started to take a step down the path and Dillon stopped her. "Wait."

Skylar stopped and turned back, a look of concern in her eyes. "Is something wrong?"

Dillon stepped forward and smiled. She put her hand on Skylar's elbow. "I just wanted to tell you that I had a really nice time this afternoon." Dillon's heart raced as she stared into Skylar's expressive eyes. "I know that's probably an inappropriate thing to say, considering the circumstances. But I just thought you needed to know."

Skylar rewarded Dillon with her killer smile; her dimples somehow seemed pronounced. Dillon tried not to stare at Skylar's lips as she spoke. "It's not inappropriate at all. It was a nice afternoon, all things considered." Before Dillon could respond, Skylar went on. "No, not all things considered. Regardless of the situation, it was a nice time. It's easy spending time with you."

"I'm sorry, again, for what happened the other night."

The twinkle left Skylar's eyes and her back stiffened. "That's done and over. We need to get back."

"Why do I always say the wrong thing to you? I'm afraid I'm not good with words."

Skylar looked at Dillon, but she didn't speak.

"I just mean I'd like to get to know you better."

Skylar's shoulders relaxed and she smiled. "Isn't that what we're doing?"

"Well, yeah." Dillon felt her face flush. "It's just I'd like to spend more time with you."

"Are you asking me on a date, Dillon Mitchell?"

Dillon fidgeted and looked away. "Yeah, I guess I am. Is it appropriate to date during an apocalypse?"

"I was going to ask if it was appropriate dating the person you're sharing a bed with."

"Oh God, I wasn't thinking about that." Dillon could feel the heat coming off her face.

Skylar smirked. "Relax. I'm just messing with you."

Dillon looked at Skylar and smiled. "So, is this a date?"

Skylar pursed her lips and looked to the sky, as if thinking. She looked back at Dillon and nodded. "Yeah, I'd call this a date. In fact, I'd call it a very nice date."

Skylar's words emboldened Dillon, who took a step forward. "Is this the end of our date then?"

Skylar gave Dillon a crooked grin. "Yeah, I think this is the end of our first date."

"Do you kiss on the first date?"

"Depends on whether I had a good time or not."

Dillon moved in closer and gently cupped Skylar's cheek with her hand. They looked into one another's eyes, but neither moved in closer. Finally, Skylar closed her eyes and moved against Dillon. Their lips lightly touched like a whisper, again and again. The kiss was soft and tender, just as their first date had been. Nothing rushed or hurried. Even though she found Skylar wildly attractive, she wouldn't let herself lose control again.

Dillon brought her lips to Skylar's a few more times before she drew Skylar against her body and wrapped her in a hug. Skylar laid her head against Dillon's chest and her arms encircled Dillon's waist. The hug was almost better than the kiss. Dillon felt the tension leave her body, as Skylar's body pressed against hers. She felt the muscles in Skylar's back relax, as well.

After several minutes, Dillon loosened her hold and pulled back to look into Skylar's eyes. She shivered when she saw the unguarded emotion burning there. Skylar blinked a couple times before she stepped away.

"Wow, I think I needed that more than I knew," Skylar said, putting her hand to her chest.

"Me too." The world was a scary place, but somehow, she'd been able to put it out of her mind when she was in the woods with Skylar.

"You know, we better get our butts moving, or we are going to be late for dinner."

Dillon took Skylar's hand. "Let's go."

Chapter Eight

Dillon put her hand on her stomach and groaned. "If I keep eating like this, I'm going to weigh a ton. But damn, that was good."

Dillon and Skylar had arrived back at the mansion with five minutes to spare. No one seemed to care about their late arrival, except for Katie, who'd shot them looks all evening.

Renee's group chose to serve tonight's meal on the balcony. Dillon suspected this would become where they'd eat most dinners. Despite its large size, the expanse maintained an intimate feel. A large reflective pool ran down the middle of the rectangular space, effectively cutting the area in half. There were four large tables in each corner, with four smaller tables near the pool. A set of double doors led into the mansion, where there were more tables set up for those who didn't want to be outdoors.

Being creatures of habits, Maria secured the same table they'd eaten at the night before. Dillon loved the location. The table was one of the large ones, situated on the left-hand side of the balcony near the railing. Before it got dark, the view from that vantage point was breathtaking. They sat four stories above the ground, which gave a panoramic view of the mansion's expanse. The lawn was perfectly manicured, but she knew it wouldn't stay that way much longer.

Their energy needed to be put into survival, not maintaining the lush grounds.

Earlier, Dillon had snapped a couple of pictures, wanting to remember what it looked like before it became overgrown. *Stupid,* but it gave her some semblance of peace. She never wanted to forget its original magnificence but feared it would fade quickly as their struggles increased. Dillon breathed in the smell of burning wood. They'd moved several state-of-the-art fire pits from the maintenance shed and installed them on the balcony. *Renee thought of everything.* The ambiance matched the five-star restaurants that Renee owned in LA.

Dillon glanced over the side rail, remembering the scene from the previous evening. Everyone had already been anxious, not knowing who or what was responsible for the deaths, so when Karen had driven an army jeep across the large expanse of lawn and only coming to a stop once she was underneath the balcony, panic ensued with everyone running for cover.

In the chaos, Tiffany and Diana had abandoned Cynthia, who'd been injured the night before. They'd run to safety, leaving Cynthia to fend for herself. Dillon, Skylar, and Jake came to Cynthia's rescue. Although it had turned out that there was no real danger, Cynthia had been hurt and angry at her friend's betrayal.

☙ ☙ ☙ ☙

Skylar admired Dillon as she stood at the end of the reflecting pool and delivered an update on the first Commission meeting. Dillon's voice remained steady, never giving away any underlying emotions. When questions were tossed her way, she answered with an easy smile and a twinkle in her eyes. Her muscular frame conveyed a sense of strength that was crucial during these times. Dillon exuded confidence. None of the women would suspect that she was struggling to come to grips with what happened three short days ago, but Skylar knew.

Watching Dillon in action gave Skylar hope. Skylar, more than anyone, understood the dangers that lurked outside the gates of the Whitaker Estate. With a community of just over thirty, they might have enough people to start over, but if they began splintering into factions, their likelihood of survival would diminish. Skylar had no illusions that things would be easy, but looking around at the faces of those listening to Dillon, she didn't think many of them understood the challenges ahead.

The delectable meal, along with the fine wine, gave everyone a false sense of well-being. She and Dillon had spoken in the woods about the fine line Dillon needed to walk between spelling out the reality of the situation, while not breaking spirits. So far Dillon seemed to have hit on the perfect balance. Everyone seemed to understand the urgency of getting to work on Commission priorities, without anyone panicking. They needed to take advantage of the calm because she doubted it would last long, once the grim reality set in.

Skylar held her breath when CJ stood to speak. *This was it.* Over dinner, they'd decided it was best for CJ to present her list of concerns, in order to allow Dillon to remain the strong positive leader.

"There are a couple things I would like to discuss," CJ said from the table.

As pre-arranged, Dillon smiled and said, "Why don't you join me up here, so we can be sure everyone hears you?"

A low murmur rose from the crowd while CJ made her way through the tables to join Dillon.

"The floor is yours." Dillon gestured with her hand and stepped back.

"Today, Anne and I were working with the computers, trying to locate more survivors. While doing so, we also did a little research. We suspect there's likely no one manning the power plants, which means we could begin to lose power at any time."

Skylar studied the crowd. She sensed some anxiety, but no outward panic.

The murmur in the crowd grew, so CJ spoke louder, and a hush fell over the group. "The good news is Whitaker was prepared and this entire place is set up with an amazing generator system, so our power supply shouldn't be greatly interrupted. Although, it's important we have a team that oversees and maintains the system."

"Hey, back off. That's Diana's job," Tiffany yelled from her table in the corner.

"I'm on it," Diana slurred and raised her glass before taking a large gulp.

"Of course," CJ said. They were apprehensive about Diana's role, but Anne and Cynthia offered assurances they could keep her in line. "I'm not concerned about our power; it is the rest of the area that I am speaking of."

Tiffany sat back in her chair, apparently appeased by the response.

"As everyone knows, we've been trying to reach

others. As the power around the country goes out, so does the Internet. Which effectively cuts us off from our means of communication. But rest assured, we have a solution. We found a wide assortment of Sat Phones in the museum along with ham radios."

"What the hell is a Sat phone?" someone called out.

"It's short for Satellite phone. Our hope is that others will pick up these methods of communication as the power grid fails. You might have remembered that Braxton Babcock's flunky mentioned having a Sat phone, as well."

So far, so good. Everyone seems to be taking the news well, which is what they'd hoped for. It was the next part of the conversation that needed to be sold without creating undo infighting.

On cue, Dillon stepped up. "You mean the power on the west coast is going to go out soon?"

"Afraid so, if it hasn't already in some places. Remember early on when we lost power and cell phone service? We still are unclear why it returned, but we suspect it will go out again," CJ answered. "But we should be fine here."

"What does that mean for the supply runs?" Dillon said, even though they'd already determined the answer earlier.

CJ turned and called across the balcony, "Anne, would you like to address that? I think you can explain it more eloquently than I can."

Perfect. Skylar smirked, but being outside of the action, no one paid attention. So far, their plan was working beautifully. They needed buy in, and more importantly help from all quarters if they were going to reach their goal. Everyone from their suite was prepared to go on the run, but that wouldn't be enough.

Anne stood up and smiled. She stayed standing at her table but spoke loudly so everyone could hear. "I believe we need to act quickly. Once the power is out, our job of gathering supplies gets much more difficult. Simple things like seeing inside of storerooms, opening doors, and operating some machinery gets much more complicated. Also, without refrigeration, much of the food will spoil, so we need to act quickly."

What Anne didn't say was that the stench from the decaying bodies would soon, if not already, make it nearly impossible for their mission to be successful. Once the power went out, they suspected the smell would worsen. After Karen's description of the accidents, downed planes, and fires in Los Angeles, there was concern with what they might find. They needed to retrieve as many supplies as possible before it became any more dangerous.

"What do you mean by quick?" Tiffany asked.

"I think we need to go first thing in the morning," Anne answered.

"We don't even know what the hell we need." Tiffany took a big gulp of her beer. "Can't we wait a couple weeks? We've got plenty of supplies here."

"Karen has it covered, babe," Anne said, putting her hand on Tiffany's shoulder.

"Whatever. I think it's stupid, so we're not going." Tiffany defiantly glared at Anne.

Skylar eyed Dillon, hoping she wouldn't let Tiffany get under her skin. They'd anticipated Tiffany's resistance; they just needed to keep her from influencing too many others. To accomplish what they wanted, they needed at least three groups with five to six people each. They couldn't afford for Tiffany to dwindle their pool of volunteers.

"Tiff, I really need to go," Cynthia said. "I want to set up a medical clinic and need supplies to do it."

"I thought the old dude thought of everything. Isn't all that shit over at the museum?"

"Surprisingly, the medical supplies were rudimentary, especially the medications. Probably back in the day, Whitaker kept a bigger stash, but the museum probably thought better of it. I went through all the displays, and they didn't have anything in them. They were just for show."

"Shit, are all the canned goods and boxed food real?" Someone called out.

"No worries," Renee said, standing up from her table. "All the food is real. We found information in the museum that once a year the food is donated to local food pantries and replaced. This means everything we found has plenty of shelf life. But we need to stockpile now, while we can. Plus, we need to think of growing our own, which will require seeds and other planting materials. I'd like to volunteer to head up the group that secures food supplies."

Cynthia raised her hand. "I've obviously got medical supplies."

"Cynthia, I think we should piggyback personal care supplies with your group," Karen said. "We'll need to go to many of the same places."

"Sounds good." Cynthia turned to Dillon. "And you need construction supplies?"

"Yep, I'll head up that group." Dillon gazed around the room. "Does anyone have any objections to Renee, Cynthia, and me putting together our own teams?"

Skylar felt her shoulders tighten, while she watched Tiffany from the corner of her eye. It appeared Anne was doing a good job of running interference, and Tiffany said nothing.

"Okay then—" Dillon started but was cut off by a voice.

"Why the fuck do you want to go to Los Angeles, when Santa Clarita isn't that far away?" Willa said.

"Great question," Dillon responded.

Wow, how did Dillon keep a straight face? The fire pits cast a strange glow on Willa's pink hair, making it look like her head was consumed by flames, while the light bounced off her various piercings, causing them to twinkle like fireflies. Skylar had to look away because the image was so disconcerting. She tuned back into what Dillon was saying.

"But there are a few compelling reasons. One, Los Angeles is much bigger and will likely have everything we need. Two, we can save the supplies in Santa Clarita for later since it is so much closer. And finally, since we are aware there are other airline passengers that landed around the same time as Karen, we might be able to make contact with other people."

"Who says we want to be in contact with others?" Willa said. "It could be dangerous."

❧ ❧ ❧ ❧ ❧

"Tomorrow is gonna come way too early," Cynthia said. She was tired and would have preferred to be in bed.

"No doubt." Dillon fumbled with the keys, trying to find the one that opened the maintenance barn. "I'm not sure why we keep locking this place;

there's nobody around to steal anything."

"Old habits." Cynthia pointed her flashlight at the lock. After Renee roped Skylar into helping with the food supply inventory, Cynthia readily volunteered to work with Dillon. She needed to get away from Tiffany and Diana for a bit. They'd been extremely drunk and belligerent during the meeting, but luckily hadn't generated enough resistance to stop the supply run, even though she'd forced them to compromise and let Willa and KC join the team.

"Finally," Dillon said, pushing the door open.

Dillon flipped on the lights, which illuminated the cavernous barn. Each bay contained a different vehicle type. Cynthia spotted what they were looking for in the third bay. They walked past landscaping equipment and tractors of various sizes, before they arrived at the section housing pickup trucks.

Dillon pointed to a black four-wheel drive truck. "I think we need one like that."

"You just want to drive that beast," Cynthia teased. "You probably can't even get in it."

"Hey now, are you making fun of my height?"

Cynthia laughed. "I could probably boost you up."

"Or you could get down on all fours, so I can use your back as a step."

"Sure, I'll think about it." Cynthia winked. "Seriously, do you want to drive that one?"

Dillon craned her neck and looked down the aisle toward the rest of the bays. "Let's see what else is in here. It looks like the vans are a couple bays down."

They didn't have to walk far to come to a section that housed ten vans of various sizes, from minivan up to one that seated sixteen people.

Cynthia approached the largest van and ran her hand over the highly polished hood. "Damn, this is gigantic. Looks like we could fit everyone that's going in this baby."

"But we probably don't want to." Dillon walked toward a smaller cargo van. "This one looks like it will carry ten people."

"Why not go in one?"

"We need the flexibility. You never know what might be out there. I think we need to take three."

"Fifteen of us, so five per vehicle?"

Dillon paused and her brow creased. "Hmmm, I guess with those numbers we wouldn't need to take a van, especially if we're going to get trucks at U-Haul."

Cynthia laughed. "Sorry, bad joke."

"Joke?" Dillon looked confused.

"U-Haul. Lesbian."

Dillon laughed. "Oh God, I must be tired. I completely missed the reference."

"Oh good, I was afraid you thought I was being inappropriate."

Dillon shook her head. "Inappropriate or not, we have to keep our senses of humor to get by."

They continued walking. Cynthia stopped at a large bay containing an assortment of electric cars. "How long before gas goes bad?"

"No clue, but I bet Tasha could tell us. She's a mechanic. Apparently, she's a wizard that can fix anything."

"Ah, okay. Good to know." Cynthia gestured at the cars. "We'll probably need these in the future."

"Good point." Dillon ran her hand over her face and rubbed her eyes, as they started walking again. "I think there's lots of things we aren't even thinking of that we'll need to do."

"Agreed." Cynthia stopped when she realized Dillon was no longer walking beside her. She turned. Dillon gaped at the bay of motorcycles they'd passed.

Dillon admired a sleek black bike and seemed oblivious to Cynthia's approach. "You ride?" Cynthia asked.

"Used to. It's been a while." Dillon knelt and ran her hand over the large chrome muffler. "Look at this beauty."

"I'm not a bike person, but that chrome is impressive."

"I think we should take a couple bikes."

"You volunteering?"

Dillon broke into a huge smile. "How'd you guess?"

"Do you think we have someone else that rides?"

"Maria does. She's a bad ass. Her riding skills put mine to shame."

"Then we probably only need a small van, since that knocks out four of you."

Dillon stood. "No, only two. Under the circumstances we'll need to ride solo. It's safer and makes it easy if we need to maneuver around things. If need be, Maria could do it with a passenger, but I'm rusty so I'm not comfortable with a passenger under the circumstances."

"So, we take one of the vans and one of the trucks?"

"Yeah, Maria and I can come back in the morning and pick our bikes."

Cynthia smiled. "Although, by the look in your eyes, I'm sensing you've already fallen in love."

"Afraid so, she's a beauty." Dillon ran her fingertips over the flames decorating the gas tank.

They turned and walked back toward the vans, neither speaking until Dillon broke the silence. "Hey, I forgot to ask you, why are the animals still alive?"

"Oh, you noticed?"

"Obviously." Dillon stopped in front of the van they'd chosen. "You've been thinking about it, haven't you? You just didn't want to say anything yet."

Cynthia smiled. "Busted. I want to see how pigs fared."

"Pigs?" Dillon's brow furrowed. "Wouldn't you want to check out apes or gorillas?"

"Possibly, but pigs are my first choice."

"Are you fucking with me?" Dillon laughed.

Cynthia shook her head. "No, seriously, I'm not. A pig's heart is the closest to a human than any other animal."

Understanding registered on Dillon's face. "So, since you think something went wrong with their hearts, you want to see if the same happened to the pigs."

"Exactly."

"Interesting. I suppose we better get these vehicles back, so we can get some sleep."

"You know tomorrow is going to be brutal. No telling what we're going to run into."

"No doubt. Do you think we're ready to deal with it?"

"Nope."

"Me neither."

Chapter Nine

The tension built as the group grew restless. The sun was barely creeping over the horizon, and there was still a slight nip in the air. Their faces were grim and there was little talking, as they waited for the last of the supply party to arrive.

Most had arrived early, to prepare for their mission. They'd run through Karen's checklist twice and finished the final preparations several minutes ago, so now they had nothing to do but wait. Some of those assembled took the opportunity to sort through the contents of the backpacks Karen's team had put together.

"What the fuck. Let's just leave without them," Maria said. "We don't have time for their shit."

Dillon glanced at her watch. "Let's give them five more minutes."

"Why? They're already ten minutes late."

"If we're down two drivers, it'll be two less trucks we'll be able to fill. The more we get now, the less likely we'll need to go back."

"Why did we have to let Tiffany's flunkies come anyway? They're just going to cause trouble."

Tasha sidled up to Maria, and gently rubbed her back. "Babe, I know it's frustrating, but we don't need to start out on the wrong foot."

"Here they come." CJ said, pointed toward the

mansion.

Willa Andrews and KC Jasper were making their way down the steps, carrying something between the two of them. Dillon couldn't make out what it was in the dim lighting.

Jake picked up his AK-47 and slung it over his shoulder. Dillon cringed. "Are you sure we need those?"

"Afraid so," he answered. "We don't know what we'll find out there. Better safe than sorry."

Out of the corner of her eye, she saw Skylar putting her gun into the front seat of the jeep. Jake, Tad, and Skylar would be the only ones carrying guns. Last night, a spirited debate raged over the use of weapons. Eventually, they decided only the three with experience would carry and ride shotgun in the three vehicles. The reference hadn't escaped Dillon.

After dropping off her weapon, Skylar made her way back to the group. She smiled as she approached Dillon and reached to straighten the collar of her jacket. "You look good in leather. The chaps are a bonus."

Dillon smiled and slowly turned in a circle. "It's been at least ten years since I've been decked out like this. I think I'm looking pretty butch."

In an exaggerated motion, Skylar looked at Dillon from head to toe. "And sexy, too."

Dillon felt her face flush. She knew Skylar was just teasing her, but it still affected her. "Thanks," Dillon mumbled.

"I just wish I was riding with you."

"That would be nice, but not a good idea today."

"I know." Skylar put her arm around Dillon and squeezed. "As long as you promise me a ride sometime when things calm down."

"I'd like that." Dillon hugged Skylar back. "Maybe we can take a ride around Lake Piru."

Before Skylar could answer, Renee's voice filled the air. "What the fuck do you think you're doing?"

Dillon turned to see who she was talking to. Willa and KC had arrived. They carried a cooler between them, and both had a beer in their other hand. Willa Andrews sported a spiked bright blue mohawk that stood nearly four inches, while the short hair on the rest of her head was dyed hot pink. If that didn't garner enough attention, the tattoos covering her neck and arms and the multiple piercings would. Willa was a talented independent filmmaker, who was creating a buzz in Hollywood. Dillon wondered if the outrageous look was a gimmick to get the right people to notice. The woman walking next to her, KC Jasper, was probably the one Dillon should ask, since she was Willa's publicist.

Since the Crisis began, they'd been two of Tiffany's biggest supporters. Dillon wasn't sure why they'd wanted to come on this mission since they'd been content doing little more than partying with Tiffany.

"Let's get this party started," Willa said, raising her beer to the sky.

"I'll drink to that." KC brought the bottle to her lips and guzzled nearly half.

"This is not a party, and you aren't taking that with us." Renee pointed to the cooler.

"Yeah, and who the hell are you to tell us what to do?" Willa stood up straighter and approached the shorter Renee.

Dillon stepped toward them before she spoke, hoping to look imposing in her motorcycle gear. "We're not having this discussion. Leave the beer or stay behind."

"Is that the Commission's orders?" Willa pretended to scan the crowd. "Can you make a Commission decision without all the members being present? I don't see Tiffany anywhere."

"Her choice," Renee said. "But the other five of us are here, and I can guarantee the vote would be unanimous."

"Fuck your vote," KC said, joining the conversation.

"Does that mean you're choosing not to go?" Dillon asked. She was getting tired of the conversation and wanted to get on the road.

KC and Willa looked at each other but didn't speak. Finally, they dropped the cooler and stalked off to the awaiting pickup truck.

Renee turned to CJ and Karen. "Sorry you have to deal with those two."

CJ smiled. "Jake's riding shotgun, maybe that'll keep 'em quiet."

❧❧❧❧

Dillon squeezed her legs against the metal and gunned the engine. It had been a long time since she'd ridden a motorcycle, but it was quickly coming back to her. She wanted to race ahead, just to feel the power of the bike, but knew she shouldn't.

Maria rode beside her and had a smile plastered on her face. The wind whipped through her black hair, causing it to fly out behind her. Dillon tried in vain to convince her to wear a helmet, but Maria insisted she needed to feel free. Hoping to appeal to Maria's commitment to her profession and the law, Dillon reminded her it was illegal to ride without a helmet. Maria laughed and said she'd take her chances. Dillon realized the absurdity of her argument. *Not like they would run into any cops.*

Dillon checked her mirror and could just make out Cynthia driving the truck behind them. She squinted, but the sun reflected off the windshield so she couldn't see Skylar sitting in the passenger seat. Behind the jeep, the two pickups followed close behind.

Since Karen and Nancy had come to the Estate from Los Angeles two days earlier, Dillon suspected they could find a clear path to the city. Although they reported some areas were nearly impassable, they'd obviously found their way around them. Dillon and Maria would be the scout team should they come upon a blocked road.

Both pickups were equipped with a winch, and the jeep had a hitch and was loaded with several chains should they need to remove an obstruction. Since the Crisis occurred sometime after midnight, they hoped the lighter traffic would make the trek easier.

Dillon was apprehensive about their decision to split up once they got to Route 170, especially since she would be separated from Skylar. It had been a contentious battle, but eventually Dillon relented. The three teams would each have different objectives. Cynthia and Skylar's team would break off from the pack first and head toward Cedars-Sinai Medical Center, which was one of the largest in Los Angeles. The other two teams would continue on Route 5 to the U-Haul center before splitting into two groups. Dillon would lead a small group to pick up building and gardening supplies, while Renee would head up the largest group, which would go in search of food.

Was this a mistake? She began to second guess their decision to go to Los Angeles when Santa Clarita held most of what they needed. Curiosity won out. The group wanted, or more likely needed, to see Los Angeles to wrap their minds around the enormity of the situation. She feared it would be a reality check they weren't prepared for.

Despite their meticulous plans, they needed to be prepared for the unexpected. Karen, who oversaw supplies, would use this experience as a trial run. She and her team would continue making smaller trips into Santa Clarita. They planned on commandeering as many trucks as possible to haul as much as they could.

Dillon had no idea how many people remained alive in LA. While Karen was there, three airplanes had landed safely at LAX, while scores of others hadn't been so fortunate. Possibly other planes arrived after Karen and Nancy left the airport, and some of those passengers likely could be roaming LA.

Even though Jake and Skylar were adamant about carrying weapons, Dillon suspected that most people would still be in shock and wouldn't be up for causing problems. Unfortunately, it would probably be a short window before lawlessness took over.

They'd agreed to avoid contact with others, if possible. Since the group was already splintering, they didn't need to bring more people into the mix. While it was tempting to have more help to share in the work that needed to be done to survive, it was too risky under the circumstances.

Dillon pushed the thoughts from her head and focused on the road ahead. It would take nearly an hour to get to where the groups would split off, so for now she wanted to enjoy the ride.

Her leathers kept her warm from the chill in the air. When they passed the spot they'd found the carload of dead teenagers, she shivered despite the protection from the cold. The thought of the teens brought Dillon back from the Zen she'd been experiencing while riding the bike.

They'd come across the crash site in the early morning hours after the Crisis when they'd traveled to Santa Clarita in search of survivors. Somehow, the tragedy of lost youth hit Dillon hard, so she was glad Cynthia had been with to share the burden. Being someone who experienced death in her profession didn't shield Cynthia from being shaken by their discovery.

With nearly four million people in Los Angeles, she couldn't wrap her mind around what that many deaths would look like. Maybe even more pertinent was what they would smell like. They'd packed gas masks in case the stench had already grown overpowering. *Stop.* She shook her head to clear it.

Dillon gazed off to her left at the Santa Susana Mountains. As they came closer to Santa Clarita, there were a few more stalled cars, but the roadways were relatively clear. Normally, the crisp mountain air would rejuvenate Dillon, but today it made her long for the past. The past, which ended three days ago. In the distance, she could make out the roller coasters from Six Flags Magic Mountain just outside of the city.

Maria revved her engine and sped out ahead of Dillon. She wanted to follow but something held her back. Maybe it was the security of knowing Skylar was just behind her, but soon Skylar would peel off, and they'd be out of contact for the next six to eight hours. CJ had rounded up Sat phones but only wanted to use them in case of an emergency. By the time they went their separate ways, they would end up over half an hour from each other, which made Dillon uneasy. Another thing she needed to push from her mind.

Too soon, they arrived at the point the group would split. So far, they'd not had to stop and move any vehicles off the road, but a couple times the pickups and jeeps were forced to travel through the ditch to make it around a pile of cars.

Dillon and Maria pulled to a stop near the off ramp, and the rest of the convoy pulled in behind them. Dillon turned off her bike and dismounted. Her legs and back were stiff, and she'd only been riding for an hour. More evidence of how long it had been since she had rode. When she approached the jeep, she hoped she wasn't as bow-legged as she suspected.

Skylar smiled when she got out of the jeep. "Hey cowgirl."

"Ugh, am I walking that bad?"

Maria came up beside Dillon and laughed. "Afraid so, old woman."

Dillon crinkled her nose and frowned.

"It's okay. You're still cute." Skylar put her arm around Dillon.

"Puppies are cute. I was going for studly." Dillon winked at Skylar.

"We'll pretend you're studly as long as you don't walk."

"How's it goin', pardner?" CJ said in her best John Wayne voice.

"You guys are so funny," Dillon said, pretending

to be irritated. "Do you think we can get back to the business at hand?"

Jake walked up with a serious look on his face. "Do you guys have a minute?"

"Sure, what's up?" Dillon asked.

"I think Tad and I need to switch groups."

Dillon laughed. "Very funny. So, you don't want to be seen with me either?"

"It's not that." Jake, who was usually quick with a smile, remained stoic. He glanced around and lowered his voice. "Those two are going to be trouble," he said, flicking his eyes toward Willa and KC.

"He's right," CJ said. "It was an excruciating drive. I felt like we had two mini-Tiffany's in the backseat."

"They certainly seem to have their heads up Tiffany's ass," Jake said. "I think they're up to something, and I don't want to put Tad in that position. He's a great kid and always been a leader with his peers, but I think they'll be too much for him."

"Definitely. They'd prey on him, and we don't need that shit," Dillon said. "Renee's group has a big enough job, without having to deal with a couple of idiots."

"Yep, I'll deal with them, so she won't have to. I'll let Tad know we're switching." Before walking away, he put his hand on Skylar's shoulder. "You've got all your ammo, right?"

Skylar nodded.

"Okay. You be careful out there, promise?"

"Would you guys stop worrying about me?" Skylar said. She gave Jake a quick side hug. "I've got this."

Jake flashed a smile and his eyes twinkled. "Okay

then. I'll see you in a few."

Dillon watched Jake walk away and smiled. They'd gotten lucky finding him and his family. He was a good man. In the few short days she'd known him, they'd already bonded. Between him and Tad, they'd have a good gene pool to start with. *Wow, where did that come from?*

"I suppose we can't stay here forever," Dillon said, taking Skylar's hand. "You know I don't like this."

"We're going to go check our equipment one more time," CJ said, putting her arm over Karen's shoulders. They walked away, leaving Dillon and Skylar alone.

Skylar smiled. "I'm afraid they won't win any acting awards, but it was sweet they gave us a minute."

"No doubt." Dillon looked into Skylar's eyes. "I just want to tell you…" Dillon caught movement out of the corner of her eye. "Oh, fuck."

Skylar's eyes widened. "What?"

"Sorry, here comes Katie. So much for alone time."

As Katie approached, she glanced at Skylar before turning her full attention to Dillon. She ran her hand over Dillon's leather sleeve. "Nice. Whitaker had expensive tastes. And you look fine in it."

Dillon tensed but didn't want to come off cold. For survival's sake, she knew a rift between her and Katie would be bad. She smiled and said in her most enthusiastic voice, "Big day. Are you ready for it?"

Katie beamed, seemingly not put off that Dillon ignored her compliment. "Ready as I'll ever be."

Dillon reminded herself that Katie was once her wife Jane's best friend, which entitled her to Dillon's compassion. She just wished Katie would accept that she wasn't interested in a romantic relationship.

"I'm sure we're in for a jolt, but hopefully we can get in and get out," Dillon said. "I need to go have a word with Cynthia and Maria before we take off. Can you let CJ know I'll be there in just a minute?" Dillon smiled, hoping Katie wouldn't feel dismissed, even though that was her intention.

"Certainly," Katie said. She ran her hand over Dillon's chaps, licked her lips, and squeezed her thigh. "I just wish I could ride with you."

"It's not safe," Dillon said, taking a step back. "Don't forget to let CJ know I'll only be a minute." Not waiting for a response, Dillon took Skylar's hand and turned toward the jeep.

"Unbelievable," Skylar said under her breath.

"I know. Don't let her get to you." Dillon picked up the pace to put distance between them and Katie.

Cynthia leaned against the jeep's fender, clipboard in hand. Her focus was so complete she didn't hear them approach, so she jumped when Dillon said her name.

"Sorry, didn't mean to scare you," Dillon said. "What's Dr. Frankenstein cooking up over here?"

Cynthia smiled and held up her clipboard. "Just going over our list one more time to make sure we haven't forgotten anything."

"She's been over it three times already," Skylar said to Dillon. "She made me read it aloud on our drive."

"Bummer, so sad I missed it. I'm sure it was riveting."

"It was like listening to a bedtime story," Skylar said. "Tasha fell asleep before we hit Lake Piru."

Cynthia laughed. "Come on, it wasn't that bad."

Skylar grinned. "Seriously, did you add anything else?"

Cynthia handed her the list. "Just a couple things. Hopefully, you'll know where to find them."

Skylar's eyebrows raised slightly, but they quickly returned to normal. She nodded and flipped through the pages. "Yeah, I'm pretty sure I know where to find most everything."

Cynthia looked at Dillon. "Skylar is going to save us so much time, since she's familiar with Cedars-Sinai. With only four of us, we're going to need to hustle."

Skylar looked at the list again. "No worries. I'm betting we finish early. My goal is to hit a couple of the clothing stores in the area, especially that cool place that only sells scrubs."

"God, I'd kill for some scrubs," Cynthia said.

"They make them in your size?" Dillon winked at Skylar. "Or do you just wear waders?"

"It's sad when short people are bitter and jealous," Cynthia said, pretending to ignore Dillon while she talked directly to Skylar. The corner of her mouth turned up slightly. "I'll probably have to buy the unisex ones."

Dillon laughed. "Do you think they take credit cards?"

Cynthia looked at her blankly, until the light bulb came on. "Wow. Old habits die hard. I guess I won't be buying them, will I?"

"It's a pretty big store. I think we'll find some that'll fit your figure." As she spoke, Skylar's hands moved as if outlining a curving body.

Dillon tried to hide her smirk when Cynthia

blushed, but she was unsuccessful.

"Don't you have a motorcycle to ride, or something?" Cynthia flipped her hand as if to dismiss Dillon.

"Fine," Dillon said. "I know when I'm not wanted." Dillon's face suddenly turned serious. Her gaze met Cynthia's. "You guys be careful."

"We'll be fine," Cynthia said, brushing off the concern.

"Seriously," Dillon persisted. "Be careful and don't take any chances. If you see anything suspicious, there's always UCLA's Medical Center, or the hospital in Santa Clarita." When neither Cynthia nor Skylar responded, Dillon continued. "I mean it. No heroics. Tonight, just the three of us are going to sneak down to the library with a bottle of wine. I want to hear all about your day."

"It's a deal." Cynthia pulled Dillon toward her, and they bumped chests in the move that had become their signature hug over the last three days. "I'm going to make sure Maria is set before we take off."

Cynthia walked off, leaving Dillon alone with Skylar.

Dillon pushed a piece of hair out of Skylar's eyes.

"Stop looking at me that way. And stop worrying," Skylar said. "I've got my gun, and I know how to use it."

Dillon cringed. *Not reassuring.*

Skylar crinkled her nose. "That didn't help, did it?"

"Not exactly."

"You can't be worrying about us. You need to stay alert. If you're distracted, it's dangerous. Are you listening to me?" Skylar scowled and pointed at

Dillon's chest. "I want you to come back safe too."

Dillon slowly nodded. "Fair enough."

"Give me a hug, then get out of here," Skylar said, stepping into Dillon's arms.

Chapter Ten

Dillon missed Maria riding beside her. When she looked into her mirror and saw only the two pickups, her heart clenched. Skylar's words came back to her. She knew she needed to focus on what she was doing, or she might miss something important. She took a deep breath and realized the morning air had begun its warm up.

It wouldn't be long before their caravan reached the U-Haul center in Burbank, where the two groups would split. Dillon regretted she couldn't help Jake and Renee with Willa and KC, but it was impractical. She was the only one who knew what building materials she needed. Her crew was small – CJ, Karen, and Tad – but the lists were developed strategically, so they could split up and get more done.

Even though she'd located several home improvement stores along the route, she hoped they could get what they needed in the first stop or two. This would give them extra time, so CJ could raid the nearby computer stores.

Despite the plan being developed with Jake in mind, she was confident Tad could get the job done. She felt sorry for the seventeen-year-old, who was being forced to grow up way too fast. There would be no college parties and the typical teenage mistakes. In three days, he was already being asked to take on adult responsibilities. It was a tribute to his upbringing that he rose to the challenge, but she knew it would likely be a struggle. She'd developed a soft spot for him, so she was happy to have him on her team.

She downshifted when she banked into the off ramp. The trip into Burbank had taken longer than planned because they'd been forced to remove several cars that had blocked their path. They'd considered backtracking and going around but had decided having a clear path in and out of Los Angeles might prove valuable in the future. Only once did they have to go around a section of the highway because of five tractor trailers mangled together under an overpass.

They'd moved quickly, intentionally avoiding looking into the cars, after Katie had made the mistake of opening the door of the first car they moved. She'd screamed and ran to the side of the road, losing her breakfast. Dillon kicked the door shut, hoping to block out the stench.

Katie was even more pale than usual when she had returned. Dillon had noticed some of the contents of her stomach had landed in her long blond hair, but before she had reacted, Renee was there to wipe it off. Dillon had breathed a sigh of relief, glad that Renee had been there to comfort Katie.

Finally feeling in control of her motorcycle, Dillon intentionally fishtailed when she turned into the U-Haul lot. Her eyes scanned the lot, as she counted the trucks. *Perfect, there were more than enough.* Her group would need two trucks and Renee's planned on taking five.

She pulled up near the office door and cut her engine. With a flick of her foot, she pushed down the kickstand and hopped off. She doubted the door would be unlocked, but she tried it anyway. *No luck.*

The others parked the pickups and piled out. A loud voice drew her attention.

"I don't give a fuck whether you want to ride together or not," Renee shouted.

Here we go. Dillon turned and immediately spotted Willa's blue hair bobbing as she talked.

"Who the fuck put you in charge?" Willa shouted.

Great. Dillon casually walked toward the group. "What's going on over here?" she asked, keeping her voice casual.

Willa stammered before shouting. "And what the fuck's your problem?"

"No problem here." Dillon raised her hands with her palms out. "Just came over to see what trucks we want to take."

"KC doesn't want to drive one of those big ass trucks, so she's riding with me." Willa glared at Renee.

"I don't blame you for being scared," Dillon said to KC. "I remember how terrified I was driving one for the first time."

"Who says I'm afraid?" KC glared at Dillon.

"Whoa, sorry, my mistake. I thought that's what Willa meant." Dillon sighed and hoped her face conveyed longing. "I'm bummed I don't get to take one out for a spin, since there's no traffic to fight. A rare thing in LA. Hey, you don't ride a motorcycle, do you?"

"No! Why?"

"Never mind, I'm just being stupid. I thought maybe you and I could trade; I'd love to be able to fly down Highway 5 with one of those." Dillon pointed at one of the biggest trucks for emphasis.

"That would be a rush, wouldn't it?" Renee said, joining the conversation. "But I'm driving the pickup."

Dillon tried to hide her smile; obviously Renee had picked up her cue. Nothing like a little Tom Sawyer trickery to get what you wanted. "Hey, maybe KC would trade with you. At least you could drive one since I can't."

"That would be awesome," Renee said, her eyes lighting up.

"Now I'm jealous," Dillon said. "You don't happen to ride motorcycles, do you?" Out of the corner of her eye, Dillon caught KC staring but continued talking as if she didn't notice. "What a trip it would be to have the open road in front of you with one of those."

"No doubt," Renee answered. "Living in Los Angeles, there's not much chance for gunning it on an open road like that."

"Back off," KC said. "You're not taking my truck. Either of you."

"Aw, come on," Renee said. "You didn't want to drive one anyway."

"Bullshit, I want that one." KC pointed at the truck Dillon pretended to eye earlier.

"What the fuck," Willa said, grabbing KC's arm. "You said you were riding with me."

"Not anymore." KC marched away toward her truck with Willa chasing behind.

Dillon stifled a laugh, until they were out of earshot. "Wow! I am so sorry you'll have to deal with that all day."

"No worries," Renee answered. "Thanks for bailing me out. I was ready to throttle them."

"I doubt if it'll last long, but at least you'll have

the full complement of trucks."

Jake walked up with a huge smile on his face. "Look what I found." He held up a handful of keys.

"How'd you get in?"

"I think that friend of yours used to be a lockpick in a former life."

Dillon laughed. "CJ has all kinds of mad skills."

"No, not CJ, Katie."

Dillon's eyes widened. "Katie, seriously? Impressive. Definitely something I wouldn't have guessed."

"Hey, where is everyone?" Renee asked.

"Pitstop." Jake pointed to the building.

"Smart. I think I'll join them," Dillon said.

"Me too." Renee motioned toward KC and Willa. "Jake, you've got babysitting duty."

Jake groaned.

※※※※

Dillon gave Tad a thumbs up before pulling out of the lot. He tried to play it cool as he waved from behind the wheel of the twenty-six-foot truck, but his smile gave him away. She gunned the bike and skidded onto the road. The front wheel lifted slightly off the ground before she pushed it down, causing the tire to grip the surface. Shooting ahead, she scanned the streets, searching for the best path. The last thing they wanted was to be forced to turn two trucks around in limited space because of a blocked street.

As she suspected, the main thoroughfare was passable; it was the exits and side streets where they would most likely hit a snag. The trucks were tiny spots in her mirror when she roared into the exit. She followed the curve around until she saw the intersection just beyond the ramp. She braked hard when she arrived at the massive collision that blocked the intersection. *Fuck!*

If they had to go to the next exit and circle back, it would take them quite a distance out of their way. Besides, there were no guarantees another exit would be any clearer. Dillon surveyed the scene. A bus and semi had hit head on in the middle of the intersection, blocking part of the right lane. The semi-trailer had spun around, taken out a traffic light, and filled the entire left lane. A crumpled car pressed against the side of the trailer.

In the rest of the right lane, an SUV had struck the other traffic light, and a tiny red sports car had rammed into the side of it. If they removed those two vehicles, she determined the two trucks should be able to pass through.

Dismounting her motorcycle, she flipped open the saddlebags and lifted out the backpack Karen had given her. She pulled out a gas mask and tightened it around her face before she slid protective gloves over her hands. She squared her shoulders and made her way toward the two cars that could most easily be moved.

She approached cautiously, then chastised herself. *Stupid.* It wasn't like anyone would jump out at her. She just needed to get in, throw the car into neutral, and get out. Then Karen should arrive with the pickup to tow them out of the way.

She went to the flashy red sports car first; for some reason it seemed like a safer bet. She took a deep breath before she lifted the door handle. When the door popped open, she tried not to look at the gray-haired gentleman sitting in the driver's seat.

She reached over him and pushed the gearshift into neutral and slammed the door shut.

So far so good. The truck engines slowed as they made their approach to the exit ramp. Butterflies danced in her stomach as she walked toward the SUV. Her pace quickened. *Just get it over with.* She grabbed the handle and pulled. Adrenaline coursed through her body, so the door flew open harder than she'd expected. In her surprise at the errant door, she looked directly at the woman who was once driving. Dillon jerked her head away, not wanting to look at the eyes that stared sightlessly at her. She realized her mistake when her eyes landed on the two car seats in the back. *Oh shit, twins.* She felt her stomach lurch and she stumbled back from the SUV.

The door was still open. She needed to close it, so she didn't have to look at the babies anymore. They were nearly the same size. One dressed in bright yellow, the other blue. *How old were they?* They couldn't have been more than six months old, if that. She needed to get the car in neutral and close the damned door. She peeled her eyes away from the backseat and reached for the gearshift.

The woman was slumped over just enough to make it difficult to move the gearshift. Dillon closed her eyes and pushed the woman back, hoping to give her a clear shot at putting the car in neutral. She opened her eyes and peered inside. The woman leaned against the back of her seat, no longer blocking the gearshift. With the last of her resolve, Dillon shoved the SUV into neutral and jumped back as if it had bitten her. She slammed the door, back-peddled away, and didn't stop until getting twenty feet away.

"What are you doing?" Karen yelled from across

the intersection.

"Just getting the cars into neutral, so you can pull them out. It's the only way we can get the trucks through."

"Are you okay?"

"Yeah, I'm fine." Dillon lied. "I just want to keep moving. Pull the truck over here. We'll move this one first." She pointed toward the SUV but didn't look at it.

෪෪෪෪

Dillon wanted to throttle down and speed away from the haunting images. At least there were a couple positives: they'd been able to get the trucks around the wreckage, and she hadn't puked. Relief washed over her when she spotted the bright orange sign of the home-improvement store.

She had two hopes. One, that they'd find no one in the store, and two, they could get everything they needed here. The thought of going into a second store seemed overwhelming, and she'd not been in the first one yet. Being in the city gave her an uneasy feeling.

The trucks pulled in behind her, and she motioned them to follow. She led them to the back of the store where the docks were. Hopefully, they could find a couple forklifts to make the job easier. Of the four docks, only one had a truck pulled up to it, which would make things easier on them.

CJ eased her truck into one of the empty bays. After several attempts, Tad was able to do the same. He emerged from the cab, his cheeks red with embarrassment.

"You did great," Dillon said. "When I first

started driving, I wouldn't have been able to back a car into that spot, let alone a huge truck."

"Thanks," he mumbled.

"At least we don't have to break in," CJ said, moving toward the open dock door.

"Careful, that probably means someone was unloading the truck," Karen said.

"Fuck," Dillon said when she entered behind CJ. Two men were off to the left, lying on their sides on the floor. Dillon peeked into the trailer. "Looks like they hadn't started unloading either."

"What's in it?" Karen asked, approaching.

"Wow, it's full of lumber. This just saved us a boatload of time. Can one of you drive a big rig?" *Really! Is this who I've become?* Two men laid dead on the ground, and she coveted their load. She knew she was being practical, but dead people on the ground had become commonplace already. Unfortunately, this would probably be their new normal for a while.

"You better ask the Texas girl, this city girl is already freaking out driving the twenty-six-footer," CJ said, running her hand through her hair.

"What are you asking me?" Karen said, approaching them. She walked past them carrying a large tarp and reverently draped the tarp over the two bodies.

Maybe there was hope. Karen hadn't forgotten her humanity. Dillon took note. Being a leader meant doing what had to be done to survive, but it didn't mean being an unfeeling robot. Leadership still needed compassion.

"Thank you." Dillon smiled at Karen and nodded her head in the direction of the bodies. "CJ says you can drive this monster."

"CJ doesn't know what she's talking about. I'm a farm girl, not a truck driver. Can't you drive one?"

"Yeah, when I first started my business, I did it all. I'm afraid I can't drive a truck and a motorcycle at the same time."

"We can load the bike in the back of one of the trailers," CJ said. "Maybe one of the others can either drive the bike or the truck when we meet up."

"Let's do this, so we can get out of here," Dillon said.

ﷺﷺﷺ

Jake gritted his teeth. *Why did I volunteer for this shit?* If Willa and Renee didn't end up in a fist fight before this was all over, he'd be amazed. He'd finally gotten them separated after the second yelling match in the past fifteen minutes. At this rate, they'd never make it to the three stores they'd intended. Their goal was to fill six trucks with food, so they would need to be efficient, but with Willa and KC he feared it would put the bulk of the work on the rest of the crew.

After Willa and KC stomped off, he cautiously approached Renee. "Hey, do you have a second?"

"Not really," she snapped.

"What are you thinking, Jake?" Katie said. She nervously looked at Renee, who focused on the box of meat she worked on.

"I know they're useless pains in the asses, but without food, we're screwed. This might be the most important mission there is, so we can't let them cause us to fail."

Renee snapped her head up. "So, what are you saying? That I'm fucking things up?"

Katie lightly put her hand on Renee's arm. "That's not what he's saying. We need you, so you can't let them get under your skin." Renee's shoulders dropped and the tightness in her jaw relaxed.

Renee gave Katie a smile, but it faded when she looked at Jake. "Fine, what do you propose?"

"Katie's right. You're the expert, and we need you. We know we can't count on them, so we give them a truck to fill, without expectation. The rest of us divide up your lists and get to it."

"I know you're right. They just piss me off." Despite the red face, Renee finally smiled at him.

"I promise, I'll do my best to keep them away from you. But I can't make any guarantees."

"Come on, girl. Don't let them get to you," Katie said in her extra perky voice. The voice he'd seen Dillon run from, but it seemed to work on Renee.

Renee's genuine smile transformed her entire face.

"Okay." Renee squeezed Katie's arm. "If Jake keeps them away, and you stay with me, I can do this."

"All righty then." Katie smiled and looked at Jake. "You know what to do."

"I'm on it."

Jake headed to the back of the store. Sid and Dee had made a beeline to the storeroom, which was a great plan. They could quickly load up the boxes still on pallets, without being slowed down by having to repackage goods that were already on the shelves. The crew would still need to pick some items off the shelves, but hopefully it would be minimal.

Dee was atop the forklift, moving a large pallet toward the awaiting trailer. Sid examined a wrapped pile of boxes. She nodded as she looked at her list and marked a large X on the outside before moving to the next.

"How's it going?" Jake asked.

"Great," Sid answered. "I think if we hit three or four stores, we should be able to get all of the canned and dry goods we need in back."

"That'll make things so much easier. It'll give us more time to help Renee and Katie with the fresh stuff. Have you seen Willa and KC?"

"Oh yeah." Sid rolled her eyes. "The Bobbsey Twins were here a few minutes ago. They took a bunch of boxes and a couple hand carts."

"Wow, surprising. At least they're doing something."

"Probably loading up on chips and candy."

Jake laughed. "As long as they stay away from Renee, they can do whatever they want."

"No doubt. I have no problem working harder if it means not having to deal with those two."

"I agree. I'm going to grab some boxes and a forklift and see if I can load up the fresh food that Renee and Katie are sorting through."

"Thank God we have Renee. I'm sure she'll know how to freeze, can, or preserve most of that stuff, so it'll last us awhile."

Chapter Eleven

Cynthia looked down at her hands that clenched the steering wheel. Her white knuckles reminded her that she gripped it much too tightly. She took a deep breath, hoping to steady her nerves. They were going further into Los Angeles than the others, so they had been traveling carefully. The further into the city they went, the more edgy she became. She was comforted when she glanced at Skylar sitting ready, with a machine gun in hand.

Good lord. When did she become someone that was comforted by someone holding a deadly weapon? It amazed her how quickly circumstances could change someone.

Skylar's eyes were intense and alert. Her gaze shifted from right to left, not once looking at Cynthia. Cynthia was convinced that scouring for danger wasn't a new experience for Skylar. *Odd thought. Where did that come from?* Now wasn't the time to analyze herself or Skylar. She needed to keep her guard up.

It took much more time than they'd expected to get to the hospital because of the blocked roads. They were driving slowly, while Maria went ahead to find alternative routes. The further downtown they went, the more crowded the roadways were. Many cars had jumped the curbs and crashed into the storefronts. It would have been a looters paradise had there been any people left.

Cynthia steered around two cars blocking her lane and avoided looking into their windshields. She came to a crossroad and on instinct slowed and looked both ways. She braked when she saw heavy smoke blanketing the street. Squinting, she was able to make out the fire that burned probably two blocks away.

"Fuck, is that a plane?" Skylar pointed down the street.

"Holy shit," Tasha said from the backseat. "Karen said there were several downed planes. I never thought what that would look like."

Cynthia cringed. Images of 9-11 flooded her brain. *Was this what it was like to be at ground zero?* She felt tears welling in her eyes. The realization that every city across the US, possibly the world, had scenes just like this one threatened to immobilize her.

Skylar reached out and put her hand on Cynthia's knee. "You okay?"

Cynthia's eyes met Skylar's compassionate gaze, and she felt grounded again. She took a deep breath before answering. "Yeah, thanks."

"Hard to see, isn't it?"

Skylar understood. It freed Cynthia to be honest, to be vulnerable. "Just when I think I have my mind wrapped around what we're dealing with, I'm reminded that I'm not even close. I saw all the plumes of smoke rising up from the city when we drove in, but somehow I didn't register what it meant."

Tasha pointed at the fire rising along the side of one of the buildings in the distance. "If that building topples before the fire peters out, it's gonna keep spreading. Do you think there will be anything left of LA in a week?"

Skylar's eyes were riveted to the scene. Without turning, she said, "Please, Cynthia, let's go."

Cynthia let up on the brake. "We've got a job to do, and Maria is going to wonder where the hell we are."

They'd just begun moving when Maria came speeding around the corner, waving her arm and frantically motioning them to go back.

"What's she doing?" Tasha said and leaned forward, trying to see out of the front windshield.

"Looks like she wants you to turn around." Skylar gripped her gun tighter.

Cynthia slammed the jeep into reverse and turned the steering wheel hard to the left. The jeep instantly spun in a circle, so they were facing the direction they'd just come. Maria shot around them and motioned for them to follow. Maria increased her speed, so Cynthia hit the gas.

At the next intersection, Maria took a right-hand turn and sped down the nearly empty street, weaving around the few cars that littered the roadway. She went several blocks before she took another right and pulled to the curb. Cynthia eased up beside her and rolled down her window.

"What the hell's going on?" Cynthia asked.

Maria's hard-set jaw and furrowed brow added to the tension. "Sorry, didn't mean to scare you."

"Baby, you okay? You look like you saw a ghost," Tasha said.

"Now I'm embarrassed. I think I'm just getting jumpy."

"What happened?" Cynthia asked.

Color returned to her face, in the form of a blush. "There were about ten guys hanging out back there. I don't think they saw me, but something about them gave me the creeps."

"What were they doing?" Cynthia asked, concerned about what she may have seen.

Maria let out a nervous chuckle. "Nothing."

"Nothing?" Tasha said.

"Yeah, dumb, huh? I rode away like a bat out of hell and scared the shit out of you guys, and they weren't doing anything. What the hell is wrong with me?"

Cynthia's heart went out to Maria. From the impression Dillon gave her, Maria was a tiger in the courtroom and she wasn't one to spook easily. "Always listen to your gut. It's never failed me. If something felt wrong, it felt wrong. Don't second guess yourself."

Maria smiled. "Thanks, Doc."

"Seriously, never apologize for putting everyone's safety first." Cynthia felt she needed to stress this to Maria. They couldn't afford any one of them getting machismo because a mistake could be deadly.

"You're right." Maria visibly relaxed. "Looks like we'll need to take a different route to get to the hospital."

❧❧❧❧

"We rock," Dillon said and slammed the door on the trailer and latched it. Her shoulder muscles relaxed. Getting this job done eased some of the tension.

"Just under two hours," CJ said. "Gives us plenty of time to hit the tech stores."

"Oh goody." Dillon rubbed her hands together,

feigning excitement.

Karen slid up next to CJ and wrapped her arm around her waist. "She's sexy when she gets her geek on."

"Sure, I'll take your word for it." Dillon called out, "Hey, Tad. You did a great job. We couldn't have done it without you."

Tad beamed and looked down at the ground. "Thanks. What do you need me to do next?"

"We're gonna go a little further into town. There's a few electronics stores that CJ wants to check out. We'll leave the two full trucks here. Do you want to drive the other truck or the pickup?"

"Do you mind if I drive the truck?"

"Catch." CJ tossed the keys toward Tad.

He snatched them out of the air with his mitt of a hand, his smile broad.

"I'm gonna take the bike, so you love birds will be alone in the pickup," Dillon said. "Behave yourselves; we have a job to do."

"Weren't you listening? She thinks I'm sexy when I'm geeking out." CJ raised her eyebrows several times.

"Stop! You're making me queasy." Dillon shook her head and turned away.

Their job so far had been easy, but Dillon wasn't sure what they'd find when they went further into LA. From where they were, they could see several points where smoke billowed into the sky. It was a sight they'd seen many times with the wildfires that ravaged California, but she'd never seen it coming from downtown Los Angeles.

Her mind shifted to Skylar and she felt her stomach lurch. She'd tried to focus on the task at hand, so she didn't worry about Skylar and the rest of her friends. Now they were back in the forefront of her mind. She was having trouble shaking the uneasy feeling that gnawed at her.

"Hey, are you listening to me?" CJ asked.

"Huh?"

CJ frowned. "Are you ready to go?"

"What? Yeah. Sorry." Dillon glanced one last time at the tarp where the fallen bodies laid. *Should we do something with them?* She wasn't sure what they could do, so she turned away, fighting her discomfort.

⚜⚜⚜⚜

"Un-fucking-believable," Renee said.

"We need to move on to the next store." Katie stepped in front of Renee.

Again, Jake was grateful for Katie. They'd been hard at work for nearly two hours, Willa and KC forgotten. He wished he could say that now.

Willa and KC sat on the bumper of Willa's truck with their feet up and drank a beer. Luckily, they were across the parking lot, so Renee would have time to cool down.

"What the fuck have they been doing?" Renee said under her breath.

"They've been out of our way, so does it matter?" Jake asked.

"What if they're too drunk to drive?"

"It's not like there's anyone on the road they can hurt." Katie offered. "We'll make them drive ahead of everyone, just in case."

"Do you think they've loaded anything? Or have they been sitting out here the whole time?" Renee asked

Sid put her hand on Renee's shoulder. "We saw them moving boxes."

"And we only gave them Willa's truck to load. We've been handling the rest. Just ignore them," Dee said.

Renee took a deep breath. "Fine. Jake, you're going to have to get them moving." Renee turned and went to the pickup. She got in, turned over the engine, rolled down her window, and turned the music up loud.

Jake trudged across the parking lot, muttering under his breath. *Calm. Calm.*

༄༅༄༅

Cynthia glanced at her watch; they needed to make up time. With their multiple detours and a stop along the way at a drugstore, they were behind schedule. Luckily, the U-Haul lot was only about five minutes from Cedars-Sinai, where she hoped they could find most of the supplies they needed.

She fired up the engine of her fifteen-foot truck, while Tasha did the same. Originally, they'd planned on taking two of the larger trucks, but after the nerve-wracking trek across the city, they settled on the smaller ones. Medicine and medical supplies weren't large or bulky, so there should be plenty of space in the faster, more maneuverable vehicles. They spoke of needing to be able to drive around the stalled cars on their path, but no one mentioned the possibility of having to outrun danger. The reality was in the forefront of Cynthia's mind, but she chose to keep it to herself.

Cynthia followed, as Skylar led the way. Having been a nursing student for the past two years, Skylar knew her way around the sprawling Medical Center, which would be invaluable if they were to regain the time they'd lost.

Skylar brought the jeep to a stop in front of the ER. When she stepped onto the pavement, she had her gun firmly in hand. Tasha pulled in behind Cynthia, and Maria rode her motorcycle near the entrance.

Taking a deep breath, Cynthia opened the truck door. It concerned her that Maria and Tasha wouldn't be prepared for what they might encounter. With Skylar's training as a nurse, Cynthia had confidence she would be better equipped. The others were going to stores that should have been closed when the Crisis happened, so there should be few to no people in them. Hospitals, however, never closed, which meant there would be dead bodies inside.

"Are we ready for this, ladies?" Maria asked.

"Where's your backpack?" Cynthia said.

"In the jeep, why?"

Skylar had a knowing look on her face. Cynthia waited for Tasha to join them before she answered. "We need to put our gas masks on."

Maria looked around at the buildings. "I don't see any fires. We didn't use them back there. Why would we want to wear them here?"

"They aren't for smoke." Cynthia pulled her mask from her bag and pulled on the straps to adjust them.

"What the hell are they for then?" Before anyone could answer, Maria said, "Oh God."

"There's probably many people inside. We need to get all the first aid supplies, medical equipment, and medications that we can. There will likely be patients and medical personnel near where these things are located." Cynthia struggled to keep her voice matter of fact. The others needed her to remain calm.

"Got it," Maria said. She opened the door to the jeep and grabbed her backpack.

They helped one another secure their masks, pulling the straps tight to ensure an adequate seal. Cynthia pulled out the lightweight Tyvek coveralls and heavy-duty latex gloves from her backpack. Despite Maria and Tasha's complaints, Cynthia insisted they don all the equipment.

Cynthia knew the smell of death, but she questioned how she would handle this level of carnage. There were over eight hundred beds in Cedars-Sinai, and she suspected thousands of employees. The electricity seemed to be out in many parts of the city, but she hoped the hospital had been spared. The warmer temperatures would speed decomposition, only exacerbating the stench.

"We need to get in and out as quickly as possible," Cynthia said. "I won't lie to you. It's gonna be bad in there. If at any time you need to leave, just go. We'll all understand."

The others greeted her words with nods, but nobody spoke. Maria nervously shifted from foot to foot, while the other two stood rigidly at attention.

"We want to raid as many of the supply cabinets as possible. The medicine in the ER and OR will be critical. We can get basic medications anywhere else, but the heavy-duty pain medications and anesthetics we'll need to find here."

"We need to just get our asses in there before I crawl outta my skin," Maria said.

"Okay, let's roll." Cynthia said, sounding more confident than she felt.

The doors swished open when they approached. *Good sign. Power is still on.* A blast of air hit them when they entered. A fetid smell hit her senses, but it had to be her imagination since they wore masks.

Cynthia steeled herself, knowing the others would take her lead. Her gaze surveyed the scene. *Friday night. Full moon. After midnight.* The nearly full waiting room made sense, especially when she looked at the patrons. They were mostly young, with a couple families sprinkled in. She wondered what their stories were but quickly pushed those thoughts from her mind.

Skylar moved into the room, but Maria and Tasha stood just inside the door, not moving. Cynthia had witnessed fear and grief many times on the faces of her patients and their loved ones, but this was different. Despite the masks covering most of their faces, the look in their eyes could only be described as horror.

Cynthia had only seen looks this intense one other time in her life. Late one evening, when she had been out for a jog, screams and gunshots rang out. Fifteen minutes later, she found herself aiding the fallen. She later learned that a lone gunman had opened fire on a crowd of people waiting to attend a free outdoor concert in the park. The same looks she'd seen then were on her friend's faces. At least here, there was little blood to add to the shock.

"Maria and Tasha, I need your help," Skylar said in a distorted voice.

Cynthia flinched and spun around before she realized her mistake. The voice diaphragm from the mask Skylar wore gave her voice an eerie quality.

Maria shifted her gaze away from the waiting room and shook Tasha's shoulder. "Come on, Skylar needs our help."

"I'm gonna get these two set up cleaning out the supply room, then I'll be back to help you," Skylar said.

Cynthia nodded.

ॐॐॐॐ

Jake smiled as he pushed the last box into the remaining space on the truck. He was covered in sweat but felt good about what they'd accomplished. These women were workers, all but two of them, but luckily, Willa and KC had made themselves scarce. A couple times, he'd thought of checking on them but decided it was better not to know. He'd have plausible deniability should Renee ask.

"Did we get everything?" Jake asked.

Renee flipped through her list once more before answering. "And then some."

"Shall we celebrate?" Katie reached into the box she carried and held up a pint of ice cream. "I've got an assortment of flavors." She dug around and held up spoons.

"You thought of everything." Renee peered into the box.

"I figured we better eat it before the power goes out." Katie's expression turned sad. "Imagine all of that glorious ice cream melted."

"You look like you just lost your best friend," Jake said.

"Ice cream and I have had a very long and emotionally satisfying relationship." With an exaggerated motion, Katie caressed the pint and kissed the lid.

Renee laughed. "Come on. I don't believe it. You should look like me, instead of having a figure like yours." Renee blushed. "I mean you certainly don't look like an ice cream junkie."

"Looks can be deceiving." Katie playfully bumped her hip against Renee's. "And stop talking trash about yourself. Everyone can't be a size two. I was graced with a good metabolism, that's all."

Renee looked Katie up and down, but then quickly looked away. "Hey girls," she called to Dee and Sid, who were resting against the side of the truck drinking a bottle of iced tea. "Katie's scored a treat for us."

"Should I go find Willa and KC?" Jake asked.

"I'm not ready to deal with Tweedle Dee and Tweedle Dumb. Can't we just save them some?" Renee said.

Nobody answered as they all dug into the box, searching for their favorite flavor.

❧❧❧❧

"Are you okay?" Dillon asked CJ. Something in CJ's demeanor seemed off.

"Yeah, why?"

"You just shivered. Excited about all the geek equipment we just loaded up?"

CJ shook her head and gave Dillon a wry smile. "No."

"Hey, what's wrong?"

CJ looked toward the other truck where Karen and Tad were packing the last boxes. She spoke in a low voice, so the others couldn't hear. "I'm starting to get the creeps. I just want to go back to the mansion, but we should probably make one more stop."

Dillon had known CJ for a long time, and she was never one to overreact or be melodramatic. Earlier, an uneasy feeling had assailed Dillon, but she'd pushed it back. "No. I think we should go."

"I'm sure it's nothing." CJ looked toward the apartment complex to the west. "But it's oppressive."

Dillon looked in the direction CJ stared and frowned. "What's oppressive?"

"All the death. We're surrounded by it. I swear I can smell it, even with these masks on." Tears welled in CJ's eyes. "You know how much I loved this city."

Dillon patted CJ on the back and smiled. It wasn't lost on her that CJ said loved, not love. "Yep. I've never known a bigger city girl. I can't believe it was only a few days ago you were weirded out by Lake Piru."

"There's nothing like the energy of four million people living, working, and playing together. I never got it when you wanted to get away to some godforsaken place." She shook her head sadly. "Now this is the most godforsaken place I've ever seen. Four million people decaying together."

Ouch. Even though CJ was right, it wasn't a good place for her head to be. They needed to get out of here. She too thought she smelled death all around them, despite the masks. Dillon suspected that soon, once all the power flickered out and the heat rose, the stench would be so powerful that it would be impossible to get within miles of the city without vomiting.

She'd once read that a dead body smells like

rotting meat sitting out in the hot sun for three days, sprinkled with sickeningly sweet perfume, but much worse. Living in Indiana, she remembered the putrid smell of a dead and bloated raccoon along the side of the road. It amazed her how much it assailed her senses, even driving past at sixty miles an hour. And that was one tiny animal. *What would four million people smell like?* She swallowed hard, not wanting to activate her gag reflex.

Before Dillon could respond, CJ said, "I feel like I have worms crawling inside my veins. Part of me wants to run screaming through the streets and break into every single apartment just to see for myself. I know they're in there, but the buildings look so normal."

"It's okay, CJ." Dillon squeezed her arm.

"I wish I'd never seen it like this. I want to imagine the way it was, teeming with life."

"This isn't healthy for you. We need to get you out of here."

CJ looked Dillon in the eye. "Am I being weak?"

"God, no! You're being human." Dillon gave CJ a half smile. "Finally, you're showing signs that you're not a robot."

CJ grinned. "Thanks. I just needed to know it's okay."

"It's okay. We'll take turns falling apart."

"Deal." CJ put her arm around Dillon and pulled her close.

Dillon returned the hug. "Should we get rolling?"

CJ nodded.

"Hey, Karen," Dillon called. "Are you guys ready to head back to meet the others?"

Karen closed the back of the truck and walked

toward them. "I thought we were going to make another stop."

"Nope, we decided not to," Dillon said.

Karen's eyes narrowed when she turned to Dillon. Understanding registered on her face when she shifted her gaze to CJ. She laid her head against CJ's chest. "Let's go home."

☙☙☙☙

Cynthia put a steadying hand on Skylar's shoulder when she noticed Skylar struggling to get out of her Tyvek suit. "Let me help."

Skylar dropped her arms to her side, letting Cynthia lower the zipper on her suit. The bulky gloves made it difficult for Skylar to slide her sleeves over. It would be easier if Skylar took the gloves off first, but Cynthia suspected she didn't want to touch any part of the suit with her bare hands.

It had been brutal inside the hospital. While Cynthia encountered death regularly, this was on a scale she struggled to accept. Pride welled in her chest. Their team worked well together. Maria and Tasha were troopers, despite having no medical training. They'd gone about the task in a methodical way, ensuring Cynthia obtained everything she needed to set up a clinic back at the Estate.

Skylar wiggled out of the suit and let it fall to the ground at her feet. She shuddered and kicked it away from her. "Do you need any help?"

"Please," Cynthia replied.

Once Cynthia discarded her suit on top of Skylar's, they moved away from the pile. Only then did they remove their masks. Cynthia peeled off her gloves, but noted Skylar continued to wear hers. An excessively steaming hot shower was the only thing that might possibly make her feel clean again, but she wasn't sure if that would even do it.

Tasha and Maria had already stripped out of their suits and masks and were huddled near Maria's motorcycle, talking quietly.

"Should we check on them?" Skylar asked.

Cynthia shook her head. "Let's let them be for a little while. I think we could all use a little breather before we head back."

"Will we have time to hit a couple more drug stores on our way?"

Cynthia looked at her watch. "Yeah, I think so. I'd love to stop at the scrubs store too if we have time."

"How do you think the others are faring?"

"Worried about Dillon?" Cynthia smiled.

"Am I that transparent?" Skylar's dimple deepened when she smiled. "I hope they didn't run into anything like this."

"They shouldn't have. I can't wait to get back home." Cynthia laughed. "Freudian? In less than a week, I'm already calling it home."

"Something tells me it will be our home for a long time."

"Hey, guys," Maria called. "Are we about ready to hit the road?"

"Whenever you're ready," Cynthia answered.

"We want to go past the Hollywood sign."

"You want to do what?" Cynthia walked toward them, thinking she must have misunderstood.

"We want to drive past the Hollywood sign," Maria said in a louder voice. "It'll be a long time, if ever, that we come back here. And even if we do, without someone maintaining it, it's hard to tell what it will look like later."

At first, Cynthia thought it was a strange request, but then she thought of iconic images she held in her head of New York City. If she would have known she wouldn't see the city ever again when she'd flown to Los Angeles a few short days ago, she would have wanted to do the same.

"Okay. Let's go. You lead the way."

⁂

"Walk away," Jake said to Renee under his breath. "We're just about done."

"Seriously? A whole fucking truck full of alcohol?" Renee answered.

"They did remember the toilet paper, so they were of some use." Katie winked at Renee, which elicited a smile. "Imagine if we'd gotten home without any."

Jake laughed. Without Katie, the day would have gone much worse. Renee seemed to be accepting Willa and KC's irresponsibility, as long as Katie kept her laughing.

"How many beers do you think they've had?" Renee asked.

"Does it matter?" Jake said. "We're not leaving any of our trucks behind."

"We need to keep them away from Dillon and Maria on her motorcycle," Katie said.

Renee frowned and crossed her arms over her chest. "I suppose it's a wrap then. Let's head to our rendezvous point."

≈≋≈≋≈

Dillon downshifted the semi as their convoy began to slow as it approached the meeting place. Even though they were nearly twenty minutes early, they appeared to be the last ones to arrive. Her gaze searched the parking lot, hoping to see Skylar. *No luck.*

She downshifted further and swung her truck around to the far end of the lot. Her truck was bigger than the rest, so she didn't want to block anyone. The truck came to a stop, and she killed the engine.

It had been a trying day, and she was sure Skylar's must have been much worse. She ran her hands through her hair and rested her head on the steering wheel, needing time to regroup. When she breathed in deeply, she immediately regretted it. The smell of death seemed to be everywhere, or maybe she imagined it. More than likely, she'd smell it for days. Her hand resting on her thigh trembled slightly, so she put her other one on top to steady it. As she stared at her fingers, she fought the overwhelming urge to run to the nearest restroom and wash them. Would she ever get them clean?

Dillon closed her eyes. She'd just sit here a little longer. Maybe she'd drive the truck back, instead of riding the motorcycle. As shaky as she felt, it would be unsafe for her to ride, and with the sun heading toward the horizon, the temperature would soon drop. They could load Maria's motorcycle into the back of the truck if she didn't want to ride alone. Dillon just wanted to go home, but that would require her lifting her head, which seemed like a tall order.

A noise came from outside her truck, which forced her to look up. Skylar and Cynthia rushed toward the truck, calling her name. *Meditation time is over.* She took a final cleansing breath before she used her foot to push open the door.

She'd barely hopped to the ground before being engulfed by Skylar and Cynthia's hugs. Dillon wrapped her arms around both. A warm feeling flooded her chest. Now, they could go *home.*

Chapter Twelve

The next month was a whirlwind; the initial shock had worn off, leaving everyone raw. The truth of the situation weighed heavily on the mansion. The grief was palpable as everyone wrapped their minds around the depth of their losses. They'd come to the realization that everyone not here with them was probably dead. The grief gave way to anger and fear. The anger led to mounting tensions, resulting in several screaming fights, with a few leading to physical altercations. The fear simply led to inactivity and lethargy.

The group divided into two. The first group rolled up their sleeves, pushed aside their emotions, and got to work. Others folded like lawn chairs, letting their fear and grief get the best of them. It wasn't uncommon for the most conscientious of the group to be up at dawn, working solidly until the last of the light faded in the evening. The members of the Commission found they were not only tasked with providing leadership, but they spent an inordinate amount of time being counselors and cheerleaders as the malaise set in.

The quest into LA to get supplies had been successful, and since then, Karen had led several smaller trips into Santa Clarita. Most of the women weren't ready for what greeted them outside the mansion gates. In their defense, many hadn't been involved in the initial supply run, so it was the first time they were seeing what their world now looked like. The smell of decaying bodies was also beginning to be an issue, driving the supply party away from some areas in Santa Clarita. Even with state-of-the-art gas masks, the stench was nearly unbearable. The group took to putting Carmex in their nostrils to block the smell. They burned their clothes upon their return to the mansion, feeling that no amount of washing them would ever get the scent of death out. Cynthia assured them the toxic smell would eventually dissipate, but it would take time.

Braxton Babcock's group had continued to believe Jake and CJ were alone with their children in North Carolina. Brother Marcus had begun to put more pressure on them to come join the ministry in Colorado, but so far, Jake had convinced them he was afraid to travel across the country with his young children. Jake had convinced them it was safer to stay friendly with the group, so they would be privy to any new developments around the country. Thus far they'd heard of none.

༄ ༄ ༄ ༄

Dillon knew she was fortunate to be the leader of the construction crew instead of the supply team, but she was still unhappy. She stepped back and looked at the tower in disgust. It was over two-thirds built, but it should have been completed already. In a pinch, they could use it, but they needed to enclose the primary entrance and complete the secondary escape.

The primary entrance was a simple staircase that wound in a tight spiral up the center of the tower.

They'd completed building the stairs, but anyone using them would be visible to enemies on the ground, which would make them sitting ducks. The thought of letting any of her friends use the tower before being enclosed made Dillon uncomfortable. Keeping the group safe rested in her hands.

Dillon had chosen the area directly behind the mansion for the structure because it provided the most safety. The escape stairway would enter through the conservatory roof and end just outside the bunker doors. This was imperative in case of emergency; anyone manning the tower could get to shelter quickly should the need arise.

Dillon wiped the sweat from her forehead with her forearm before she hoisted the pile of boards onto her shoulder. Jake manned the circular saw and only had a small stack of wood left to cut, so she needed to take him more.

On her way, she walked past Skylar, who stained the wood balanced between two sawhorses. Dillon felt Skylar's gaze on her.

"Damn, those shoulders are getting tanned and ripped. I might need to run my hands over them later." Skylar ended her flirtation with a whistle.

Dillon blushed but still turned around and winked at Skylar. She secretly enjoyed it when Skylar commented on her physique. Over the past month, the manual labor had hardened her body. Recently, she noticed carrying supplies had become easier. Maybe she wasn't in quite the shape she had been in her early twenties, when she worked with the crew every day, but given time, she would be.

Despite being nearly five o'clock, the heat and humidity hadn't diminished. The slight breeze felt more like a blast furnace than anything to cool them. Dillon wanted to finish building the wall they were working on before quitting, but as was becoming customary, her work crew had shrunk. Her workers were supposed to start promptly at eight a.m., which she'd thought was too late, but she'd relented. Recently, over half her crew were in the habit of showing up at ten o'clock. Then at noon they took an hour, or sometimes longer, lunch before they cut out at three to enjoy cocktails by the pool.

Dillon smiled affectionately at her die-hards; Skylar, Cynthia, Tasha, Jake, and Tad, who were still working, despite the heat. All the crews were having the same problem. Renee and Karen complained constantly about not having enough help to get the job done.

"Face it, Dillon, it's not going to happen tonight," Tasha said, the annoyance evident in her voice.

"Come on, Tash, where's your spirit?" Dillon said, trying to sound upbeat.

"The jackasses that left early took it with them."

"You're right." Dillon sighed and her shoulders drooped. "There's no sense killing everyone trying to get this done. It can wait."

Skylar put her arm around Dillon, obviously sensing her frustration. "It's all right, Babe. You're doing the best with what you've got."

"That's the point, look at us." Heat rose up Dillon's neck as she glanced around at her tiny work crew. "What's wrong with this picture?"

"I know it's frustrating," Cynthia said. She moved up beside Dillon, put her arm across Dillon's shoulders, sandwiching Dillon between her and Skylar. "It's not like we're on a deadline. I'm afraid we're going to be here for a while."

"I know. I just have an uneasy feeling. I'd like to get the watch tower done, so we can keep an eye on what's going on around us. I'd feel like we were safer."

"Won't matter." Jake sauntered over to join the conversation. "We won't be able to defend ourselves anyway."

"Not helpful, Jake," Skylar said.

"Seriously Skylar, you know we aren't ready."

Dillon sighed, knowing Jake was right. With the help of Skylar and Tad, he'd developed a weapons training program. To date only five people attended regularly. They'd tried to encourage participation by changing the schedule. It hadn't worked.

"We'd be slaughtered," Tad said. In a couple short months, he had grown into a man. He even looked taller to Dillon. He'd definitely lost his baby fat, and his body was chiseled like only a young man could be. He tanned to a golden brown and would have had the girls flocking to him had there been any straight girls there. Although, Dillon had noticed that Nancy's fourteen-year-old daughter hung on his every word.

Skylar shot Tad a dirty look before she spoke. "Well, we can sit around and complain about it, or we can do something about it."

"Point taken." Dillon smiled at Skylar. "We have a Commission meeting tomorrow afternoon. I'd say that's as good a place as any to take up a conversation about it."

"Shit, is it Friday already?" Jake asked. "If it is, we need to get our butts moving."

"Why?" Dillon asked.

"The big party tonight," he answered. "Lily will

shoot me if I'm late."

"Since she's one of the few going to defense classes, she'd probably be able to hit you," Dillon said.

"Thanks." Jake laughed.

☙ ☙ ☙ ☙

Dillon swept the crumbs off the counter into the palm of her hand and deposited them into the garbage can. She sighed; the garbage needed to be taken out again. It was evident that eight people were living under the same roof. They'd done okay together, but sometimes the cozy living quarters were too much, especially when little things got under her skin.

Dillon hated crumbs and found them everywhere. It was a losing battle, but she still waged it. She constantly wiped off the counter, the table, and sometimes even the couch cushions, but more appeared. Maria would say she had no right to complain since Dillon's bad habit drove Maria crazy. Oftentimes she'd leave her glass sitting wherever it was she last had it. It puzzled her where this newfound behavior came from since she never used to do it at home. *Freudian?* Was it retaliatory against the crumb dropper?

The door creaked and Dillon looked up from her mission to eradicate all the crumbs in their suite. She watched Skylar as she emerged from the bedroom they shared with CJ and Karen and couldn't help but admire her body. She was dressed in a tight low cut black shirt that hugged her breasts and showed off her full cleavage. Being outside working every day had given her a golden tan, which only increased her beauty. Dillon tried not to stare but failed miserably, feeling the familiar ache every time Skylar was around.

"Damn, I forgot to brush my teeth," Skylar said and retreated.

They hadn't slept together since that first night. Actually, they slept together every night, but they hadn't had sex again. Sometimes lying in the dark next to Skylar was nearly unbearable. She would lie there for hours with her thoughts in overdrive, and the ache between her thighs begging to be sated. She'd never had insomnia before, but recently that had changed.

Dillon's gaze went to Skylar's perfectly shaped butt as she exited the room. Dillon's thoughts returned to the previous night.

❧❧❧❧❧

There was a full moon, so the brightness filtered in through the curtains. Skylar came to bed after taking a long shower, and a subtle smell of sandalwood clung to her. She wore only a t-shirt and a skimpy pair of underwear. Flushed, Dillon quickly looked away. Skylar crawled under the covers on her side of the bed, as she'd done every night. They were both careful not to touch one another.

"Are you awake?" Skylar said. Her raspy voice was even sexier when she whispered.

"Yeah," Dillon answered, her voice hoarse.

"Do you dream about things the way they are, or how they used to be?" Skylar asked, staring at the ceiling.

"What do you mean?"

"Early on when I dreamed, everyone was still alive, and the world was like it always was. But lately, I've had more dreams with it being like it is now."

"The old world is starting to fade." Dillon turned to face Skylar in the dark.

"Exactly." Skylar shivered.

"Are you okay?"

"Yeah, just a little frightened," Skylar answered.

"Would you mind if I came over by you?"

"Of course not, come here."

Skylar slid over next to Dillon and laid her head on her shoulder. Dillon wrapped her arm around Skylar and hugged her. A contented sigh escaped Skylar, and her body relaxed. Careful to touch her only in a comforting manner, Dillon gently ran her hand through Skylar's hair and down her back. Skylar's breathing soon evened out and sleep took her, while Dillon lay awake, enjoying the feeling of Skylar in her arms.

⁂

"Dillon!" Skylar said. Tightness gripped Skylar's chest. The Crisis weighed on her whenever someone didn't answer right away. She shuddered, thinking how Leslie must have felt finding her wife, Denise, dead.

"Huh?" Dillon shook her head as if trying to clear her mind.

"You were a million miles away. I called your name three times."

"Just thinking," Dillon stammered.

"It must have been pretty engrossing."

"You could say that." Dillon wrapped her arms around Skylar.

They hugged tightly, and when they separated, Dillon found Skylar's lips. Their kiss was hungry and intense, and both were breathless when they parted. Skylar looked into Dillon's flaming brown eyes and saw everything she needed to know. Dillon obviously wanted her as much as she wanted Dillon. Even though Dillon's restraint and the respect it showed touched Skylar, her body yearned for more. Last night she'd heard Dillon's sharp intake of breath when she'd pressed her body against Dillon. But Dillon had simply rubbed her hair and back, until she fell asleep to Dillon's labored breathing.

Skylar stepped back, knowing another kiss may make it impossible for either of them to go to the party. As much as she would love to stay in the room, alone with Dillon all evening, she couldn't do that to Renee. The party was Renee's attempt at improving morale, so it would be in poor taste if everyone on The Commission wasn't there to support the effort.

"We better go," Skylar said breathlessly.

"Yeah, everyone else already went down." Dillon took a deep breath.

"Did CJ ever come up to the room?" Skylar absentmindedly straightened Dillon's shirt.

"No, she's the only one unaccounted for. Karen couldn't pull CJ away from her lab."

"Is Karen pissed?"

"No, she's used to CJ getting absorbed in a project."

"What's she working on?"

"I'm not sure. I don't understand ninety percent of what CJ is talking about when she gets her geek on. Mouse and monitor about sums up my knowledge. After that, I'm lost."

Skylar laughed. "Are you ready to escort me to the party?"

"It would be my pleasure." Dillon held out her arm, and Skylar looped her arm through Dillon's and leaned into her.

Chapter Thirteen

Dillon sat back from the table, lost in thought, only half listening to the conversation around her. She tilted her head back and gazed up at the stars. A pang of sadness hit. She'd almost forgotten how much she enjoyed being outdoors in the evening since the lights of LA obscured the night sky. If it weren't for the loud conversations and music playing in the background, she guessed she would be able to hear crickets chirping.

She gazed over at Skylar's empty chair. When Skylar recognized that Renee's diminished crew struggled to keep up with serving the meal, she jumped in to assist. Dillon marveled at Skylar's boundless energy.

Skylar had become a valued member of multiple groups, while Dillon felt inadequate by comparison. Jake had recruited Skylar as an instructor for his defense classes since she was one of the few who had ever fired a gun. Her calm demeanor had proven to be invaluable in working with the women who had an aversion to firearms. She'd also teamed up with Cynthia to establish a medical clinic.

If those duties weren't enough, she'd insisted on learning the building trades, so she could work alongside Dillon. They'd spent many evenings discussing design ideas and drafting future building plans.

Dillon smiled to herself, remembering CJ's surprise when she had discovered Dillon's attraction to Skylar. Dillon sensed then that there was something special about Skylar, and she hadn't been wrong. Skylar had proven herself to be one of the most valuable members of the group because of her versatility. If anyone didn't measure up, it was Dillon, whose only real skill was construction.

With a feeling of pride, Dillon watched Skylar across the room. When Skylar caught Dillon admiring her, she flashed a smile and winked. The look went straight to Dillon's heart. Under the circumstances, Dillon shouldn't be so contented. She continually wrestled with her feelings of happiness, but she had begun to accept the paradox.

Dillon gazed around the room, hopeful that Renee's plan was working. Dillon hadn't witnessed so many smiles or as much laughter for several weeks.

Katie stood by the dessert table, serving those indulging in seconds. Dillon rose. She needed to give Katie her compliments on the success of the evening.

"Amazing meal," Dillon said with a smile. "You two outdid yourself."

"Thanks." Katie's huge smile quickly faded when she looked up.

The abrupt change didn't go unnoticed. Dillon grasped for something profound to say to save the moment. She knew her relationship with Skylar was painful to Katie, who spent less and less time in their suite or with the group. Dillon wished there was something comforting she could say to ease the pain but was at a loss.

"You and Renee make quite a team." Dillon

picked up another piece of cheesecake, even though she wasn't hungry.

"Yes, I guess we do. At least someone here appreciates me." Katie handed Dillon a fork.

Dillon winced. *This isn't going well.* Should she thank Katie for the cheesecake and walk away, or should she say something more? Pretending not to notice the dig, she forged on. "Renee told me she couldn't do any of this without you." Fearing her words were coming out too stiff and formal, she tried again. "You guys have been working your butts off. I barely see you around."

"Did you ever think maybe that was by design?" Katie busied herself with wiping down the already clean table.

"I'm sorry." Her guilt sat heavily on her shoulders. It pained her to witness what her actions did to Katie. There wouldn't be any healing until the issue was addressed head on. But how could she do it?

Katie's gaze locked on Dillon. "Sorry for what?"

Dillon pretended to chew the bite of cheesecake she'd already swallowed. Anything to give her more time to come up with a response. Katie wasn't going to make it easy for her. "I'm sorry for whatever I did to make you upset with me." Immediately, Dillon knew it was the wrong thing to say when Katie's face flushed, and her eyes hardened.

"Don't give me that innocent bullshit. You know perfectly well what you did." Katie slammed the serving platter onto the table and stormed off.

Wonderful. That certainly didn't go as planned. Dillon watched Katie stomp inside. Part of her wanted to follow and try and make Katie understand, but she feared it would only make things worse. How could she explain that Skylar was able to re-open Dillon, in ways that Katie hadn't been able to in years? She needed to try. Dillon set the piece of cheesecake on the table and walked to the door in search of Katie. As she was about to enter the mansion, CJ burst through the door, nearly knocking Dillon to the ground.

CJ didn't seem to notice and shouted, "I've found someone in New York."

With those words, pandemonium ensued, and Dillon's plan to talk with Katie dissolved.

᪥᪥᪥᪥᪥

"Would you guys stop asking me questions, so I can talk?" CJ said. The women quieted and CJ continued. "I've been running an algorithm that I developed to work with my ham radio and…"

Oh God, not full-on geek. Dillon held up her hand. "CJ, stop. I know you're excited about your techie stuff, but nobody wants to hear it. We want to know about the people."

"She's right, honey." Karen put her arm around CJ's waist and rested her head against her shoulder. Karen's touch brought CJ from under her technological cloud and her eyes softened.

"Oh yeah, right," CJ stammered.

"There are sixty-four people in the group, who call themselves the Heroic People of the East or HOPE for short," CJ said. "The members of HOPE met in New York City. Most hadn't known each other beforehand, but they came together out of necessity. They encountered two other groups, but they didn't join forces. They have already lost touch with both, which they claim is for the best. One of the groups seemed hell bent on destruction, and HOPE wanted no part of their methods."

"Are you sure we can trust them?" Dillon asked.

"I think so. Here's the most exciting part." A huge smile lit up CJ's face. "They've been able to locate a group outside of Chicago, another in Boston and a third in Florida. They're hopeful they'll find more. HOPE has made it their mission to locate as many people as possible."

"Did you tell them we're in contact with Braxton Babcock's crazies?" Dillon asked.

"Yep, they've talked to them too and are just as wary as we are. Maybe more so. Apparently, one of HOPE's members got into a verbal altercation with Babcock's minion, who threatened hellfire and damnation on them."

"What the hell," Dillon said. "Didn't Brother Marcus tell you they haven't found anyone else?"

"Yep. Sneaky bastards, just like we suspected."

"Exactly why we shouldn't still be talking to them," someone shouted from the crowd.

Not this again. The argument kept arising even after the Commission voted to continue their communication with Babcock. As distasteful as it was, Dillon voted in favor of doing so. *Keep your friends close and your enemies closer.*

Every week, Jake checked in with them. Of course, they wanted to talk to the man. *Misogynists.* The message was always the same. Come to Colorado and join the ministry.

"Who cares about Babcock?" Maria said. "I want to hear about the HOPE people."

CJ spent the next fifteen minutes filling them in on what she'd learned. The room was silent, except for CJ's voice, but as soon as she stopped talking, the room erupted as everyone began talking at once and shouting questions at CJ.

⁂

Once the pandemonium started, Cynthia left the balcony and went inside to get away from it. Her mind was in overdrive, and she needed a quiet place to think. She leaned against one of the tables and closed her eyes.

"Cynthia," a voice called. She opened her eyes to see Anne rushing toward her. "This is so exciting."

Cynthia couldn't help but smile at Anne. Already someone who exuded such positive energy, her enthusiasm was not only overflowing but contagious. "Best news we've had in some time," Cynthia said.

"Have you seen Tiffany? I have to tell her about this."

"I think she went with Diana to find some more wine, but I haven't seen them in quite a while."

Dillon and Skylar walked through the door from outside. So much for having a moment to herself, but she didn't mind. Given a choice, these were the three people she'd most want to share such a moment with.

"Hi ladies," Anne said. "I don't mean to be rude, but I have to find Tiffany so I can tell her the good news." Anne quickly gave all three a hug before she hurried off.

"What are the odds you know someone from HOPE?" Dillon asked.

"When CJ told the story, my stomach did flip flops," Cynthia answered.

"We thought of you as soon as we heard about

New York." Skylar excitedly grabbed Cynthia's arm.

"And then did you do the math?" Cynthia sighed and blinked back tears.

"Unfortunately." Dillon frowned.

"Come on, you two, maybe the odds aren't the greatest, but there is still a chance," Skylar said.

"Sometimes that's all we have." Cynthia had already ridden the rollercoaster of emotion in her mind and settled on not allowing herself too much optimism. Could she handle the disappointment?

"I have connections," Dillon said. "Let's go see if CJ can get us some names."

When they arrived, they found CJ pushed against the dessert table, as all the women surrounded her. The six-foot, four-inch CJ towered over the group, but they continued to press in around her.

"It looks like the Lilliputians might overwhelm poor Gulliver," Dillon said.

Cynthia laughed, imagining CJ tied up with tiny ropes.

"Be nice." Skylar playfully slapped Dillon's arm.

CJ spotted them. Her eyes widened and she shot Dillon a pleading look. "Dillon, there you are," CJ said loudly. "Did you need me?"

Cynthia smiled at the mischievous gleam in Dillon's eye. She knew Dillon was tempted to say no, just to watch CJ squirm a little longer.

Dillon took her time answering. "Actually, I do need your help."

"Duty calls." CJ took Karen's hand and parted the crowd to get to Dillon. As soon as CJ slipped through the group, they seemed to instantly forget her and excitedly talked amongst themselves.

"Come on." Dillon motioned them to follow and

led them inside.

CJ clutched at her chest. "I thought they were going to trample me."

"What are you whining about? I thought they would smother me. Disadvantage number 5,943 of being short," Karen said.

CJ's gaze darted around the room before she spoke. "Did you really need something, or were you just rescuing me?"

"Hell, I'd have left you there if I didn't need something from you." Dillon laughed.

"Figures. So, what is it?"

"Actually, it's for me." Cynthia raised her hand and stepped up next to CJ.

"Good, I didn't want to have to do something for Dillon anyway." CJ winked. "What can I do for you?"

"I know this is gonna sound stupid, but I hoped maybe I'd know someone in New York."

"We can check it out." Without saying anything more, CJ turned and headed toward the stairs.

"I'm assuming she's going down to her equipment, or her mother planet is finally calling her home," Dillon said.

Karen laughed. "Dillon, you should know better than anyone when CJ's on a mission, all her social graces fly out the window."

"Wow, you're generous. You actually used CJ's name and social graces in the same sentence."

Karen shook her head. "You two. We better get moving if we plan on catching up with her."

CJ already sat at her equipment, tapping on a keyboard when they arrived. She looked up at Cynthia and said, "Do you mind if I give them your name?

They might be reluctant if I start asking them too many questions right away."

"Go ahead, unless there's a reason I shouldn't give it."

"No, your name should be fine. I'm just not willing to give out our location at this point."

"Why not? You don't think they're creepy like Babcock's group, do you?" Karen asked.

"You've watched *The Walking Dead*. There may be some unbelievably bad people out there."

"Seriously, you're going to base your decisions off of a television show?" Karen rolled her eyes.

"Unfortunately, I think she's right." Dillon put her hand over her face. "I can't believe I just said that."

"Very funny." CJ shot Dillon a look before returning to her screen. "It's a different world now." CJ continued tapping on the keyboard and clicking the mouse, with a look of concentration on her face. "We don't know who we can trust."

"How sad is that?" Karen looked dejected. "I'd like to believe people are still good. I have to believe that, or I'm not sure I could get out of bed every morning."

"I agree," Skylar said. "But unfortunately, it only takes a few bad people to destroy everything."

Cynthia looked at Skylar out of the corner of her eye. Somehow, she thought the statement was more personal than philosophical.

"Trust has to be earned, we can never forget that, or we put everyone here in danger," Dillon said. "This is our home now. Our family. We need to protect it at all costs."

Karen nodded and cast her gaze to the floor.

CJ still tapped her keyboard and turned knobs

on her radio. A text box popped up into the middle of her screen. "Okay, we're connected. Here goes." CJ typed rapidly and after a few seconds said, "Jason says he will check with the others. It might take a few minutes."

Cynthia stared transfixed by the blinking cursor, willing it to bring her good news. The others made small talk. They must know she was crawling out of her skin and were doing their best to keep her distracted. The elevator bell dinging broke her concentration.

The doors had barely opened when Anne pushed through the crack and ran across the atrium. She was nearly upon them when her eyes widened in recognition. Without a word, she veered off, picked up her pace, and ran out the entrance doors.

"What the hell was that about?" CJ said.

"Did you see her eyes?" Cynthia asked. "It looked like she was crying. Something was wrong. I should check on her." Cynthia turned to follow Anne.

"It's dark out there," Karen said. "I don't think you should go wandering around by yourself."

"What do you think Tiffany did this time?" Dillon asked. Cynthia shot her a warning look. Dillon held up her hands in a gesture of surrender. "I'll go with you."

"I'll go too," Skylar said.

"I haven't got an answer for you yet." CJ looked up from her screen.

"It'll have to wait. I don't like the thought of her out there by herself."

"Karen and I will stay here and wait," CJ said.

The three ran across the atrium, heading for the door.

Chapter Fourteen

A s they pushed through the over-sized doors, blackness greeted them. Cynthia loved the lack of lighting because it allowed her to see the stars that she was unable to see in New York City, but the darkness wasn't their friend tonight.

The power had gone out long ago, and everything ran off a generator now. To conserve energy, they didn't power any of the outside lights.

"I can barely see my hand in front of my face," Skylar said.

"Sound's our best weapon." Cynthia began shouting Anne's name.

They methodically spread out, taking turns calling out to Anne. After ten minutes, they were nearly fifty yards from the mansion when a faint sound came from the darkness.

"Over here," Dillon said. "I think she's off to my left."

"Keep talking," Skylar shouted. "We'll try to follow your voice."

Dillon rambled about nothing until the two stood beside her. Cynthia called Anne's name again, and they followed her answering call.

"I think it's coming from the path going to the hotel," Dillon said.

Once they arrived at the path, with a reference

point under their feet, they were able to pick up the pace. Periodically, they called Anne's name until her voice came from nearby.

Dillon had been leading the trio, so when she stopped abruptly, it created a chain reaction. Skylar plowed into Dillon's back, followed by Cynthia, who ran into Skylar.

"Sorry," Dillon mumbled. "I wanted to get my bearings."

"Warn us next time, will you?" Cynthia said.

Dillon screamed.

"Okay, never mind," Cynthia said.

Dillon and Anne burst out laughing.

"I wasn't screaming at you. Anne just grabbed me and scared the shit out of me."

"Anne?" Cynthia said. "I can't see you."

A blinding light cut through the darkness, causing all three to turn their heads and squint. Anne held up one of the high-tech lanterns they'd found in the museum.

"Why didn't you turn it on earlier? It would have made it much easier to find you." Cynthia blinked her eyes several times, trying to vanquish the spots dancing in her vision.

"Sure, but where's the fun in that?"

Cynthia gazed at her for the first time. She looked awful. Pale and with red puffy eyes. Despite trying to appear casual, she'd obviously been crying. "What's going on, Anne?"

The light turned off and darkness enveloped them.

"Nice try, but we already saw," Cynthia said. "Do you think you could turn that back on?"

Anne took two deep inhalations before light

filled the night again. "There's not much to tell."

"What happened?" Cynthia asked. *Tiffany, obviously.* What had she done this time?

"Tiffany being Tiffany," Anne said elusively.

"Would you like us to leave the two of you alone to talk?" Skylar offered.

"No, I'm sure everyone will find out soon enough, but thank you."

When Cynthia saw the tears streaming down Anne's face, she instinctively went to her. She'd comforted Anne more times than she could count over the years, whenever Tiffany did something thoughtless, which was often. She put her arm around Anne's shoulders.

"Why did I think this time would be any different in the middle of a crisis? God, I'm a fool." No one spoke as they waited for Anne to continue. "I went to find her to tell her the good news…" Anne took a deep breath but didn't continue.

"And?" Cynthia said when the silence drug on.

"And…she was in bed with Willa and KC." Anne's face contorted in pain.

"Are you fucking kidding me?" Cynthia's jaw tightened, and her stomach rolled. "I'm gonna kill her."

"Don't." Anne grabbed her hand. "Please, just don't."

Cynthia paused and took two deep breaths. She looked Anne firmly in the eyes. "Anne, you said you thought this time it would be different. Are you saying she's done this before?"

Anne looked to the ground, her eyes full of dejection. "I've lost count of how many times," she whispered.

"I'm going to kick her ass." Blood pounded in her ears, and her fists clenched. What the fuck was wrong with Tiffany? Anne deserved so much better.

"No, it's as much my fault as it is hers." Anne handed Skylar the lantern and put her hands over her face.

"It's not your fault," Skylar said, raising her voice. "Stop blaming the victim."

"I'm no victim." There was venom in Anne's voice. "Maybe the first time I was, possibly the second time I was just naïve, but now I'm an enabler."

"Don't blame yourself for her shit." Cynthia's anger rose, but she tried to keep it out of her voice. In that moment, she hated Tiffany and wanted to shelter Anne, so Tiffany could never hurt her again.

"I appreciate your support, I really do." Tears streamed down Anne's face. "But I've let it happen. I've never called her on anything she's ever done to me. I've been sweeping it under the rug for years."

"Don't let her off the hook that easily." Cynthia's frustration rose, but she bit back the angry words she wanted to say.

"Who said I'm letting her off the hook?" Anne said with conviction. "This time, I'm done."

"That's the spirit." Dillon finally joined the conversation.

Impressive. Cynthia knew Dillon's feelings toward Tiffany, but she'd kept herself in check the entire time.

"When I saw them tonight, something in me snapped. Kinda crazy that it took the end of the world for me to finally decide enough was enough." Anne let out a sardonic laugh. "If I've learned anything these past couple months, it's that everything can change in an instant. It's about time I change too. I love her, probably always will, but I can't live like this any longer." She took several deep breaths before she continued. "I might have six months or sixty years left, but before my time in this world is over, I want to be loved, really loved. Is that stupid? The world's collapsed, and all I want is love. How selfish is that?"

"It's not selfish at all." Skylar put her hand on Anne's arm. "In the end, I think love is the only thing that's kept us going. And it's not just romantic love. It's the friendships that have been forged in fire that will never be broken." Skylar looked at Cynthia, as she delivered the line. "I believe you will eventually find the love you're craving, but, in the meantime, never believe you aren't loved."

"Amen to that." Cynthia squeezed Anne. She needed the hug nearly as much as Anne did. "You know I love you."

"Stop, or I'm never going to stop crying." Anne struggled to take a breath.

"Okay. What can we do to help?" Cynthia asked.

"I need to move out. But that's easier said than done since our suite is the only one with any room."

"I know." Cynthia snapped her fingers. "I'll come with you. We could move over to the other wing."

"No!" Dillon said. "That's way too dangerous. If something happened, you two would be all alone. I'll fight you on this."

"Our suite is overcrowded." Skylar looked at Dillon before continuing. "Maybe we could come with you."

"You don't want your own space?" Dillon asked.

"No, I'd like the two of us to have our own

room." Skylar looked down at her hands when she spoke. "I love CJ and Karen, but I'd prefer not sharing the same bedroom with them."

"Really?" Dillon's smile lit up her entire face. "I'd like that too."

"Okay, you two get a room already," Cynthia said. "Oh wait, that's what you're trying to do."

The joke broke the tension, and they all laughed.

"I bet CJ and Karen would come too. We could stay in the big suite that has three rooms," Anne said. "That's if you wouldn't mind sharing with me, Cynthia."

"I'd love to room with you."

"Are you sure?"

"To be honest, there have been times that I lay awake in my room feeling alone, wishing there were someone else there." Cynthia couldn't believe she'd just said that. Something changed in her when the Crisis struck. She'd never been this open with anyone before. She shrugged. "It will do us both good."

"So, what's our game plan for getting Anne out?" Skylar asked.

☙☙🙚🙚

Cynthia took a deep breath before she pushed open the door. The others filed in behind her. At first, Anne resisted bringing an entourage, saying it wouldn't be fair to Tiffany. *Fuck Tiffany.* She'd brought this on herself.

Cynthia figured it would be a toss-up whether Dillon's presence or Jake's would make Tiffany the angriest. *Oh well.* She didn't much care.

Tiffany sat at the bar in their suite, her hair still

messed up from her romp in bed with Willa and KC. She took a large drink of rum straight out of the bottle when they entered.

Anne marched up to Tiffany. "I'm here to get my belongings."

"What the fuck are you talking about?" Tiffany slurred. "And what the fuck are they doing here?"

"They're here to help me get my things." Anne kept her voice controlled, even though her hands trembled. She turned and walked away from Tiffany toward their bedroom.

"The fuck they are!" Tiffany rose from the barstool. She walked with a swagger as she crossed the room. She came to a stop only inches from Anne and glared down at her. "You're not going anywhere."

Cynthia had watched Tiffany intimidate people over the years with her height but didn't appreciate Anne being on the receiving end, so she moved up beside her. Everyone else hung back.

Anne grabbed Cynthia's hand before speaking. "I'd appreciate it if you would leave the suite for a little bit. It shouldn't take long for me to clear out."

"Did you hear me?" Tiffany's face was red, and spittle flew from her mouth. "I said you aren't going anywhere. I don't know what your problem is."

"My problem," Anne said, raising her voice. "Are you serious? My problem is you sleeping around on me."

Tiffany laughed and brought the bottle of rum to her mouth. She took a large swig before she responded. "Is that what you're upset about? I just needed a little tension release. No big deal."

"It is a big deal to me. And in case you haven't been listening, I'm leaving you."

Without warning, Tiffany threw the bottle of rum across the room, and it shattered against the refrigerator, sending rum and glass flying everywhere. She started raging incoherently at Anne, until Cynthia stepped between the two.

"Enough." Cynthia raised her voice. "Tiffany, knock your shit off." She looked at Anne and said, "Why don't you take Karen and Skylar into your room and get your things together?"

"Thanks, Cynthia." Anne turned away. Tiffany grabbed her arm and yanked her back. Anne's eyes widened and she gasped. She tried to pull her arm away, but Tiffany squeezed harder.

Cynthia gaped, too stunned to react. She'd never known Tiffany to be aggressive with Anne.

"Ouch, you're hurting me." When Anne tried to step back, Tiffany pushed her against the bar. Her back pounded against the edge.

Cynthia caught movement out of the corner of her eye. She'd been so focused on Anne and Tiffany she'd forgotten the others in the room.

Dillon grabbed Tiffany's wrist, the one holding onto Anne's arm. Tiffany's grip immediately released. Before anyone could react, Dillon slammed Tiffany against the closest wall and pinned her there. Jake and Tad jumped in and tried to pull Dillon off, but it took Cynthia and CJ's help to finally break them up.

During the mêlée, Cynthia motioned for Anne to gather her things. Skylar and Karen joined her, and they disappeared into Anne and Tiffany's bedroom.

Tiffany tried to follow, but Jake and Tad stood outside the door, blocking her entry. At first Tiffany tried to rush them, but soon figured out she was outnumbered. She stepped back and began an incoherent tirade. Despite the thick walls, Cynthia suspected anyone on the floor would hear her. Hopefully, nobody came to investigate. They didn't need a bigger scene than they already had.

When Anne exited the bedroom, her gaze immediately went to Tiffany, who was slumped on a barstool, looking forlorn. As soon as she saw Anne, tears streamed down her face.

The tension in the room grew when Skylar and Karen carried several bags out. Dillon, Jake, and Tad moved in behind Anne, on high alert, ready to spring into action if needed.

Anne walked over to Cynthia, who stood closest to Tiffany. "I've got all of my belongings now, Tiffany. I'll be going."

Tiffany looked at Anne with such anguish that Cynthia feared Anne would waiver, but Anne abruptly turned away.

"Please, Anne," Tiffany said. "Don't leave me." Tiffany's silent tears had turned to sobs. "I can't live without you."

Anne stopped with her back still to Tiffany and didn't turn around. "I have to go. You've hurt me one too many times."

"No," Tiffany cried. "I'm sorry, Anne. I love you."

Anne's shoulders slumped and her gaze met Cynthia's. The deep pain in her eyes made Cynthia's heart ache. "Hey, Skylar and Karen, could you give that stuff to CJ and Dillon and come here?" Cynthia said.

"I'll never do it again." Tiffany continued pleading. "You have to give me another chance."

Skylar and Karen complied with Cynthia's request, handing off their load before they hustled over to where Anne stood.

Cynthia put her hand on Anne's shoulder and looked into her eyes. "Skylar and Karen are going to take you to the suite. We'll be right behind you with the rest of your things."

Anne nodded and gave Cynthia a half smile.

Skylar linked one of her arms through Anne's, and Karen did the same.

Anne squeezed their arms, raised her head up high, and walked toward the door. Tiffany screamed. The others moved behind her to prevent Tiffany from following. Anne never looked back.

❧❧❧❧

Anne dropped onto the couch with a heavy sigh. Leaving Tiffany proved more difficult than she'd imagined. Cynthia sat down beside her and patted her leg. Anne rested her head against Cynthia's shoulder and closed her eyes.

She felt as if she'd aged ten years in the last few hours. At thirty-seven, she normally felt youthful and energetic, but she knew she looked haggard and tired now. The move had taken a toll on her, and she couldn't stop from playing the scene over and over in her mind. What would Tiffany do when she found that Anne had removed her ring and left it on the nightstand?

Anne had held her emotions together until she was away from Tiffany, and they had settled in their new suite. Now that it was safe, she broke down. The pain of Tiffany's infidelity and selfishness came out in waves as she cried. Skylar and Karen comforted her, encouraging her to talk and let out all the years of betrayal and hurt. The release left her exhausted, so now all she could do was rest against Cynthia like a rag doll.

Jake and Tad were gone, so it was down to just her new suitemates. CJ and Karen snuggled against each other on the opposite couch.

Dillon popped the tops off several beers. She held out two bottles to Cynthia and said, "Anne, I think a beer would do you some good."

Anne took the bottle and smiled up at Dillon. "Thanks."

"Hey, I'm sorry I lost it earlier," Dillon said.

Anne took Dillon's hand. "I thought it was sweet. It's nice to know I have someone that will stand up for me." While she held Dillon's hand, she noticed the fingerprint bruises that were forming on her arm. She looked around the room, fighting back her tears. "I appreciate all of you guys being here for me."

Cynthia squeezed her leg. "Who would have thought?"

"Thought what?" Anne asked.

"Who'd have thought two months ago that it would be the six of us sitting here together? Not just sitting here, but that we'd be so..."

"So important to each other." Karen finished Cynthia's sentence.

"Yeah, and that we would depend on each other so much. It's weird, I didn't even know any of you, except for Anne."

"I'm sorry that we didn't turn up anyone you knew in New York," CJ said.

"It was a long shot." Cynthia sighed. "I'd hoped someone I knew survived. But I'm glad I found you guys. I can't believe how much we've all bonded."

"A crisis can do that," Dillon said. "You have to

sort out who you can trust to have your back."

"It's nice having this family feeling," Skylar said. She quickly added, "Not that I wanted something like this to happen to get it."

Dillon put her arm around Skylar. "We get it. Before this, we were all so wrapped up in our own world that we didn't have the time, or more like didn't take the time for each other. There were always so many distractions, which in the end meant nothing. All that's important is this, being here for each other. It's a shame it took something so drastic for us to figure it out."

"Is it wrong that I'm enjoying the slower pace?" Karen asked.

"No," CJ said. "Is it wrong that I'm happy to have Dillon back?"

"I'm sorry." Dillon glanced down at her hands. "Thanks for not throwing me out when I was being a jerk."

"You weren't a jerk. You were grieving, but I did miss you," CJ said. "Just don't tell anyone I said that, or I'll deny it."

"Okay, so do we need to kill the witnesses?" Dillon chuckled.

"Naw, we'll let them live as long as they swear that they weren't listening."

"Listening to what?" Cynthia said.

They all laughed.

❧ ❧ ❧ ❧ ❧

Dillon yawned and stretched her arms over her head. She glanced at Anne, who kept nodding off. *Poor thing.* She had to be emotionally drained. The evening had taken its toll on everyone.

They barely made it through two beers before deciding to call it a night. Dillon shut their bedroom door, and her heart raced when she realized they were alone for the first time. Skylar smiled and slid up to her, wrapping her arms around Dillon's waist.

"Alone at last." Skylar had a flirtatious look on her face that was impossible to miss, no matter how hard Dillon tried.

"Um…do you want to use the bathroom first?" Dillon asked.

"I'm not going to bite." Skylar laughed. She abruptly stopped. "Sweetheart, what's wrong?"

"Long day." Dillon untangled herself from Skylar's embrace. She turned away and began putting her clothes in the dresser drawers. She worked with her back to Skylar, while she weighed her words.

"Please talk to me," Skylar said. "I promised I'd talk to you when something bothered me. I need you to do the same."

Dillon stopped arranging the shirts and her arms fell to her side; slowly she turned to Skylar. No matter how many times she blinked her eyes, she couldn't stop the tears from rolling down her cheek.

Skylar stiffened and clenched her hands at her sides but didn't say anything.

"I don't want to screw this up," Dillon said.

"What are you afraid of screwing up?"

"The first time went so wrong."

"Oh Babe." Skylar moved toward Dillon. "You don't have to be afraid." Skylar's warm gray eyes welcomed Dillon, but Dillon remained rooted to where she stood.

"It would hurt too much if it went wrong again."

Dillon felt exposed and wanted to turn back to her task but didn't.

"Is that why night after night you leave me aching so much, I can barely sleep?" A smile played on Skylar's lips. "I'm not sure how many more cold showers my body can withstand."

Dillon didn't smile. She picked through her clothes and pulled out a pair of shorts and a t-shirt. "Sorry, I'm afraid I don't find it funny. I need a shower."

She was almost to the bathroom door when Skylar's voice stopped her. "Please Dillon, I wasn't laughing at you. I was just trying to cut through some of this tension."

"What do you want me to do?"

"I want you to talk to me. I want to understand what you're thinking. What you're feeling."

"Terror. That about sums it up."

"Why?"

"Why? Because I like you," Dillon said. "Oh, for God's sakes, now I sound like a fucking Mouseketeer."

"Am I allowed to laugh now?" Skylar tried to hold back her smile.

A grin broke out on Dillon's face, and it soon turned to laughter. Skylar joined her.

Skylar moved toward Dillon and put her hand on the side of Dillon's face. She looked into her eyes and moved against her. Skylar's breasts brushed against Dillon.

Dillon gasped and took in too much air, almost causing her to choke. She exhaled loudly, trying to calm her racing heart. It had been months since their animalistic passion, and Dillon wanted to move slower even though her body screamed out for release.

Dillon wrapped her arms around Skylar and drew her closer. Their bodies rubbed against one another as Dillon found Skylar's lips. The kiss started out soft and sweet, but the desire soon turned it more urgent.

Skylar kneaded the muscles in Dillon's shoulders, while Dillon enjoyed Skylar's softness. Tentatively, Dillon touched Skylar's breast and was rewarded with a throaty moan. Gently, she ran her finger over Skylar's hardening nipple, letting the sensation course through Skylar's body. Dillon kept up the gentle pressure, as Skylar pushed into Dillon.

"We've had a couple months of foreplay, I'm not sure how much more I can take," Skylar said, her voice husky.

Dillon grinned, the mischievousness back in her eyes. "But I want our second first time to be special."

"Our third first kiss was good. I think this will be too." Skylar ran her hand up the inside of Dillon's thigh. Dillon tensed when Skylar's hand reached its destination. Dillon pushed against Skylar's hand and increased the pressure she put on Skylar's nipple. With her other hand, Dillon unbuttoned Skylar's jeans and slid the zipper down. Once she had access, she ran her hand inside Skylar's underwear. The wetness surprised her, and she grinned.

"I warned you." Skylar moaned. "You've been driving me crazy for weeks."

"I think I can probably help you out with this little problem of yours." Dillon slowly rubbed Skylar's clitoris.

"Please," Skylar said, pushing against Dillon. "Oh God, Dillon, please."

Chapter Fifteen

Skylar opened her eyes and smiled. She laid half on Dillon, their naked bodies intertwined. Dillon's chest rhythmically rose and fell beneath her. Gently, Skylar ran her fingers through Dillon's thick hair. Dillon murmured but didn't awaken.

She'd lost count of how many times Dillon brought her to climax, but she knew she'd never felt so satiated before. *Unbelievable.* It astonished her how completely she'd given herself to Dillon, and how good it felt to do so. Never in her life had she opened up so completely to anyone. Now, watching Dillon sleep, she wanted to do it again.

She slowly moved down Dillon's body and lightly brushed Dillon's nipple with her lips. Dillon shifted in her sleep. Skylar slid Dillon's nipple into her mouth and gradually increased the sucking motion. Dillon moaned, and her eyes opened.

Dillon greeted Skylar with a smile. Skylar met her gaze and flicked Dillon's nipple with her tongue. With surprising speed, Dillon flipped Skylar onto her back and pinned her to the bed. Without hesitation, she slid down Skylar's body and her mouth found Skylar's ache. Skylar started to protest, but when Dillon flicked her tongue, Skylar forgot her protests and opened her legs further so Dillon could have all of her.

After last night, Skylar figured she'd be sore or too satiated to come. She'd been wrong. Dillon's warm tongue soothed her and excited her at the same time. She closed her eyes, laid back, and enjoyed the sensations coursing through her body.

※※※※

"We thought we were going to have to come in there and get you," Karen said when Dillon and Skylar exited their bedroom.

The others were sitting around the table, enjoying their morning coffee; the smirks on their faces gave away their thoughts. Skylar blushed, and Dillon tried her best to look dark and brooding.

"Busted." CJ laughed and pointed. "Check out the looks on their faces."

"Don't you have something more important to discuss than our sex life?" Dillon tried to maintain a scowl, but her eyes danced.

"Who said anything about sex?" CJ said. "I do believe you just outed yourselves."

"You walked into that one," Cynthia said with a laugh.

"God, I'm going back to bed." Dillon regretted her choice of words as soon as they'd left her mouth.

The group continued mercilessly teasing them while they searched for something to eat for breakfast. None of them wanted to go down to the main dining area for a meal, so they scrounged the few things they'd moved from their old living quarters.

After a delicious meal of dry cereal and pop tarts, the conversation turned more serious. "Your meeting isn't going to be pleasant," Anne said. "I'm sorry I've put you in this position."

"It's not your fault. We're big kids, it'll be fine." Cynthia tried to sound upbeat, but worry lines creased her forehead.

Tiffany would be hurt and angry, a lethal combination. The Commission didn't need drama, considering the challenges they faced. They needed to refocus and work on the projects that would help ensure their survival.

"Let's hope she's pouting, or better yet, doesn't show," Dillon said.

"I know her. She'll show. She's ready for a fight. I feel awful." Anne looked down and swirled the coffee left in her cup. "I'm sorry. I don't want my personal drama to interfere with us getting back on track."

"It's not your fault." Skylar patted Anne's hand and waited for her to look up before she continued. "You need to stop apologizing because of the things she's done. Besides, I have all the confidence in the world in our able-bodied Commission."

"Skylar's right. Well, at least about you having no need to apologize." Dillon stood. "Well girls, shall we head to the lion's den?"

Karen sighed, got to her feet, and gave CJ a kiss.

"Let's do it." Cynthia clapped her hands together. "I'm ready for whatever the day brings."

Dillon wished she shared Cynthia's certainty.

※ ※ ※ ※

Tiffany already sat stoically glaring when they arrived at the meeting. The air sizzled with tension, as they took their seats. Dillon had hoped Tiffany would be humbled by what happened, but it was apparent that her anger seethed just under the surface. Renee stared at her papers, engrossed in reviewing her notes. *Had she heard what happened last night?* Judging by her calm demeanor, she hadn't.

Jake wandered in last. *Rough night?* He looked like he'd gotten little sleep.

"Since we're all here, shall we get started?" Cynthia said.

"Why the fuck not?" Tiffany slapped her hand on the table. "I've got some things I'd like for us to discuss."

Here we go. Any hope that Tiffany would rise above was gone. No doubt, it would soon become personal. Dillon braced herself for the worst.

"Well, I guess I'll start." Tiffany glanced around the table with a dangerous smirk. Not a sign of remorse or humility. "Let's talk about betrayal, shall we?"

"I thought that's a topic you'd want to avoid," Dillon shot back. "Quite frankly, I'm more concerned about the critical work we need to do than your pathetic personal problem."

Cynthia grabbed Dillon's leg under the table and gave her a pleading look.

"Oh really, so you think I'm the only one here with personal problems?" A satisfied glint came into Tiffany's eyes. "Maybe you should pull off those fucking rose colored glasses and take a look around you."

"Come on, ladies," Jake chimed in. "We have some important things we need to get done. Can't we table this until later?"

Tiffany rose from the table and approached him with a sly smile. "Ah, Mr. Jake, the man of the house. Care to tell everyone how much of a man you truly are?"

Jake looked at her, confused.

"Oh, going to play innocent, are you?" Tiffany let out a cruel laugh. "Maybe you should tell your wife and your girlfriend to be a little more discreet when they're discussing your sexual prowess."

Jake's face fell and he squirmed in his chair. Dillon suspected he wanted to find an escape. He briefly gazed at Dillon, but when their eyes met, he turned his head and studied the painting on the wall.

"Maybe that's why you look so tired. Trying to keep two women satisfied must be taking its toll."

"What the hell is she talking about?" Dillon said, turning to Jake, but he diverted his gaze and doodled on the pad of paper in front of him.

"Jakey here, he's decided to start his own harem." Tiffany clapped her hand on Jake's shoulder. "Or maybe, it's just that all the lesbians have made the two ladies horny for each other, and they decided to let Jake join in."

"It's not like that," Jake finally said. He tried to squirm out of Tiffany's grasp, but her hand remained firmly on his shoulder. "It's different now. Everyone needs someone, some physical comfort, and Nancy was alone. It was Lily's idea."

"Why didn't you say anything?" Dillon suspected her face showed the disgust she was feeling.

"Don't look at me like that. It wasn't anyone else's business. I don't hear you running around telling me what you and Skylar are doing." Jake defensively crossed his arms over his chest.

"He's right, Dillon, this isn't our business," Renee said.

"You go girl." Tiffany released her hold on Jake

and spun toward Renee. "Why don't you tell Dillon the reason you hate her?"

"I don't hate Dillon," Renee snapped.

"Right." All eyes watched Tiffany as she prowled around the table toward Renee, with a smirk on her face. "But isn't she the reason you can't get laid? Aren't you sick of hearing Katie go on and on and on about Dillon? Apparently, Katie's not interested in a soft roly-poly woman, with pasty white skin. She wants a real woman with muscles and a tan, like our ever-popular Dillon."

Silently, Renee stared at the table, fighting back tears. Dillon opened her mouth to speak when Cynthia slammed her hand onto the table.

"Shut up." Cynthia glared at Tiffany.

"My dear old ex-friend, maybe you and Katie can start a club. You could call it, 'I want Dillon in my pants, but she won't bite.'"

Cynthia winced. Tiffany smirked, apparently enjoying the pain she inflicted.

Dillon shifted her gaze between Renee and Cynthia. By the pained expression on their faces, Tiffany's words hit a nerve. Now wasn't the time to figure it out; she needed to find a way to stop Tiffany's onslaught.

"Tiffany, attacking everyone else isn't going to fix your mess," Karen said, joining the conversation. "Maybe you should take responsibility for yourself. Try and fix what you did and leave everyone else alone."

Tiffany let out a cruel laugh and turned to Karen. She kept her gaze glued on Karen as she walked around to Karen's side of the table. "Are you going to take responsibility when you find your best friend, Leslie, with her wrists slit?"

"What the hell are you talking about?" The muscles in Karen's neck bulged and her jaw was set, as she stared up at Tiffany.

"Cut the outrage." Tiffany rolled her eyes and flicked her wrist in Karen's direction. "When Dillon lost her precious Jane, you guys couldn't do enough for her, but what about poor Leslie? All of you have been treating her like she has the plague."

"You don't know what you're talking about," Karen shouted, but Dillon recognized the doubt in her eyes.

"You don't have a clue what she's been up to, do you?"

Karen glared but didn't respond.

Tiffany laughed. "I didn't think so. Don't you feel guilty slobbering all over CJ, knowing Leslie lost Denise? Did you think twice about moving out of the suite, leaving her to handle her own grief? Why should I care! You're the one who will have to look yourself in the mirror when she turns up dead."

"Enough!" Dillon hit the table with her fist.

"I'm almost done." Tiffany leveled a cold gaze at Dillon. Her lips curled into a smile, and she let out a cold laugh. "Poor naïve Dillon, do you want to hear who your bar wench really is? I bet she never told you what she does on her knees."

Without warning, Cynthia stood up and knocked her chair over. "God damn you, Tiffany. Shut the fuck up, already." Tiffany looked at Cynthia, shock registering on her face. "All you do is destroy everything you touch. You had it all. You could have had anything, but you pissed it all away." Cynthia pointed at Tiffany. "You had your second chance and you're fucking it up again. Anne is an incredible woman and God knows why she stood by your side for so long."

Tiffany started to respond, but Cynthia cut her off. "No, you're going to listen for a change. This was your opportunity to be something different. Your daddy's gone, so you don't have to run around trying to please him anymore. The company you hate is gone; you could have become what you always wanted to be, but no, you're gonna fuck this up too. I brought all those canvases and paints back for you when we went on a supply mission, but have you used them? No, they're still boxed up in your suite. You had the opportunity to change, to be somebody else, someone good. But here you are trying to tear everything and everyone down, to destroy everything in your path, but this time I won't let you."

Everyone in the room stared, stunned by Cynthia's outburst. No one dared to say anything. Tiffany's shoulders sagged and it was as if she was being deflated. The look of angry arrogance was replaced by defeat. Without warning, Tiffany abruptly turned and stormed out of the room.

After Tiffany left, Dillon stared at the door for several seconds. No one spoke. Eventually, Cynthia bent down and picked up her overturned chair. She plopped into it and put her head in her hands, the tirade seemingly draining all her energy.

The room was silent. Everyone looked down at the table, sneaking glances at one another and then quickly looking down again. Dillon suspected that everyone was weighing whether they should take Tiffany's lead and walk out as well. A million thoughts rushed through her head, but she needed to focus on keeping the Commission together.

"Well, wasn't that fun?" Dillon said, breaking the silence. "Come on guys, heads up." Most everyone around the table glanced up but kept their heads down. Cynthia continued to keep her face buried in her hands. Dillon got up from her chair and stood behind Cynthia. She gently put her hands on Cynthia's shoulders and lightly kneaded them. "We've come too far, built too good of relationships to let her bring us down. You guys are my family now, all of you. We've worked well together, and we still can. Please don't let her win."

They were all looking at her now, but still no one spoke.

"Jake, you're my buddy. You have been since the first day I nearly ran you over. Sorry about my reaction earlier. She caught me off guard. You need to do what's right for you and your family. None of us should be judging. Hell, lesbians of all people should know how shitty that feels. Are you still with me?"

"Yes," Jake said with a half-smile.

"Good. What about you, Renee?"

"We're good. Sorry if I ever took my frustration out on you."

"No problem. You know..." Dillon started to say, but Renee cut her off.

"Dillon, please I'd prefer not to talk about it here."

"Fair enough. So are you ready to get down to work?"

"You know I am," Renee said with a smile.

Dillon returned the smile before shifting her gaze. "Karen, you know Tiffany was right. We should probably be thanking her for pointing it out to us."

"I know." Karen looked back down at the table.

"So, are you going to sit around and feel sorry for yourself, or are you going to do something about it?" Dillon challenged.

"I guess I'm going to have to do something about it."

"Great, so are you in?"

"Definitely," Karen answered. "But first I need to invite Leslie to have lunch with me, just the two of us."

"So that just leaves you." Dillon hugged Cynthia around the neck. Cynthia put her hands on Dillon's forearms and squeezed back. "Nothing will ever break our summer camp bond. You hear me? Nothing." Dillon couldn't see Cynthia's face, but by the uncomfortable shuffling from the others, she suspected Cynthia was crying. "Hey guys, can we take five?"

She didn't have to ask twice; the remaining Commission members sprang from their seats and scrambled from the room. Dillon pulled a chair beside Cynthia and sat facing her. Cynthia picked at her cuticle. Several tears trickled down her face and landed on her jeans. Dillon reached up and wiped one off her cheek.

"Cynthia, it's okay," Dillon said, not sure what else to say.

"She's trying to drive a wedge between us." Cynthia swiped at the tears streaking down her face.

"Then don't let her. She can't do anything to us unless we let her."

"But didn't you hear what she said?"

"I heard."

"And?"

"And, what?"

"Doesn't it make you uncomfortable?"

"Should it?"

"Dammit, Dillon." Cynthia raised her voice. "You tell me."

"I'm thinking by your reaction there may be some truth in what she said."

Cynthia gave a slight nod but said nothing. The old Dillon would have avoided the conversation, but she knew to survive there could be no secrets. The tough conversations had to be had. Honesty was the only way to ensure they could trust one another implicitly. "Well then, I'm flattered. And no, it doesn't change anything."

"It's not like that, really," Cynthia said. "I just really, really like you. We have fun together. We laugh a lot, so in one of my weaker moments early on, I told Tiffany that I wished I'd met you before Skylar did."

Dillon put her hand under Cynthia's chin and lifted it, so she gazed into Cynthia's eyes. She looked so vulnerable, which only enhanced her beauty. "Maybe I shouldn't say this, but I'm going to anyway. If we're going to have a completely honest friendship, then everything needs to be on the table. I won't lie to you. If there were no Skylar, you would, without a doubt, be the woman I'd be most interested in."

A look of pain shot through Cynthia's eyes before she closed them.

"Did I say too much?" Dillon asked.

"No," Cynthia answered, opening her eyes. "I appreciate your honesty, it's one of the reasons I love you. I just don't want to lose your friendship or Skylar's. It's not like I would ever cross any lines or betray Skylar. And I don't want you or Skylar to think..." Cynthia stopped, not knowing how to finish.

"Don't worry, I don't think most of the time," Dillon teased. She got a slight smile from Cynthia, so she continued. "Seriously, you're my friend and nothing is going to change that. Actually, you and CJ are my best friends, and I couldn't imagine my life without you. Besides, despite my obvious charm and personality, you're getting the best end of the deal. You don't have to live with me. Oh wait, you still have to live with me too. It sucks to be you."

Cynthia laughed. Dillon hoped their natural playfulness would break through her discomfort. "Don't flatter yourself. Didn't you catch the operative words, 'weaker moment'?" Cynthia jabbed back.

"Does that mean you've already dumped me and set your sights on new prey?"

"Ancient history, baby," Cynthia said. "Haven't you heard this is the new lesbian Mecca?"

"I must have missed the memo." Dillon smiled broadly. "Are we okay?"

"We're good." Cynthia leaned over and hugged Dillon, who tightly returned the embrace.

❧❧❧❧

Even without Tiffany, once they'd resumed the meeting, it took nearly two hours to agree on a plan to get the group back on track. After a heated debate, they decided, for now, the Commission wouldn't impose rules on the group; instead, they would try to get everyone on board through persuasion. They would present their plan as a recommendation, not an edict.

The Commission unanimously selected Dillon to speak to the group after dinner. While honored, she was also apprehensive. Since the group had gotten so far off-track, she wasn't sure she was up for the challenge. The speech weighed heavily on her when she left the meeting, not wanting to let the Commission down since they'd put their trust in her.

Chapter Sixteen

Dillon dove into the cool blue water and swam under the surface until her lungs could take no more. She shot out of the water, taking in the fresh air. After a couple quick breaths, she kicked back under, enjoying the tranquility. The pond seemed to clear her jumbled mind. She'd been distracted trying to come up with the words she needed for tonight's speech. Under the surface, with the world blocked out, her sentences started to coalesce, and the speech took shape. She dove again, hoping for more inspiration.

Dillon had wanted to spend the afternoon preparing her speech, but her friends convinced her otherwise. Skylar had been the catalyst. She'd reminded Dillon that over preparation oftentimes was worse than being under prepared, and Dillon didn't want to come off as wooden or robotic. It was imperative that Dillon's natural sincerity shine through tonight.

She'd still not been fully convinced until Skylar pulled out a black and white two-piece swimsuit that left little to the imagination. Seductively, she slid the bottoms up her evenly tanned legs. Dillon's hands trembled as she hooked the top and ran her hand down Skylar's flat stomach. Skylar smirked when she turned and looked into Dillon's eyes. All Dillon could manage was, "You win."

They'd discovered a small, crystal-clear pond a

few weeks ago and had shared the location with their closest friends. Now, the small contingent frequently snuck away to the secluded area to enjoy a little privacy from the larger group. They almost missed it when they explored the grounds with it being nestled deep in the trees. It took about ten minutes to get there on the ATVs, so none of the others had discovered it yet. They'd named it The Cove, and it quickly became their sanctuary.

The others, after a quick dip in the pond, straggled to the sandy area and lay on the towels spread haphazardly on the beach. Dillon bobbed her head up again and her gaze immediately went to Skylar, who caught her staring and gave her a playful wink. Dillon slightly nodded her head and slowly licked her lips before she remembered where she was. She glanced around, checking to see if anyone else noticed.

Skylar stood and, with a seductive sway in her hips, made her way to the pond. Before she dove, she bent low enough to give Dillon a good view down her bikini top. Dillon's heart raced. Before Skylar hit the water, Dillon swam to meet her.

When they came together, Dillon wrapped her arms around Skylar's waist and pulled her against her body. Skylar let Dillon draw her in and her lips found Dillon's. The kiss started slow and soft but gained in intensity. Dillon's leg slid between Skylar's, and she moved it seductively back and forth. With one hand, Dillon kept them afloat and the other gripped Skylar's buttocks and pulled her more firmly against her leg. Rhythmically, she pushed Skylar back, only to pull her forward again, increasing the pressure between Skylar's legs.

"No," Skylar said weakly. "Not fair, Dillon. You

can't get me this worked up, with no chance of release. That's mean." Skylar looked back at the beach, where their friends lay oblivious to them.

"Who said you can't have a release?" Dillon winked. Her passion welled up, but she tried to keep her demeanor playful.

"Not here, for God's sake." Her words were cut off by a moan as Dillon's leg brushed across her again.

"Come on." Dillon swam toward the bend in the pond.

They were about twenty feet from the curve that would lead them to the wooded area when a voice stopped them.

"Hey, where are you two going?" CJ called.

"Just exploring the rest of the pond," Dillon said. She hoped she sounded innocent.

"Carry on," CJ said.

As soon as the trees obscured them, Dillon guided Skylar to the edge of the pond where they could both stand with their feet touching the bottom. Their lips met and their tongues soon entangled. It stunned Dillon how much she wanted Skylar, but she didn't have time to question it now. Her hand snaked up under Skylar's swim top and brushed her nipple. Skylar moaned softly and straddled Dillon's leg.

Skylar's breath caught when Dillon squeezed her nipple. They were both so aroused that Dillon knew this wouldn't take long. They continued to kiss, as their hands roamed each other's bodies. Without warning, Dillon snaked her hand down Skylar's bottoms and found her mark. Skylar gasped and ground against Dillon's hand. She buried her mouth against Dillon's shoulder, trying to muffle her cries. She pumped against Dillon's hand, while at the same time finding Dillon's swollen need. They resumed their kiss as they rhythmically brought one another to ecstasy.

They clung to each other, trying to catch their breath before Skylar suggested they return. When they came around the bend, they made extra splashing noises to alert their friends to their arrival.

"Damn, I was sure you two were up to something," CJ shouted when they got closer to shore.

"Can't we check out the terrain without you getting suspicious?" Dillon called back. "Besides, I need a snack. I'm ravenous."

Skylar poked her in the ribs, and Dillon jumped. "Really?" Skylar whispered.

Dillon stifled a laugh, knowing they'd avoided detection. There were some advantages to how quickly Skylar excited her.

They swam to where the bottom became shallow and walked the rest of the way out of the water. Their suits clung to them and dripped water onto the sand. Their hair was slicked back and immediately started drying in the soft breeze. They talked quietly as they walked hand in hand.

Cynthia and Anne were stretched out on their towels with their eyes closed, possibly asleep. Now that CJ had lost interest in what Dillon and Skylar were doing, she laid nearby with her nose in a book. Maria rummaged through the remains of the picnic, while Tasha had her hand buried in a bag of Doritos. About twenty yards down the waterline, Karen and Leslie sat on beach chairs, engaged in an intense conversation.

Dillon smiled at the scene before she plopped down on her towel.

CJ looked over her book. "I thought you were

hungry."

"I'm not going to wrestle those two for leftovers." Dillon's gaze shifted toward Tasha and Maria.

Dillon rolled onto her back and shut her eyes, letting the sun warm her. Skylar dropped down beside her and took Dillon's hand. Their fingers intertwined. She should have opened her eyes, but instead she felt herself drifting off.

❧❧❧❧

Skylar enjoyed the feel of Dillon's large hand enveloping her much smaller one. She tried to nap, but sleep escaped her. She inhaled deeply twice, but still struggled to catch her breath. Fear gripped her. *Is this what a panic attack feels like?* It was frightening to be this happy, to let someone into her heart so completely. She'd had lovers before, if she could call them that. More like sex partners, but she'd never let them have any part of her heart. What if Dillon discovered how unlovable she was? *Would Dillon disappear?*

Her mind raced ahead. All the available women. Surely, one or more of them would be interested in Dillon. Her stomach lurched, and she battled another round of breathing difficulties. She squeezed her eyes shut. Maybe it would stop her thoughts.

"Are you okay?" Dillon said softly.

"Sure, why?" Skylar stammered.

"You have my hand in a death grip."

"Oh, sorry." Skylar relaxed her hold. "Go back to sleep."

❧❧❧❧

The sun had moved across the sky, indicating it was time to return to the mansion. The groans and heavy sighs from her friends matched Dillon's feeling. The afternoon went much too quickly, but it was cathartic. While still being nervous about her speech, the tightness in Dillon's shoulders had lessened.

Her friends were right. She needed more moments like this, instead of being focused on work all the time. Skylar reminded her frequently that they were given a second chance to get things right, and they shouldn't squander the opportunity.

While they were packing their belongings, Dillon leaned down and whispered to Skylar. "I think Cynthia's struggling. Mind if I have her ride back with me?"

Skylar smiled and nodded. "It would do her good."

"I think your back should be healed by now," Dillon said to Cynthia. "What do you say you ride back with me?"

Cynthia looked at Dillon and then to Skylar.

Skylar smiled and said, "Be my guest. You're the only one crazy enough to ride with her when she's got that glint in her eye."

"Are you sure?" Cynthia said, her voice tentative.

Before coming to the cove, Dillon filled Skylar in on what had happened at the Commission meeting. Skylar earned more respect when her only reaction had been one of concern for Cynthia. She didn't appear to be upset or feel threatened. During such uncertain times, they needed all the friends they could get, so no way would she let this derail their friendship.

"Why don't you go get your chariot?" Skylar

said to Dillon.

Dillon cocked her head, and her eyes narrowed when she looked at Skylar. Realization dawned. Skylar wanted to talk to Cynthia alone. "Oh right, sure thing."

❧❧❧❧

Cynthia fidgeted with her towel to keep her hands steady. Obviously, Skylar wanted to get her alone. Her sending Dillon away hadn't been subtle. *But why?*

Skylar watched Dillon jog off before meeting Cynthia's gaze. "It's okay." Skylar put her arm around Cynthia.

"Dillon told you about the meeting?" Cynthia said and looked down at Skylar.

"Yes, she did. And it's fine." Skylar smiled.

"It wasn't like that. You must believe me; I never wanted you two not to be together. I was just feeling lost."

"You don't need to explain."

"But I do. Tiffany was trying to stir up trouble."

"Big surprise there," Skylar said, with a smile.

"I can't even remember exactly what I said to her." Cynthia looked into Skylar's sympathetic eyes, which somehow made her feel worse. "But it was before I got to know you."

"It's okay. You can't help your feelings," Skylar said. "This has been one hell of a ride, and Dillon is amazing."

"You have to know though; I was just hurting and scared." Cynthia knew she tended to ramble when nervous, but she wanted to say something to fix the situation. "Dillon is so damned solid and reliable.

She's someone I could count on. And during the worst of times, she made me laugh. And I made the mistake of talking to Tiffany, and she twisted everything around."

"So, you weren't attracted to Dillon?" Skylar asked.

Cynthia paused and for a split-second thought of lying, but instead reluctantly said, "Yes, I was attracted to her." *Idiot, keep your mouth shut.* Her rambling would only cause more problems. Feeling defeated, she dropped her head and stared at the ground.

"And that's exactly why I'm not worried." Skylar touched Cynthia's arm.

"I'm afraid I'm not following you." Cynthia couldn't meet Skylar's gaze. She'd just admitted that she'd been attracted to Skylar's girlfriend, but Skylar still had a smile on her face.

"Anyone else would have lied to me. It would have been easy to deny everything and blame Tiffany. Then we could all go on pretending that nothing happened, but it did happen."

Cynthia fought back tears. "I understand; it's all my fault. We can't just act like it never happened. Not that it makes a difference, but I am sorry."

"No, don't apologize."

"You're right." Defeat washed over Cynthia, and her heart felt heavy. She blinked back tears. "I'll let Anne know that I'm moving back to the other wing."

"Why?" Skylar squinted, as if she were looking into the sun, but it was at her back.

"I get it, sometimes an apology isn't enough." Cynthia was unable to hold back her tears any longer.

"Don't cry." Skylar wrapped her arms around

Cynthia. "That's not what I meant. I don't want you moving out."

"You don't?" Cynthia clung to Skylar and struggled to catch her breath.

"Of course not. I trust you both, completely." Skylar hugged Cynthia tighter. "You and Dillon chose to tell me the truth when a lie would have been so much easier. That tells me everything I need to know."

"You don't hate me?" Cynthia felt a flicker of hope.

"Oh God, no. I love you. We both do." Skylar hugged Cynthia again. "Big deal, you have feelings for Dillon, it happens all the time. Most people just aren't honest enough to admit it."

"It doesn't bother you?" Cynthia asked, wanting to make sure she understood Skylar.

"It doesn't," Skylar said. "The heart feels what the heart feels. Anyone that says they can control their feelings is lying. The only thing you have control over is your actions, and I know you would never betray me or Dillon."

"Never!" Cynthia said. "I love you guys."

"And we love you, so stop worrying so much."

"Sometimes I feel guilty because of the bonds I've developed with people here. The bonds are deeper and more intense than anything I've ever experienced in my life, including my family. Living through something like this changes people."

"There's nothing to feel guilty about."

"Do you ever feel closer to this group than you did with your own family?"

"Without question." Skylar avoided Cynthia's gaze and stared at the pond.

Before Cynthia could comment, the roar of an

engine cut off her words. Dillon soared over a small
hill, catching air, and landed about twenty feet away.
Cynthia and Skylar stood with their arms around each
other, smiling as they watched Dillon bearing down
on them. Dillon skidded to a stop a few feet away,
kicking up sand that harmlessly landed at their feet.

"She's such a child." Skylar laughed.

"Undoubtedly," Cynthia responded. She turned
toward Skylar. "We're okay?"

"We're better than okay," Skylar said. "You're
my family, and I love you."

"I love you too, Sky."

Dillon revved the engine, and Skylar rolled her
eyes. "Come on, the impetuous child is getting impa-
tient."

Cynthia laughed and walked with Skylar toward
Dillon and her ATV. Dillon leaned over and kissed
Skylar, while Cynthia climbed on behind her.

"You be nice, and don't scare the shit out of
Cynthia." Skylar wagged her finger at Dillon, who met
her gesture with a smirk. "I'm serious."

"You better hold on tight," Dillon said to
Cynthia, seconds before she gunned the engine.

Cynthia screamed, followed by laughter.

Chapter Seventeen

The sun had sunk beyond the horizon, but there was a lingering glimmer in the distance. Dillon nervously twisted the cloth napkin that was still on her lap. It would soon be dark, and the balcony would be bathed in a glow from the fire pits. The last of the dishes were being removed from the tables, and Renee's crew were setting up a podium near the end of the reflecting pool.

Dillon looked over the balcony at the shadows starting to invade the vast lawn. This had become one of her favorite places on the Estate. She loved the view and would sometimes sneak up here at night to look at the stars and listen to the crickets. It also held fond memories because of celebrations they'd had here. Renee was a genius and only used this space once or twice a month for special occasions, while the rest of the time, the meals were served in the conservatory.

Cynthia met her gaze across the table and gave her an encouraging look. Cynthia leaned over and in a loud whisper said, "Stop looking like you're going to puke. You've got this."

Dillon smiled and mouthed, "Thanks."

"Are you about ready?" Renee put her hand on Dillon's shoulder and gave a reassuring squeeze. "I think we have everything in place."

"Ready as I'll ever be." Dillon wiped the palms of

her hands on her napkin and set it on the table.

"Hold on," Renee said. "I'm going to make this official and introduce you."

Dillon nodded.

In order to get the attention of the lively group, Renee had to call out several times. Everyone seemed to be celebrating the news of finding other survivors and the champagne flowed. When the crowd finally quieted, Renee began. "I hope everyone enjoyed the meal."

The crowd burst into applause and whistles. A few women called out accolades while the rest of the group cheered them on. Renee smiled and gestured with her hands to quiet the group.

After a couple minutes of boisterous celebration, Renee continued. "As you know, we had the exciting news yesterday that there are other survivors." The crowd erupted again, many holding up their glasses and yelling cheers. Renee held up her own glass before she forged on. "Over the last couple of months, the Commission has been working extremely hard for you. Tonight, we would like to give you a state of the Estate, so to speak." More cheers rang out. "The Commission voted to have one of our members speak to you tonight. So, without further ado, please give a warm welcome to Dillon Mitchell."

The crowd cheered loudly as Dillon rose. She looked down into Skylar's comforting gray eyes. Skylar squeezed her hand, offering silent encouragement. Everyone's eyes bored into her as she made her way to the podium. The importance of the moment wasn't lost on her, but she couldn't give in to her nerves. The next fifteen minutes would set the course for the group well into the future. *Am I up to the challenge?* It was too late to question herself now.

When Dillon arrived at the podium, she hugged Renee before stepping behind it. She looked out at the crowd, letting her eyes adjust to the flickering light of the fire. The fire pits had been placed perfectly, so she was able to see most of the faces clearly.

"My friends," Dillon began. "I would like to start by thanking the Commission for entrusting me with the honor of speaking to you tonight."

Dillon stopped, smiled at the group, and took a sip of water from the glass on the podium.

"Before I stepped in front of you tonight, I planned to dive right into the practical matters at hand. We obviously have some very important decisions to make in order to move forward, but looking out at you now, I would like to go off script for a moment."

Dillon moved from behind the podium and went to the empty buffet table at the edge of the reflecting pool. She sat on the corner with one foot resting on the floor and the other leg dangling.

"For just a few minutes, I want to speak to you from my heart." Dillon tapped her hand on her chest for emphasis. She noticed her friends exchanging questioning glances with one another. They were obviously trying to figure out what Dillon was doing, since she hadn't discussed these changes with any of them, not even Skylar.

"The last couple of months haven't been easy, yet here we are. I can't speak for anyone else, but I hope you can relate to what I'm about to say." Dillon paused, looking out at the faces intently looking back at her. "Most of the time, I think I'm numb to the reality of what we're living through, because it's just too damned big for me to wrap my brain around.

Sometimes, in the quiet times when I'm alone, the emotions sneak up on me like a tidal wave. And it's usually something simple, something I never would've thought would set me off."

Dillon smiled sadly. "Just the other day, I was listening to music, and before I knew it tears were pouring down my cheeks. It shocked the shit out of me. I sat there for the longest time, trying to figure out what my problem was. Then it hit me; I was mourning. There is so much for all of us to mourn, but at that moment, I was mourning the loss of so much talent. Just like old friends, some of those voices had been with me for years. They'd been singing to me since I was a teenager, and they'd brought me comfort and joy when I needed it most. The realization was like a slap in the face – they would never sing again. Their music would forever be frozen in time. I was angry. I was sad. I was hurt. And the grief and fear choked me, making it hard to breathe. My chest ached so bad I wasn't sure I could go on, but then something happened."

Dillon stopped speaking and stood up from the table. She made eye contact with several in the audience; the looks were open and encouraging, so she continued. "I'd turned off my music because I couldn't listen to it any longer. I couldn't bear it. Then I thought I heard something, so I stood and walked toward the sound." As Dillon said this, she began walking across the room and stopped in front of one of the tables full of women.

"I came around the side of the mansion and stopped in my tracks. Renee and Sid were taking out the garbage. They were singing, and it was the sweetest, most beautiful sound I'd ever heard." Dillon looked down at Renee, and then her eyes shifted to where Sid sat. She looked back at Renee and smiled.

Renee returned the smile.

Dillon paused for a couple beats, not wanting to hurry her remarks. "Then the tears came back, but this time they were tears of joy. At that moment, I knew no matter what we'd lost, we weren't defeated. As long as we are here together, there would still be voices lifted in song. I can't tell you if either one can carry a tune, but it didn't matter. To my ears, it was the most beautiful song I'd ever heard."

Dillon stopped and looked at Renee and Sid again as if they were the only two people in the room. "Thank you."

"You're welcome," Renee said, blinking back tears. Sid nodded to Dillon and swallowed hard. Dillon turned and silently made her way across the room and didn't speak again until she was behind the podium.

"I'm not the same person I was two short months ago. I'd be shocked if any of us are. As we move forward, we probably won't be the same two months from now. I hope we'll be better. What we do now will determine that."

"I know we haven't always agreed on everything, and sometimes it has been pretty intense and ugly." Dillon looked directly at Tiffany. "I don't know if I have any family left out there." Dillon peered out over the railing into the distance for several seconds before her attention returned to the group. She scanned the crowd, and her gaze stopped at the table where her closest friends sat. She drew strength from them before her gaze continued around the room until it landed back on Tiffany. "But I know I do in here. You are my family now, and I hope I'm yours."

Dillon glanced around. All eyes were on her, and several women nodded.

"I'm scared and I need your help," Dillon said, her tears welling. She'd promised herself she wouldn't cry, but she was in danger of breaking her promise. Dillon's gaze locked on the gray eyes she sought whenever she needed comfort. Skylar looked at her with compassion and pride through her own tears.

Skylar smiled and mouthed, "Go on."

"My job was to stand up here and lead you in the discussion of the things we need to accomplish, but I'm afraid I can't do that." A murmur rose in the crowd, as Dillon stood not saying anything. Shortly, it died down and their attention returned to her.

"With your permission, I'd like to sit down with all of you. I'd like to have this conversation sitting around the proverbial kitchen table with my family. Right now, I'm raw and more than anything, I need to be with all of you. Standing here behind a podium, the distance is too great."

CJ leaned over and whispered to Skylar, who nodded and quickly stood. Skylar made her way to the front of the room and took Dillon's hand. Several in the group jumped up and rearranged the tables. Wordlessly, Skylar led Dillon to the head of the table and motioned for her to sit. Dillon lowered herself into the offered seat, but Skylar remained standing. The rest of the group moved around and found a seat. Dillon pulled out a chair for Skylar.

Skylar shook her head, no.

"Sky, why won't you sit?" Dillon asked.

"I'm not on the Commission; they should be the ones surrounding you."

"No, it's you I need with me. Don't you know it's you that gives me the strength to do this?"

"She needs you, Sky," Cynthia said, patting the seat between hers and Dillon's.

Skylar hesitated as she sat, searching the other's faces.

Dillon slid her chair closer and put her arm over Skylar's shoulders. "Let's get down to business."

※ ※ ※ ※

"You did it. You crazy son-of-a-bitch, you pulled it off," CJ said when they were back in their suite. "I can't believe how much you got accomplished tonight."

"No, we did it," Dillon said. Heat rose in her cheeks. How was it she felt both exhilarated and exhausted at the same time?

"Dillon, you were amazing," Anne said. "The energy in the room was incredible."

"Even Tiffany seems to be on board," Cynthia added. "Now that was no small feat."

Dillon didn't want to continue down this path. Compliments always made her uneasy, so she needed to find a way to deflect them. "I think everyone was just ripe for some direction."

"You're my hero, Rick Grimes," CJ said, batting her eyelashes. "I'd follow you anywhere."

"Really?" Dillon chuckled, thankful for CJ, who always did something to make her laugh. "You did not just make a Walking Dead reference."

"Yep, I did."

"Please tell me there aren't zombies in our future."

CJ shrugged and held her hands out at shoulder level with her palms up.

"I, for one, found your leadership sexy," Skylar said.

"Damn, my secret's out. The only reason I did it was to get laid," Dillon said, pulling Skylar onto her lap.

"It worked." Skylar winked and ran her tongue slowly over her lips. She ran her hand through Dillon's hair and leaned forward, finding Dillon's lips. The kiss started out tenderly but intensified quickly.

Dillon broke the kiss, her face flushed, shocked by the surge she felt between her legs. "I'm not going to be able to have a civilized conversation with everyone if you do that again."

Karen laughed. "Be careful, Sky, she's a lightweight. We don't want her erupting right here."

Everyone laughed, while the heat rose up Dillon's neck onto her cheeks.

Chapter Eighteen

It had been nearly two months since Dillon's speech. In that time, the group had made tremendous progress. They'd finished the lookout tower, so now they could see over the tree line to the road leading to the mansion. Dillon knew it was a false sense of security, but after finishing it, she felt better. She was still driven to get things done, but the urgency had left her, and she was able to relax and enjoy the developing relationships.

Dillon glanced around the room, as Jake gave his report to the Commission. Even Tiffany was focused and nodding as he spoke. In fairness, Tiffany had made the greatest transformation, which still astonished Dillon.

"Everyone has finished the first level of weapons training?" Cynthia asked.

Jake nodded. "Yep, all but two. Unfortunately, they have a serious phobia when it comes to guns."

"I'm not sure they'll ever be comfortable," Dillon added. "Skylar's been working with them, but it's been slow going."

"But they're trying," Jake said. "The good news is about half the group have become pretty proficient." Jake tipped his head toward Dillon. "This one has become a regular sharpshooter."

"Maybe during target practice." Dillon laughed.

"As soon as the target moves, I can't hit a damned thing."

"But you can assemble, disassemble, and load an AK-47 blindfolded." Jake beamed at Dillon like he was a proud father.

Dillon playfully slapped at his arm. "Stop."

Tiffany laughed. "In a pinch, I think you'd do fine. You have a steady hand."

"Don't you think we should talk about the elephant in the room?" Karen said, her face more serious than the rest of the Commission members sitting around the table.

Renee sighed. "Can't we talk about our gardens? They're growing like crazy and quite impressive."

Karen patted Renee's hand. "I'd love to hear about them. Better yet, I think we should have a meeting at the gardens so we can see them firsthand. But we need to talk about the growing number of people out there and whether they're a threat."

"Last night, Anne told me that they'd located another group. What's that bring us up to now?" Tiffany asked.

"CJ gave me the numbers this morning." Karen pulled out a notebook and flipped it open.

Cynthia stood from the table and went to the giant whiteboard, where they kept tally. There were twenty-four groups listed on the board, with the largest being HOPE, from New York, that consisted of ninety-seven people, and the smallest being two people in the Appalachian Mountains in West Virginia.

"They located another group in Florida with eleven people," Karen said. She waited for Cynthia to write the group on the board before continuing. "Also, the group in Chicago added four more to their community."

Cynthia changed the number next to Chicago. "Any others?"

"Nope, that's it."

Cynthia reached toward the total but stopped. "Have they heard from the group in Missouri lately?"

Karen shook her head. "CJ says it's been nearly three weeks with no contact."

Cynthia began to erase the group name and the six people listed.

"No," Dillon said louder than she intended. Everyone's head snapped around. "Sorry. I just don't think we should be erasing people until we know for sure what's up."

"Okay." Cynthia nodded and let her hand with the eraser drop to her side, while she rewrote the number six with her other. "With the new group in Florida and the four new people joining the group in Chicago, that brings the population to 889."

Cynthia erased the old number and wrote 889 and followed it with an exclamation point, hitting her marker hard against the board when she made the dot. They clapped as they did each time the census was added to.

"Any more insight on whether Babcock's numbers are accurate?" Jake asked.

Karen shook her head. "Nope. HOPE is wary of them too, so at least we have an ally should things go south."

"CJ mentioned that Braxton Babcock has taken to communicating for himself, instead of relying on one of his groupies," Dillon said. "Apparently, it's working."

"How so?" Cynthia asked.

"He's been trying to get the clusters to join him in his mountain sanctuary. To date, HOPE reports that three small cells have been persuaded and are making their way to Colorado. I'm not clear on how they know this, but CJ seems to think the intel is good."

"Is he still trying to convince you?" Cynthia turned to Jake.

He nodded. "'Fraid so, but so far I've been able to hold him off."

"How soon before Babcock's population surpasses HOPE?" Cynthia said.

An involuntary shiver coursed through Dillon's body. She tried to hide it, but by the way Cynthia stared at her, she hadn't been successful. "Do we have to keep talking about him? It creeps me out."

"We need to talk about what happened in Amarillo last week," Jake said. "I think we need to have a serious discussion about manning the lookout tower twenty-four seven."

"Seriously?" Renee said. "Who's going to sign up for that?"

"I think he's right." Tiffany said.

Dillon resisted the impulse to turn and stare at the new Tiffany. It had been nearly a month since she'd started seriously participating with the group, but Dillon was still cautious and waiting for the old Tiffany to come out.

"Any reason to suspect Braxton Babcock had a hand in it?" Cynthia asked.

"Naw, I don't think so," Jake said. "CJ talked to the leader from Amarillo pretty extensively. He was understandably shaken up, but from his description, I don't believe they're involved."

"I've heard several different versions of the story. What's true?" Renee asked.

"From what we've been told, it was a gang of young men carrying heavy assault weapons. They had two large SUVs and the rest were riding motorcycles. They snagged four teenage girls and two adult women."

"How did they manage to snag them?" Cynthia asked. "Didn't they hear them coming?"

"They think they'd been watching them for a few days, and when the women went to work in the fields, they grabbed them." The crease in Jake's forehead deepened as he continued speaking. "When the rest figured out what was happening, a group of their best fighters gave chase. They drove into an ambush around a sharp bend in the road. The sons-of-bitches opened fire. It was over in minutes; everyone in both trucks died in the blast when one of the gas tanks exploded."

"Brutal." Dillon ran her hand over her face. "Hasn't everyone experienced enough loss? I can't even imagine how they must feel. But how do we know it wasn't Babcock?"

"We don't for sure, but my gut tells me it's not." Jake said.

"We're going to start making decisions on hunches?" Karen's face showed her skepticism.

"Long term, I wouldn't put it past him, but it's still early in the game." Jake said. "He's a classic narcissist. He believes he can charm anyone, so that's the angle he's working. He doesn't get to this level of dangerous, until he figures out his methods aren't working."

Everyone around the table nodded, although Karen still looked doubtful.

"Do we man the watchtower twenty-four seven then?" Cynthia asked.

"I'm not seeing the point," Renee said. "It would destroy morale, and things have been going pretty well lately."

"I have to agree," Karen said. "The girls would rebel. Besides, where would people escape for a little privacy?"

Everyone laughed. A couple weeks ago, two women decided to have a rendezvous in the watchtower. It had been a nice night and most of the mansion windows were open. The sex-crazed lovers hadn't realized how far sound carried in the still night air. Nearly everyone was treated to the moans and screams, as they brought one another to climax multiple times.

"Speaking of the need for privacy," Dillon said with a smirk. "We should have our first four individual living quarters done in a month or so."

"We never did determine who gets the first ones," Karen said.

Renee groaned. "Do we have to do that today? My brain hurts from all this talk of bad guys closing in."

Dillon held up her hand and shook her head. "No reason to do it now. We have plenty of work to do before they're ready."

"Does that mean we can go?" Tiffany glanced at her watch.

"Hot date?" Cynthia asked.

"Maybe." Tiffany looked down at the table. Dillon detected a slight blush.

She'd recently started dating Anne again. After Anne moved out, Tiffany had withdrawn. She'd disappear as soon as the workday was over and had stopped attending cocktail hour. She had emerged just in time for supper, but once the meal was over, she had left again. It was nearly three weeks before they'd discovered she'd been slipping off to use her paints and canvases, the ones that Cynthia had brought back for her. Her work was amazing, so two weeks ago, the Commission had convinced her to paint a large mural in the atrium to depict The Crisis. She'd reluctantly agreed, but now that she'd started, she was absorbed in the work.

She'd left one of her paintings, depicting Anne bathed in sunlight staring across a still lake, at the door to Anne's suite. She'd attached a note asking Anne out. The gesture had touched Anne, and she'd agreed to the date. Tiffany had been surprisingly chivalrous; each night, when she walked Anne home, she'd give her a sweet kiss before saying her good nights. Anne joked she was starting to get a little frustrated but was secretly flattered by Tiffany courting her again.

"Tiffany has a date," Cynthia said. "I guess we better adjourn this meeting then."

Despite the levity, Dillon sensed pain behind Cynthia's words. She'd done her best to be supportive of Anne and Tiffany, despite her own loneliness. Recently, it had been rumored that she was seeing two different women, but she hadn't shared that with Dillon. All Dillon knew was sometimes she didn't return to their suite until late at night. She and Skylar had discussed whether they should talk to Cynthia but decided against it. Cynthia was an adult, and the decision was ultimately hers.

"Meeting adjourned." Cynthia pounded the gavel on the table.

Chapter Nineteen

The sunlight streamed in the southern bank of windows of the Athens room. They'd given the room off the library that sported the gigantic mural of The School of Athens that nickname. It was reserved for quiet reflection and had become a sanctuary for when they wanted to read or do research.

When the patio door flew open, CJ looked up from her book. Katie stomped in, with a dark cloud accompanying her. *This can't be good.* CJ braced for trouble. Katie had been distant, almost sullen, and at other times seemed openly angry and hostile. CJ hoped she'd be over it by now, but lately she seemed more upset with Dillon and Skylar's relationship. The old Katie wasn't the type to say anything, but CJ feared the new Katie might.

A disgusted look crossed Katie's face when she saw Skylar lying with her head in Dillon's lap, while Dillon ran her fingers through Skylar's hair. Dillon studied a blueprint, and Skylar read a medical textbook. Neither looked up from the material they were intently studying.

"How sweet," Katie said.

Dillon looked up and smiled. CJ cringed, realizing Dillon missed the sarcasm in Katie's tone.

"Hi Katie," Skylar said cheerfully.

"Oh, I didn't know you were paying attention.

I thought you were having a nibble. After all, I hear that's what you're good for."

"What?" Dillon said, finally seeming to notice Katie's bad mood.

"I'm sure it's nothing she's told you about," Katie said.

Skylar sat up on the couch but said nothing. CJ put down the book she held and nonchalantly made her way across the room. She hoped Katie would say her piece and leave.

"Is there something bothering you, Katie?" Dillon asked.

"Ya think?"

"Katie, you seem upset," CJ said, joining the conversation. "Why don't you and I go for a walk, and you can tell me what's bothering you?"

Katie pointed at Skylar. "We need to stop pretending she's one of us." She looked Dillon in the eyes. "Do you know your girlfriend's a slut?"

"That's enough." Dillon rose to her feet. "I'm not sure what your problem is, but you need to back off."

Skylar took Dillon's hand and pulled her back onto the couch. She gave Dillon a look and subtly shook her head as if to say no.

"You'd like me to shut up, wouldn't you, bar wench?" Spit flew out of Katie's mouth as her voice rose.

Dillon tried to stand again, but Skylar grabbed her arm and kept her on the couch. Dillon's face was a deep shade of red, and her eyes flashed in anger.

"Just let it go, please," Skylar said to Dillon. "Everyone's stressed out and upset."

"I'm upset that Dillon is being fooled by a whore

like you." Katie glared at Skylar, almost daring her to do something, but Skylar said nothing.

Katie turned to Dillon. "Why did you choose her? Didn't I have big enough tits?" She moved toward Dillon and shoved her chest toward Dillon's face. Dillon leaned back into the couch, trying to get away from Katie.

"Come on, Katie, your beef is with me. Please, leave Dillon alone," Skylar said.

"Don't you speak to me." Katie spun around, her eyes blazing. "I don't want my name to cross your lips. I know where they've been, you fucking tramp."

"Enough!" Dillon shouted.

Shit. This was not going well. There was a vacant look in Skylar's eyes that CJ didn't like. The situation was going downhill fast, and she feared it would soon get out of hand.

"Sky?" Dillon said softly. When Skylar didn't respond, Dillon said her name louder, but still nothing. Dillon gently touched Skylar's arm, but she flinched and turned away.

"Okay, Katie, time for you to go outside and cool down." CJ slid between Katie and the couch.

Katie ducked around CJ and stood towering over Skylar. "Tiffany wants you to stop by her room tonight. She says you're good on your knees."

"Fuck you." Skylar leapt to her feet, startling everyone, including Katie, who took several steps back.

"Hit a nerve, did I? Afraid Dillon will dump your ass?"

Dillon was on her feet now. She tried to move closer to Skylar, but Skylar pulled away. A pained look crossed Dillon's face and she gave CJ a desperate look.

CJ moved beside Skylar and tried to touch her, but Skylar pulled away from CJ as well.

"She was mine. At least she was before you threw yourself at her," Katie said, tears streaming down her face.

"What the hell are you talking about, Katie? There was never anything between us," Dillon said.

"She's too good for you," Katie said to Skylar.

"I know." Skylar looked down at the ground, her shoulders slumping forward. CJ felt Skylar's pain, hating the defeated look on her face.

"No, Skylar." Dillon put her arm around Skylar, again. This time Skylar didn't pull away, so Dillon pulled her closer. The action only served to incense Katie, who began screaming again.

"Better enjoy her touching you now." Katie sneered at Skylar. "She'll never want to touch you again once she knows the truth. Why don't you tell her?"

"Go ahead and do it." Skylar shouted. She broke free from Dillon's embrace and took a couple steps back until she bumped into the end table. "Tell her what a disgusting slut I am. Just get it over with already. The suspense is killing everybody." Skylar angrily swept her arm back across the table, sending the vase of flowers crashing to the floor.

Everyone momentarily froze, stunned by Skylar's outburst. Dillon's eyes welled with tears, as she stood immobilized.

CJ finally reacted. "That's it. The party's over."

Katie opened her mouth to speak, but CJ pointed at her. "I don't want to hear another goddamned word out of you."

CJ walked to where Skylar stood and put her

hands on Skylar's arms just above her elbows. Skylar tried to pull away, but CJ held her tightly. She bent down so she looked directly into Skylar's eyes. "I don't know what's going on, but I know you and Dillon need to talk."

Skylar held CJ's gaze but didn't speak, so CJ continued. "You're the best thing that's happened to Dillon. I trust that whatever this is, you two can work it out." CJ wrapped her arms around Skylar and was encouraged when Skylar returned the hug.

Katie started to protest, but CJ turned and glared in her direction. When CJ released Skylar, she turned to Dillon. "Take care of her."

CJ took three long strides across the floor and hooked her arm through Katie's. "You and I are leaving now." CJ practically dragged Katie from the room.

❧❧❧❧

"Sky, please sit down and talk to me," Dillon said.

Skylar's first inclination was to bolt, but she knew Dillon deserved better. She bent down and started picking the glass off the floor. Dillon knelt beside her and carefully plucked up the bigger shards and held them in her hand. Skylar glanced at the flowers that she so recklessly scattered and began to cry. Gently, she gathered them together.

Dillon jumped to her feet and grabbed another vase full of flowers off another table. She handed the vase to Skylar. The gesture touched Skylar, and more tears flowed as she put the flowers in the vase and rearranged them.

Dillon brought a garbage can over and used an old magazine to sweep the glass into the trash. Skylar felt her heart opening, as she watched Dillon patiently cleaning up, without saying a word or trying to force Skylar to talk.

No, dammit. She couldn't let her guard down. *Not now.*

Once they'd finished cleaning up, Dillon took Skylar's hands between hers and said, "Skylar, would you please tell me what's going on?"

"Do you really want to know?"

"More than anything, but only if you want to tell me."

"I don't want to tell you, or anyone else for that matter. But if I don't, I'm sure Katie will. I guess it's best if you hear it from me."

"Let's sit down." Dillon led Skylar to the couch. After sitting, Dillon turned, putting her knee on the sofa so she faced Skylar, but Skylar sat facing straight ahead with her legs folded under her. She gazed down at her own hands and picked at her fingernail.

"It's okay. It can't be that bad," Dillon said.

Skylar knew the words were meant to be soothing, but instead they hit a nerve. "No, Dillon. The world isn't always a nice fucking place, and the little birds don't always come out singing a happy tune, making everything all better. We don't always get a fairy-fucking-tale life. And people aren't always who you think they are."

Dillon sat with her hands in her lap. She didn't move or speak but continued to look at Skylar.

"Do you want to know who I am? Do you really want to know?" Skylar gazed at Dillon for the first time.

Dillon nodded.

"Katie's right; I'm a bar wench. I fooled myself into believing I could be something different, but in the end, no one changes who they really are. I was born to shit, raised in shit, and I became shit." Bile rose in Skylar's throat. "I was one of the stupid ones. I believed. I believed I could start over, that I could make something of myself. I came to LA because I wanted to be a nurse. What a fucking joke. I thought I could help people, and maybe make a difference in someone's life. In the end, I couldn't even make a difference in my own pathetic existence."

"You've made a difference in mine, a huge difference."

The emotion in Dillon's voice cut into Skylar and threatened to bring down her walls. Skylar was tired – no, exhausted. She'd spent so many years hiding from the world, from everyone. Dillon had made her believe in the goodness in people, but what if Dillon couldn't handle what she was about to tell her? Would she be able to handle a look of disgust on Dillon's face? *Will I survive it?* That's who she was before, a survivor who went it alone, but she didn't want to be alone anymore.

Despite the fear she felt and the tightness in her chest, she looked at Dillon. "We'll see if you still feel that way after I tell you what I did." Skylar's eyes filled with tears and she looked away. She couldn't meet Dillon's eyes when she told her story.

࠾ࠀ࠾ࠀ࠾

She moved to LA three years ago when she was awarded a nursing scholarship from UCLA. Her life to that point hadn't been easy, but she felt this was her big break.

She ran away from her foster home at sixteen and ended up living on the streets in Nashville for a couple of years. Eventually, a social worker saw her potential and took a liking to her. Through a state program, the social worker helped her get a job and a tiny apartment. The program also set her up with the local junior college, so she was able to get her GED. There, she discovered she loved learning and began taking night classes, while working two jobs. It was slow going, but she received her associates degree. Then she sent out applications to several nursing schools, never expecting to be accepted. The letter of acceptance came. She was both excited and frightened.

She moved to LA in the late spring and was to start school in the fall. She struck gold when she found an affordable student apartment near the campus and got a job at The Blue Moon. She was on her way to becoming a success story, until the letter came in the mail a week before she was to start classes. Apparently, she hadn't read the fine print on the papers she'd signed. She needed to pay a little over $1,500 in fees before the first day of class.

She wasn't worried, figuring it was a mistake, since she was a scholarship student. She called the school and found it was no mistake. If she couldn't pay the fees, her classes would be dropped on Monday. She pleaded with the admission counselor to help her work something out. If the school agreed to float her the money, she'd pay it back before the semester ended. She offered whatever interest rate it required, but the bureaucrats turned her down. If she couldn't pay, she'd have to reapply to the nursing program, and it could be years before she was accepted again.

She went to the bank and even the payday loan service, but no one would help. Her money came mostly from tips, so no one wanted to lend her money. She had nothing to sell or pawn. She came to LA with only the clothes on her back and a few outfits in her suitcase. Since she was new to The Blue Moon, she hadn't built up her regulars yet, so tips had barely paid for her rent and food.

The Friday before classes were to start, she'd been working at The Blue Moon and had run out of options. It was a rotten Friday night at the bar. Her tips were down because she'd been distracted and on edge, which hadn't played well with the customers. At closing time, to make matters worse, Tiffany was in her usual state, too drunk to drive home. She called Anne to pick up Tiffany and left her slumped over a table while she went about her nightly closing routine. Skylar was in the back room restocking the cooler and thinking about school.

Tiffany staggered in and witnessed tears streaming down Skylar's face. In a weak moment, she spilled her story to Tiffany. She tried to fight back the tears but found they only flowed harder. Tiffany had seemed genuinely concerned. When Skylar finished telling her story, Tiffany reached into her pocket and pulled out her wallet. Skylar watched in shock as Tiffany peeled off fifteen one-hundred-dollar bills. Tiffany offered the money to her but pulled it back when Skylar reached for it.

❧❧❧❧

Dillon tensed, not liking the direction the

story was taking. Her temples throbbed. More than anything, she wanted to reach out to Skylar, but knew she needed to let her finish her story uninterrupted.

"It was like a switch flipped in her. All the kindness I'm sure I saw earlier disappeared. Tiffany got this shit eating grin on her face." Skylar grimaced. "Then she said she should get something in return. She unlatched her belt, unzipped her jeans, and dropped her pants to her ankles." Skylar clamped her eyes shut and ran her hand through her hair. "I will never forget it. She looked me in the eye, and without a word, she put her hand on my head. I'd like to tell you that she forced me to my knees, but she didn't."

Skylar stopped, took a deep breath, and opened her eyes before continuing. Dillon's heart clenched. seeing so much pain on Skylar's face.

"I willingly dropped to my knees, and she pulled my head into her," Skylar said, with a look of disgust on her face. "It only took a few minutes. She pulled up her pants, zipped them, fastened her belt, and stood looking down at me. I was still on my knees, stunned by what I'd just done."

"I tell myself if it had ended differently, maybe I'd be okay. Maybe I could convince myself it wasn't what it was. If she'd touched me or hugged me, or just showed me an ounce of affection, maybe I could have fooled myself into believing it was simply a one-night stand. When she zipped up, I didn't even feel human anymore."

Skylar wrapped her arms around her knees and sank into the corner of the couch.

"Then she took the money from her pants pocket and looked at it as if it were the filthiest thing she'd ever seen, filthier than me. She stared at the money for a couple seconds, and then tossed it down on the floor in front of me. She didn't say anything or even look at me. She just turned and walked out of the room. If she'd laid the money on the bar or slid it into my pocket, maybe then I could still look at myself in the mirror. But she threw it on the dirty floor, to the dirty person kneeling there. I've always wondered if she felt as disgusted as I did."

Dillon sat in stunned silence, wanting so badly to reach out to Skylar but was afraid how she would react. Taking a deep breath, she tried to fight back the anger that burned inside her. If Tiffany were to walk into the room right now, Dillon was afraid of what she might do.

"And I stayed there on my knees and sobbed, until I heard Tiffany leave the bar. Once she was gone, I picked up the bills, and scrubbed my face nearly raw before I went home."

"I'd been on the streets nearly three fucking years, and I'd never sold myself. But there I was, on my knees like a fucking street whore."

Skylar finally looked at Dillon.

What do I do or say? Looking into Skylar's eyes, she saw the depth of her pain. Dillon tried to hide the expression she knew must be on her face.

"Don't look at me like that." Skylar jumped to her feet. "I see the repulsion on your face. Well, guess what, Dillon? I'm so disgusted with myself that I have no fucking room for your contempt."

Dillon opened her mouth to speak, but Skylar cut her off.

"I took that money, and I went to nursing school. I was one fucking month away from graduating, and then the world, as we know it, ended. How fucked up is that? After everything, it didn't matter because now I'll never fucking graduate. So, there you go. That's what Katie wanted you to know. I went down on Tiffany in the back room of The Blue Moon, for money. So now what do you think of me, huh?" Skylar yelled.

Dillon opened her mouth again but didn't get the opportunity to speak.

"Fuck you, Dillon. Who gave you the right to judge me? It's your own damn fault. Maybe you should have done a better job figuring out what kind of person you were getting involved with. That's what happens when you're drawn in by this." Skylar ran her hands down her body and shook her breasts. "I know what you're thinking; it's written all over your face, so just leave me the hell alone."

"Can I say something for myself?" Dillon asked.

"Go ahead, hit me with your best shot."

"I love you," Dillon said softly.

"What the fuck did you just say to me?"

"I love you."

"No, Dillon, no, you can't say that kind of shit to me." Skylar's voice cracked.

"But it's true."

"The first time you say it, it's supposed to be special."

"What better time for me to say it, than when you really need to hear it?" Dillon asked, approaching Skylar. Dillon wanted to take Skylar in her arms and erase the pain in her eyes, but she held back, unsure if Skylar was ready for that.

"Damn you, Dillon." Skylar glared at Dillon. "I can't…" Skylar said, her voice trailing off.

"Can't what?" Dillon asked. Skylar shook her

head but didn't answer. "What can't you do?"

"Believe," Skylar answered in a whisper.

"You have to believe I love you. You have to know it."

"But what about everything I just told you?"

"It doesn't matter. None of it does. I know who you are and love you for it. Nothing you told me changes that. If anything, it makes me love you more. I've always suspected you've walked through fire to become the incredible woman that you are. And now I know."

Dillon reached out her hand and Skylar took it.

"Tell me one more time," Skylar said with tears running freely down her face.

"I love you, Sky."

"I love you too, Dillon. I need for you to show me."

"Here?" Dillon's eyes widened and her voice came out higher than she'd intended.

Skylar looked into Dillon's startled eyes and laughed. "I think I can wait until you take me back to our room."

"Now?" Dillon asked.

"Please."

Dillon looked deep into Skylar's eyes and suddenly realized how much of herself Skylar was giving. With that one word, she laid herself bare, completely vulnerable to Dillon.

"Anything for you." Dillon gently put her hand against Skylar's cheek.

Skylar closed her eyes at Dillon's touch and said, "Thank you."

Dillon took Skylar's hand and they walked in silence to their suite.

Chapter Twenty

Skylar held her breath when Dillon pushed open the door. *Everyone was out.* Her pulse quickened. She wanted to be alone with Dillon, but now that they were here, fear gripped her. *Seriously?* It wasn't like she was a virgin, so why was she feeling this way?

She took a relaxing breath when Dillon took her hand, led her to their bedroom, and closed the door behind them. The walk across the suite seemed like miles considering all the thoughts that raced through Skylar's mind. *Get a grip.* At this rate, when Dillon finally touched her, she'd run screaming from the room.

Just inside the door, Dillon stopped and gazed into Skylar's eyes. Dillon's body jerked. *Did Dillon just shiver?* The vulnerability and fear in Dillon's eyes matched Skylar's.

Skylar put her hand on Dillon's cheek. "Show me. I need to feel it."

Dillon trembled again. This time Skylar was sure of it. "Okay." Dillon took a step forward and drew Skylar to her.

Their lips met, retreated, and came together again. The kiss was soft, almost tentative. Skylar longed for more urgency, but she knew Dillon would move slowly. Be gentle. Skylar would have to be the one to push things along when her need became too great to wait.

The kiss intensified, and Skylar slipped her hand under Dillon's shirt and ran it across the smooth skin of her back. Skylar moaned when Dillon lightly sucked Skylar's lower lip. Her body screamed out for more, so she let her hand move toward Dillon's breast. With her thumb, she rubbed Dillon's nipple through her bra.

"No," Dillon said, breaking the kiss. She ran her fingers through Skylar's hair and gazed into her eyes. "Please, let me show you how much I love you."

For a split second, fear threatened to overwhelm her, but when she looked into Dillon's eyes, it subsided. She had no doubt that Dillon loved her, even if she wasn't worthy. Skylar didn't speak, but she dropped her arms to her sides. A shiver coursed through her body, despite the heat coming from Dillon's body.

Dillon stiffened and her breath caught. "What's wrong?"

"What if I don't know how to be loved?" Did she just say that? Of course, she'd felt it all along, but she surprised even herself when it spilled out of her mouth. For some reason, with Dillon, it seemed to be happening more often.

"That breaks my heart. Who hurt you so badly?" Dillon put her hand under Skylar's chin, and gently lifted it so their gaze met.

"No, not now, just prove it to me. Show me that I can accept love. I'm yours."

Dillon gave her a tentative smile. "That was hard for you to say, wasn't it?"

Dammit. How did Dillon read her so well? "Probably the scariest thing I've ever said to anyone."

Skylar could no longer meet Dillon's gaze, so she buried her face against Dillon's shoulder.

Dillon ran her hand over Skylar's hair, making several slow, gentle passes. The sound of Dillon's heart beating comforted Skylar, and she breathed in deeply, allowing herself to enjoy the sound. Dillon held her for several minutes without speaking. The feeling of being in Dillon's arms felt like home, but her body wanted more.

Skylar lifted her head and brought her lips to Dillon's neck. Slowly, she kissed her way up until she arrived at her ear. Flicking her tongue across Dillon's earlobe elicited a throaty moan. Her kiss lingered there before trailing her kisses across Dillon's cheek to her lips.

The kiss grew more urgent, while Dillon explored Skylar's body with her hands. Although Dillon avoided touching her breasts or between her legs, just having Dillon's hands on the rest of her caused electricity to course through her body.

Dillon raked her fingers slowly across Skylar's stomach. She longed to be touched in other places, so she took Dillon's hand and moved it toward her breast. When Dillon cupped Skylar's breast and ran her thumb over her nipple, Skylar's breath caught in her throat.

Skylar nibbled on Dillon's lips and kneaded the hard muscles in her shoulders. As their touches grew more urgent, Dillon snaked her leg between Skylar's and pressed against her. She moved her leg rhythmically. Every time Dillon pulled back, Skylar found herself pushing forward, not wanting the pressure against her swollen clitoris to be broken.

"Can I…" Dillon didn't continue.

"What is it, Babe?" Skylar asked.

"Would it be okay if I undressed you?"

Skylar grinned. "I certainly hope you will after what you've been doing to me."

"I just want to make sure you're okay."

"So sweet. So considerate." Skylar touched Dillon's cheek. "When I'm with you, I'm more than okay."

Tentatively, Dillon unbuttoned Skylar's shirt. After undoing the last button, Dillon ran her hand up Skylar's stomach to her breasts still encased in a black bra. Dillon brushed her thumb over the silky material, contacting her erect nipple.

Dillon kissed her way down Skylar's chest to the spot where her breasts formed a deep cleavage. Skylar moaned and put her hand on the back of Dillon's neck. Dillon thrust her tongue between Skylar's breasts.

"God, Dillon, I'm gonna go crazy if you keep up this pace."

"Do you want me to slow down?" Dillon teased and withdrew her tongue.

"Only if you want me to hurt you." Skylar pressed her body against Dillon. "Would you mind getting these clothes off me already?"

Dillon found Skylar's lips while she slid Skylar's shirt off and unhooked her bra. Once it fell to the floor, Dillon lowered her head and ran her tongue over Skylar's large areolas, careful not to touch her nipple. Skylar contorted, trying to get Dillon's mouth to contact her need, but Dillon moved with Skylar and evaded touching the spot that screamed for her attention. Finally, Skylar grasped her own breast and guided her hardened nub toward Dillon's mouth.

Dillon flicked her tongue lightly over the stiff peak a couple times, but her passion took over and she devoured them. Dillon sucked in and out, moving between her breasts. Each time Skylar moaned, Dillon increased her tempo.

Every nerve ending in Skylar's body felt every flick of Dillon's tongue. She needed Dillon, now. Skylar unbuttoned her own jeans. Dillon's tongue worked on one nipple, while she rolled the other between her fingers. After lowering the zipper, Skylar pushed her jeans toward the floor. Dillon helped push her jeans the rest of the way down, so Skylar could step out. The back of Dillon's hand brushed against the soft material between Skylar's legs.

That wasn't an accident. "I need you, now." Skylar panted and thrust against Dillon's hand.

Dillon groaned, but stopped and quickly flung off her own clothes, before helping Skylar out of her underwear. Both stood next to the bed naked. Dillon paused and her gaze took in Skylar's body.

"God, you're beautiful." Dillon's brown eyes seemed to darken as she studied Skylar.

Heat rose in Skylar's cheeks. She started to tell Dillon to stop with the compliments, but instead, she said, "Thank you."

Once in bed, Dillon settled on top of Skylar. She put one leg between Skylar's and gently rocked into her. Skylar's breath quickened as Dillon increased the pressure against Skylar's wetness. Dillon moved back to Skylar's nipples with her lips, and then started to make her way down her stomach.

Skylar stopped her. "No, I need you up here with me. Hold me while I come." *Unbelievable.* Since when did she become someone who said something like that? Maybe more shocking was her realization that she meant it.

Dillon squirmed against Skylar and rubbed her sex against Skylar's leg. Snaking her hand between their bodies, Dillon dipped her finger into Skylar's wetness. Both moaned in unison. Dillon slid first one finger, then a second one inside of Skylar. At first, Skylar lay still, while Dillon slowly pushed her fingers inside and gently eased them out again. Soon, Skylar couldn't hold back and thrashed against Dillon's fingers.

Dillon removed one of her fingers and ran it over Skylar's clitoris. *Oh God.* She was so close. She couldn't believe Dillon brought her this close to coming, already. Dillon's fingers sent shockwaves through her body. After a couple strokes, Skylar couldn't hold back any longer. She called out and an orgasm shot through her. Dillon rubbed her several more times, making sure she'd reached a full release before she slid her fingers back inside Skylar. A fresh orgasm rose, and Skylar thrust into Dillon's fingers as she came again.

Skylar's heart beat out of her chest, and blood pounded in her ears. Dillon rolled off her and pulled her closer, holding her while the throbbing slowly subsided. Smiling, she kissed the top of Skylar's head. First one tremble hit, then another until Skylar's entire body shook.

"Sky?" Dillon said tentatively.

Waves of emotions hit, so Skylar buried her face against Dillon's chest. She couldn't respond for fear her voice would be gone. She shivered and squeezed Dillon tighter.

Gently, Dillon lifted Skylar's chin. *How embarrassing.* Dillon would see the tears streaming down her face. She tried to speak, but her breath caught.

Sobs finally overtook her.

Dillon pulled Skylar tightly against her and said, "It's okay, Baby, I've got you. Let it out."

Neither spoke for several minutes as Skylar cried and Dillon held her. Years of pain escaped her body. *Why now?* An internal battle raged. Should she shut this down, and stuff it back where it belonged? This wasn't who she'd ever been. *Sobbing? Really?*

"I love you, Skylar. Don't fight it. Let it go."

How the hell did she know? It didn't matter. This felt right. Skylar's shoulders relaxed, and she sank into Dillon.

"Do you want to tell me about it?" Dillon finally asked.

"No, I just need you to hold me."

"I can do that." Dillon kissed the top of Skylar's head.

When Skylar's trembling subsided, Dillon relaxed her grip and ran her fingers through Skylar's hair. Skylar knew how hard this must be for Dillon, who was a talker and a fixer. What Dillon probably didn't realize is this repaired her more than any words ever could.

Eventually, Skylar spoke. "I'm sorry. I don't know where that came from."

"I hate that you've been hurt so badly. And when I find Tiffany, she's going to wish she'd never laid a hand on you."

"No, Dillon, this isn't about Tiffany. You have to promise that you won't do or say anything to her."

"You want me to let her get away with that shit?"

"Things have changed. There's something much bigger to think of than me." Skylar lifted her head and looked at Dillon. "I love you for wanting to protect me, but we have to think of the entire group now. If we're going to survive, we can't have any more infighting. Besides, she didn't force me. I did it willingly."

"But she held all the power."

"No, she held the money, and I made a choice."

Dillon cringed.

"That may be hard for you to hear and harder for me to say. But I wasn't a victim. Please, don't make me a victim."

"But I just want to..." Dillon's voice trailed off when Skylar put her finger against Dillon's lips.

"Please, Babe, don't. Tiffany's finally working with the rest of the group and not causing trouble. If we're gonna survive, that's what needs to happen. Call it a sixth sense, or maybe I'm just paranoid, but I've had an uneasy feeling the last couple of days. If there's danger, we can't afford to have rifts between us."

"I don't think you even realize what an amazing woman you are," Dillon said. "Do you know how much I love you?"

"You did a pretty good job of showing me." Skylar smiled. "Thank you."

"Wow, I'm not sure anyone has ever thanked me for sex before," Dillon teased.

Skylar playful slapped her on the shoulder. "You keep up whatever it was you did to me earlier and I might just thank you again sometime."

Dillon laughed and hugged Skylar to her. "I suppose I'm not allowed to say anything to Katie either."

"No, actually, I want you to talk with her. I want you to make things right with her."

Dillon groaned. "Great, and how do you propose I do that?"

"She's hurting. You need to talk to her and

figure out how to fix it."

"If that's what you want me to do, I'll do it. Damn, I must really love you."

"Good, I'm glad that's settled." Skylar ran her hand down Dillon's stomach and lightly brushed between her legs. "I'm afraid I've made you suffer."

Dillon moaned as Skylar rubbed between her legs.

"Another reason I know you love me," Skylar said, rolling Dillon's clitoris between her fingers. "You've been so busy comforting me, you'd forgotten about this."

"I remember it now." Dillon's voice caught, and she pressed into Skylar's hand.

"It's my turn to take care of you." Skylar smiled and brought her lips to Dillon's.

⁂

Skylar's body was satiated, and her heart full. She hugged Dillon from behind, while Dillon buttoned her shirt. Dillon put her hands on top of Skylar's and squeezed.

"Sometimes I feel guilty," Dillon said.

"About what?" Skylar asked and hugged her tighter.

"That I'm so happy, even though the world has fallen apart." Dillon turned in Skylar's arms. "And that I love you so much."

"The old world might be gone, but that's no reason not to live and love."

"But I'm happier than I've been in years." Dillon finished buttoning her final button and picked up her jeans from the floor.

"Would it make you feel less guilty if I told you that I'm happier than I've ever been in my life?"

"Seriously?" Dillon asked, looking into Skylar's brimming eyes.

"Yep," Skylar said. "The tough girl has taken down her wall, so please be gentle."

"Always." Dillon reached out and touched Skylar's cheek.

"And for the first time in my life, I feel like I have a family." Skylar shook her head. "No, that's not entirely true. When I was on the street, we were a family. We had to be to survive, but it was so unhealthy at times. I watched so many slip away to drugs and violence."

"Will you ever tell me what happened to you?"

Skylar waited for feelings of defensiveness to arise and was surprised when they didn't. As she looked at Dillon, she felt the genuine concern Dillon had for her. There was no morbid curiosity or judgment. In that moment, she knew Dillon only wanted to understand her better and know where she came from. "Probably over time," Skylar answered.

"I'll love you regardless of whether you ever tell me." Dillon wrapped Skylar in a bear hug.

"You're gonna make me cry again." Dillon gently brought her lips to Skylar's. When Skylar broke the kiss, she said, "And don't think you're going to get out of what you have to do."

"Oh, you noticed I was trying to get you back into bed?"

"Let's just say that kiss traveled all the way to my toes and made a couple stops along the way." Skylar smiled. "But I've got more willpower than that."

"Damn, I must be losing my touch. Fine, I'm

going."

"I love you, Dillon," Skylar said, loving the sound of the words they'd finally spoken.

"I love you too, Sky."

Chapter Twenty-one

Dillon rounded the corner, hoping to find Katie in the atrium, where she tended to hang out in the afternoons. She was so busy rehearsing what she would say to Katie that she wasn't paying attention and nearly ran into Tiffany.

"Whoa." Tiffany raised her hands, and then put them on Dillon's shoulders to steady her.

Every muscle in Dillon's body tensed. *Punch her!* Skylar's face flashed in her mind. *Dammit!* Skylar was adamant in her wishes. Dillon wasn't to do or say anything to Tiffany.

Dillon stopped and her muscles relaxed. "I didn't see you there."

"No worries. You looked like you were a million miles away. Everything okay?"

Dillon didn't detect any sarcasm or animosity. *Who is this woman, and what did she do with Tiffany?* "Yes, I was just looking for Katie."

"I saw her a couple hours ago but haven't seen her since." Tiffany smiled. "Hey, do you have a couple minutes?"

Seriously? The image of Skylar on her knees in front of Tiffany bombarded Dillon's thoughts. She clenched her fists, wanting a reason to use them.

"Hey, you don't look so good." Tiffany put her hand on Dillon's arm. "Are you sure you're okay?"

Dillon closed her eyes, sighed, and let her hands fall open. Skylar's words filled her thoughts. There was no doubt Skylar would be furious if Dillon retaliated against Tiffany. "Yeah, I just have a lot on my mind, but I have a couple minutes."

"Great," Tiffany said with obvious excitement. "I have to show you something. I think you'll love it."

Tiffany motioned for Dillon to follow. Walking behind Tiffany, Dillon's mind kicked into overdrive, again. *Just shove her.* Dillon wasn't one to take a sucker punch at someone; if she were going to hit her, Tiffany would know it was coming. Who was she kidding? Skylar had spoken, and Dillon would respect her wishes, even if she didn't agree with her.

Tiffany stopped in front of the large curtain that she'd hung to block the wall. There was paint stuff scattered everywhere, brushes, paint cans, once white rags that were now multi-colored. Dillon glanced at Tiffany, and noticed for the first time Tiffany's paint-stained t-shirt. It wasn't confined to only her shirt; the bridge of her nose was splattered, making it look as if she had freckles.

"Looks like you've been busy." Dillon nodded toward her face.

Tiffany ran her hand across her face and laughed when her fingers touched the big dollop of paint on her cheek. "I swear I get more on me than I do the wall."

"What is it you wanted to show me?" Dillon kept her voice friendly but wanted to get out of this conversation as quickly as possible.

"Ah, yeah." Tiffany grabbed the curtain and pulled it back part ways. "I thought you'd like to see this." Tiffany pointed at the section of the mural she'd unveiled.

"Holy shit, that's amazing." Dillon's animosity waned when she looked at Tiffany's work. *Beautiful.*

It was a familiar scene. Dillon's eyes scanned the picture, and she marveled at Tiffany's talent. In front of her was a likeness of Skylar knelt on the bar, performing her Sky-High routine.

The painting drew her back to the first time she'd met Skylar. She'd been mesmerized when Skylar performed her act. *So theatrical.* At thirteen past the hour, Skylar would call out, *Sky High Time,* and raise a bottle of tequila above her head while dancing seductively. The women lined up as the chant, *Sky High,* filled the bar.

Once everyone was assembled, Skylar knelt on top of the bar and straddled a plate of limes and a pile of salt. Another bartender handed out shot glasses. The patron would sit on the stool in front of Skylar with their back to her. In one fluid motion, she would fill their shot glass with tequila and tilt their head back. Skylar would let their head rest against her arm, although all would claim they were nestled against Skylar's breasts. *What an illusion.*

After they were in position, Skylar would rub the lime around their lips, pour a tequila shot in their mouths, and once they swallowed, throw a pinch of salt onto their tongue before sending them on their way.

Dillon took a step closer to the mural. Tiffany had captured Skylar's intelligent eyes, and her heart-stopping dimple. "Perfect. That's amazing, Tiffany."

Tiffany stepped up beside Dillon. "Did you notice?" Tiffany pointed.

Dillon forced herself to look away from Skylar's

picture. She burst out laughing. She was looking at a drawing of herself sitting away from the bar. Her eyes were intense, and it was obvious her sole focus was on Skylar.

"Do you like it?" Tiffany asked.

"Love it! You nailed it." Dillon gave Tiffany a real smile, before turning back to stare at the wall. "You captured her beauty, completely."

"It wasn't hard. She's a beautiful woman."

"That she is," Dillon agreed. "But not everyone could have translated that onto the wall."

"Thank you." Tiffany looked at the floor.

Dillon gaped. *Was Tiffany being shy?* "I look forward to seeing more."

Tiffany glanced up and smiled. "Thanks. I hoped you'd like it."

"I do." Dillon couldn't believe what she was about to say but knew Skylar would be proud. "I appreciate you sharing it with me."

"Any time." Tiffany met Dillon's gaze. "Thanks for taking the time. I'll let you get back to the mission you were on."

Dillon was still thinking about her encounter with Tiffany when she entered the kitchen. A cold chill greeted her when she approached Renee, which was a stark contrast from the reception Tiffany gave her. Even after Dillon met Renee with a broad grin, Renee didn't return the smile. Obviously, Katie had already been here.

"Hi, Renee," Dillon said, trying another smile.

"Hello." Renee's voice was icy.

"Have you seen Katie?" Dillon braced for her answer.

"Haven't you done enough damage already?

Why don't you just leave her alone?"

"I never meant to hurt her." Dillon maintained eye contact with Renee. "I can't help that I fell in love with Skylar."

Renee's eyes softened, but her voice still held an edge. "What did you do to her?"

"She didn't tell you what happened?"

"No, she came in here crying and said she couldn't work. Then she left. I tried to stop her, but she wouldn't listen. She wouldn't talk to me, so I figured it was you."

"I promise, I'm looking for her to try and make things better. You've watched what's going on. Can you honestly say I've done anything wrong?"

"No," Renee admitted. "I just hate seeing how much she's hurting."

"I know you do, and I hate it too."

"I believe you." Renee blinked back tears. "I think she may have gone to check on the crops."

"Thank you." Dillon clapped her hand on Renee's shoulder. "I hope one day she'll see what's right in front of her face."

Renee gave Dillon a sad smile and turned back to the mushrooms she was slicing.

࿇࿇࿇

When Dillon stepped outside, she was happy to see three ATVs parked in the lot. It would speed up her search for Katie if she didn't have to walk. She hopped on one and turned over the engine.

She sped along the path, until she arrived at the series of hills that led to the garden area. When she reached the top of the final hill, Katie sat on a big rock at the edge of the field. Dillon sailed over the last hill before she hit the flat surface and cut the engine. Instead of driving to where Katie sat, she walked across the twenty-five-yard expanse, giving Katie time to prepare for her arrival.

The garden was immaculate. Not a weed in sight. There were tiny green tomatoes on the vines that were just beginning to turn red. An entire section of the garden was devoted to herbs, which Renee used freely in most dishes she created. There were other plants in various stages of growth, but the only other ones she could identify were the pumpkins. Katie had taken to gardening and could rattle off everything that grew in their fields.

Katie's eyes were red and puffy, but she was no longer crying. Without expression, she watched Dillon's arrival.

"Hey." Dillon stopped a few feet from where Katie sat.

Katie crossed her arms over her chest and glared at Dillon but didn't respond.

"Can we talk?" Dillon tried again.

"Go ahead. I'm afraid I don't have much to say."

"I do." Dillon smiled. "Mind if I sit down?"

Katie didn't answer but slid down on the rock, making room for Dillon. As she sat, she tried to gather her thoughts. "I'm sorry if I've hurt you." *That's the best I've got?* She needed to find a more eloquent way to say it.

"Are you really?"

"Yes, I am."

"Why her?" Katie asked. For the first time since Dillon's arrival, she saw emotion on Katie's face.

"I don't know, Katie. I wish I could tell you, but

I don't have an answer." Katie glared at her, but she continued. "Honest, I don't know why. All I know is I've fallen in love with her."

"Are you trying to hurt me?" Katie's voice was flat.

"God, no," Dillon said. "You're my friend. You were Jane's best friend. I don't want to hurt you."

"What does she have that I don't?" Katie unconsciously ran her fingers through her long blond hair. The anger from earlier was gone. All that was left was sadness.

"It's not about her." Dillon picked up a handful of loose pea gravel around the base of the rock.

"So, it's just about me then? Great!" Katie shifted on the rock and glowered. "Should that make me feel better?"

"You were Jane's best friend." Dillon tossed a piece of gravel at the trunk of a nearby tree. She watched it sail wide to the left before she continued. "You were the sister she never had. How wrong would that be?" Dillon's revelation shocked even her. She'd blamed Katie's perkiness for her lack of interest, but in that moment, Dillon realized it wasn't true. She'd developed a near repulsion to Katie because of Jane.

"You're serious?" Katie said, the life returning to her eyes. "You don't find me unattractive?"

"How could I? You're beautiful," Dillon answered honestly. She threw another stone at the tree, this time missing by only a couple inches.

"It's always been about Jane?" Katie eyed her, more life returning to her eyes.

"Yes. I can't look at you without seeing her," Dillon answered and felt tears welling in her eyes. "I see the two of you sitting in our living room, drinking a bottle of wine, and laughing. Laughing about shit that I didn't understand, which made you guys laugh harder. Jane loved you so much." Dillon threw another rock, finally hitting the base of the tree.

"Why didn't you just tell me?" Katie put her hand on Dillon's arm.

"I didn't know." Dillon fought back tears. "I didn't want to think about the reasons why because then I'd have to think about Jane."

"Are you okay?" Katie asked, her face full of concern.

"I don't think so," Dillon choked out before the tears were unleashed. She dropped the rocks she held and crossed her arms over her chest. She hugged herself, trying to stop the sobs caught inside.

Katie put her arms around Dillon, and Dillon let herself be pulled against Katie's chest. Katie gently rocked her and ran her hand through Dillon's hair. The tension between them dissipated, and Katie's gesture was comforting. The realization freed her, so she let herself cry in Katie's arms. Katie held her and whispered soothingly in her ear. After several minutes, Dillon flinched and pulled away, afraid she'd given Katie the wrong impression. Just because the interaction didn't feel romantic to Dillon didn't mean Katie felt the same.

"It's okay," Katie said. "I'm not trying to get into your pants."

Dillon looked up in shock and was surprised to see a big smile on Katie's face. "I…" Dillon stammered.

Katie laughed. "Relax, Dillon. I understand."

"You do?"

"Yes, I never stood a chance. I just wish I'd known before I used up so much of my energy."

"I'm so sorry." Dillon wiped her arm across her eyes.

"I know it wasn't on purpose." Katie smiled, but there was sadness in her eyes. "So where do we go from here?"

"I probably don't have a right to ask you this." Dillon took Katie's hand. "But I would like to have your blessing."

"Why me?"

"You were her best friend. You knew her better than anyone," Dillon said. "Do you think she'd hate me, or would she be okay with Skylar?"

"Shit, Dillon. You're really asking me that question?" Katie said, but her voice was light.

"I'm sorry." Dillon's pain threatened to send her back into tears.

"She'd love Skylar," Katie answered. Dillon felt her heart leap when she realized Katie had finally spoken Skylar's name. "Jane loved you and would want you to be happy, and Skylar makes you happy. You would have Jane's blessing."

"And yours?"

"You're not going to make this easy, are you?"

Dillon looked at her hopefully, with a sheepish smile. She shook her head.

Katie took a deep breath. "You have my blessing."

"Thank you." Dillon wrapped her arms around Katie, and they held each other as they both cried.

After several minutes, Katie jumped to her feet. "Oh God, I need to apologize to Skylar. I'm sorry. I never thought to ask if she's okay."

"She's fine."

"I was such an idiot. I don't even know if what Tiffany told me was true. She told me the story right after Anne moved out. She was so angry and bitter, and saying such…" Katie's voice trailed off.

"I don't want to know what Tiffany told you," Dillon said. "All I'll say is that Skylar has had a pretty tough life, and what you did probably opened the door for us to talk."

"So, you two are okay?" Katie asked.

"Yes."

"Good," Katie said, and Dillon believed she meant it. "I'm sorry if I hurt her."

"I think lots of people have hurt her, but she's a survivor."

"Do you think she'll ever forgive me?"

"Who do you think insisted I come and talk to you and make things right?"

"Are you kidding me?"

"Nope."

"Don't let her get away," Katie said.

"I won't."

They sat on the rock for some time, talking like the two old friends they were. Dillon finally worked up her courage and said, "When are you going to see what's right in front of your face?"

"What?" Katie asked.

"Renee thinks the sun rises and sets on you, and you act like you don't even see it."

"What are you talking about?" The edge in Katie's voice returned.

"Are you saying you haven't noticed how much she cares about you?"

"Of course she cares about me. She's become my best friend, but she's been seeing several other women."

"Only because you haven't noticed her."

"I don't think so."

"I know so," Dillon countered. "You should have seen her when I went into the kitchen looking for you. I thought she was going to rip my head off."

"Renee?"

"Yes, I was a little nervous talking to her while she was holding a knife," Dillon joked.

"You mean I've had my head so far up your ass, that I missed it?" Katie grinned.

"Afraid so."

"Sounds like I have some damage to clean up," Katie said. "Would you mind giving me a ride back on your chariot?"

"It would be my pleasure." Dillon hugged Katie. "I love you."

"I love you too," Katie said. "Be happy; you deserve it."

"Thanks." Dillon jumped off the rock and held out her hand to Katie. "Let's see if we can do something about your happiness."

Katie took Dillon's hand and slid off the rock.

Chapter Twenty-two

Dillon's gaze shifted to Jake. They hadn't had this contentious of a Commission meeting in a long time. She resisted her urge to smooth things over, knowing everyone needed to say their piece before things could be worked out.

"I just don't think it's a good idea." Jake slammed his pen down on the table. "We can't let down our guard after what happened in Amarillo."

"That was nearly two months ago," Renee countered. "We're hidden in the middle of nowhere."

"All it takes is for someone to know about this place and they might come looking for it," Jake answered.

"I doubt if a bunch of bikers have even heard of Whitaker Estate," Karen said. "Renee's right. We could all use a little pick me up."

"And what about Babcock? His numbers seem to be growing every day. It won't be long before he sends out scout parties," Jake added.

"I think you're stretching, Jake," Dillon said. "You know that guy gives me the willies, but he has no clue we're here."

"Besides, from what CJ said, he's still pulling in idiots from around the country. HOPE just lost four members last week who decided to make the pilgrimage to his compound," Karen said.

"Ugh. What the hell is wrong with people?" Dillon tossed her pen aside in disgust.

"He's the new messiah and the flock is gathering," Karen said with a look of distaste. "But you've said it yourself, Jake, he's a narcissist and if they keep coming, he's not going to risk sending people out who he can't control. That'll come later."

Jake sighed. "But why Lake Piru? We aren't equipped to defend ourselves like we are here." Jake's voice relayed his annoyance.

"Can't we just do the party here?" Tiffany asked, trying to bring the sides together. Who would have predicted that Tiffany would be the one on the Commission trying to reach a compromise? Dillon kept expecting the old Tiffany to rear her ugly head, but to date, it hadn't happened.

"We could, but it wouldn't be the same. The girls are excited about doing some boating and fishing for a change," Renee answered.

"How about we send Jake and his crew to check out the location and see if they can create a secure environment?" Dillon said and looked to Tiffany, who nodded.

Jake said nothing, but his angry glare softened slightly.

"What do you think, Jake?" Cynthia asked.

"I still don't like it, but I could take a group to check out the area. I don't want the Commission to commit to a party until we do."

"How does that sound, Renee?" Dillon asked, hoping to reach an agreement, so they could move on to other business.

"Fine. I don't know why everyone is so afraid, but I'll defer to Jake on this one." Since Renee had begun dating Katie, she'd been buoyant and seemed unable to perceive the possibility of danger. Luckily, the relationship also made her too happy to want to argue either.

"Okay then, that's settled," Cynthia said.

"I'll get together a team and check it out tomorrow afternoon," Jake said, but his voice held reluctance.

⚘⚘⚘⚘

Tiffany held open the door as Anne went through. Some days the new Tiffany still surprised Anne, but with each passing day, she had begun to believe. They'd eaten their meal in a hurry, so they could enjoy a walk while it was still light outside. Darkness was about an hour away by Tiffany's estimation.

She gently took Anne's hand and looked at her cautiously. "Is this okay?"

Anne greeted her with a smile. "It's nice."

They went down the path that led to the hotel. It was tree-lined and peaceful, but not as popular as some of the other paths, which would afford them more privacy.

"What do you think of the idea of a party?" Tiffany asked.

Anne sighed. "I'm torn. We have such beautiful grounds here; I'm not sure if it's worth exposing ourselves to potential danger."

Tiffany nodded. "I don't know how I'll vote, but I'll keep your concerns in mind."

"Who knows, maybe Jake's party will decide it's not a good idea and call it off." They rounded the curve, and Anne's breath caught. Her heart raced. Willa and KC were walking on the same pathway in front of them.

Tiffany stopped and gripped Anne's hand tighter. Since she'd been caught in bed with Willa and KC, she did her best to avoid both. "Why don't we turn around and find a secluded spot near the mansion where we can sit and watch the sunset?"

"I'd like that." Anne turned abruptly, hoping Tiffany wouldn't notice her misty eyes. At first, she wanted to snatch her hand back from Tiffany, but she steadied herself. *One step at a time.*

They walked in silence until they were nearly back at the mansion. Anne finally broke the silence. "You said Jake was against the party. Don't you think he will ultimately be able to sway the rest?"

"I'm not sure. People are going stir crazy. There's been so much grief and loss. I think everyone just wants to feel normal for a change."

Anne squeezed Tiffany's hand. "I know. I'm not sure how many more tears any of us can shed."

"I used to hear stories about someone losing their entire family in a car wreck and wondered how they survived it. Now, I'm not sure how any of us have. We lost so many people." Tiffany's voice cracked.

Anne shivered. Tiffany put a protective arm over her shoulder and pulled her closer. They were near the hilly side of the mansion, where they'd continued to mow a small patch of grass so they could sit outside and enjoy the day. The rest of the overgrown lawn still made Anne sad. She knew the Commission made the right decision not keeping it up, but the pristine estate in an overgrown condition was a harsh reminder of their reality. Maybe one day when they got on their feet, they could go back to mowing at least all the front of the mansion.

"I could run in and get us a blanket," Tiffany said.

"No, I don't mind sitting on the grass. If you don't."

"As long as you're sitting next to me, I'd sit anywhere."

Anne smiled as she sat down. She patted the ground beside her, and Tiffany lowered herself next to Anne. They sat with their shoulders touching, staring off to the west at the sun that still had some time before it snuck below the horizon.

Anne nestled against Tiffany. As the sun moved lower in the sky, the temperature dropped, but having Tiffany so close made her forget any chill she might feel.

They chatted about nothing, as they watched the fiery globe.

"Is it wrong that I feel happy sometimes?" Tiffany asked.

"Where did that come from?" Anne turned and studied Tiffany's face.

"I don't know." Tiffany sighed.

"Do you think I'm gonna let you get away with that answer?"

"No. I know you better than that." She turned and put her hand on Anne's cheek. "May I have a kiss before I answer?"

Anne smirked. "Maybe a tiny one."

Their lips met. The kiss was sweet and tender. By now, the old Tiffany's hands would be roaming up Anne's shirt, but she didn't need to worry about that. Tiffany had been respectful and not pushed anything.

She believed Tiffany had remained celibate since being caught. This was probably the longest Tiffany had ever gone without sex, but Anne didn't feel pressured; in fact, just the opposite. She'd begun to long for more.

As if on cue, Tiffany broke the kiss. She took Anne's hand and gazed at the sunset.

Anne moaned slightly but turned her gaze back to the western horizon to watch the scene Tiffany did.

"There's a lot of things about the old world that I don't miss. Does that make me horrible?" Tiffany said. She didn't look at Anne; instead, she studied the sky.

"No, there's lots I don't miss either. But what is it that you don't?"

"Working in the family business," Tiffany said without hesitation. "Don't get me wrong. I don't want my family to be dead, but…"

Anne patted Tiffany's knee. She waited for Tiffany to continue, but when she didn't, Anne spoke. "I understand. It was a lot of pressure being Stanton Daniels III's only child. I saw the complicated relationship you had with him."

Tiffany looked down and studied her fingernails. "I loved him. And maybe he loved me in his own way, but I never really felt it. I hated that business, but I worked my ass off, hoping he might approve of me. But I don't think he ever did."

"It was a complex relationship. But I have no doubt he did love you. He was prouder of you than he let on."

Tiffany blinked back tears. "He just had a funny way of showing it."

"That he did." Anne snuggled closer to Tiffany. "I think we've all changed from who we were. I hope for the better."

"I'm trying." Tiffany gazed at Anne. "But I got off to a rocky start."

Anne nodded. "Yes, you did. But I still believe in you."

"You do?" Tiffany's voice was full of hope. "Do you think you'd ever consider moving back in with me?"

Anne smiled. "Maybe someday. But I'm enjoying what we have now. I don't think we need to rush anything."

Tiffany smiled and watched the last sliver of orange sink below the horizon. "I'll wait."

Chapter Twenty-three

I should be back in a couple hours," Skylar said, startling Dillon. "Sorry, Hun, I didn't mean to scare you."

Dillon stood up from her hunched position, a smile lighting her face. "I didn't hear you walk up."

"That's because you've been cussing and glaring at that drywall for the past ten minutes," Skylar teased.

"Did you see what a lousy job we did on this section?" Dillon scowled at the wall in front of her.

"I'm sure you can fix it." Skylar wrapped her arms around Dillon and squeezed.

"Careful, I'm disgusting and covered in grime." Dillon ran her hand down her arm and held it up. Her fingers came away nearly black. "See, gross."

"I don't care. I want a kiss before I head out."

"Shit. Is it that time already?" Dillon picked up a rag lying nearby and ran it over her sweat-covered brow. "You guys be careful out there."

Skylar smiled at the concerned look on Dillon's face. It was new having someone care so deeply about her, but with each passing day, it felt more natural. "We're just going to check out the lake area."

"I know, but I worry about you when you're not close by."

Skylar saw a glimpse of fear in Dillon's eye before she pulled her in. Dillon's strong arms held her tightly. It was still a feeling she struggled to accept. For the first time in her life, she allowed someone to take care of her. It was as if Dillon instinctively knew when to pull Skylar closer, and when to let her have space. Right now, Dillon hugged her tighter.

Skylar's heart leapt, as she returned the hug. "I'll be fine. We shouldn't be gone long."

"I just don't know what I'd do…" Dillon's voice trailed off.

"Do about what?" She kept her head resting against Dillon's chest, enjoying the closeness.

"I couldn't take it if something happened to you."

"I'll be fine." Skylar leaned back from the embrace and found Dillon's lips. The kiss intensified, and Dillon backed Skylar against the wall.

"Get a room," a loud male voice said.

"Jesus, Jake, can't we get a little privacy?" Dillon said.

"Yeah, in your suite, not in the middle of the construction site." Jake laughed.

Dillon rolled her eyes at Skylar. "He's so unreasonable sometimes."

"Would you hurry up and finish whatever you were doing, so we can get on with our mission?" Jake said.

"You've ruined the moment." Dillon threw up her hands in mock anger.

"Good, I hoped I had."

Dillon glared at him, but the twinkle in her eyes gave her away. "Damn homophobes," Dillon muttered loud enough for Jake to hear.

He answered her with a laugh.

❦❦❦❦❦

"Do you really think we need all of this?" Skylar said, as Jake strapped the ammunition belt around her.

"I'm in charge of security. Everyone is going to be safe on my watch." He was still angry they were doing this mission in the first place. A party at Lake Piru was something he'd put in the unnecessary column. The Commission should have deferred to his opinion when it came to safety, but he was forced to appease everyone and run this dog and pony show. Why couldn't they understand how reckless it would be for them to play out on the lake where there was little to no protection?

"Honey, if you load us down with much more, we won't be able to sit, which we have to do if we plan on driving there. I'm thinking walking would take too long." Lily playfully slapped Jake in the butt.

"Mom's right, Dad," Tad said, joining the conversation.

He's a man now. In the past five months, he'd watched the transformation. He felt both pride and sadness. Sadness that Tad was forced into adulthood too early and would never get to experience what it was like to be an adult in a normal world.

A lump caught in his throat when his thoughts flipped to his daughter. It seemed even more unfair to Kelly, who was only ten. She'd never know a regular childhood. Then again, unlike them, she'd never know any different; maybe that would be easier.

"Dad!" A deep voice jarred him out of his reverie.

Jake blinked and gazed into Tad's eyes.

"Are you okay?" Tad asked.

"Yeah, sure. Just thinking." Tad looked at him as if he expected Jake to say more, but Jake's mind was a blank. "Care to remind me what we were talking about?"

"Wow, really." Tad looked at him curiously. "Mom said to stop loading us down with so much equipment."

"Yeah, that's right." Jake felt his face go hot. He needed to keep his head in the game. He couldn't space out like that when they were at Lake Piru. Hoping to regain his authority, he said, "Go ahead and throw the rest of the gear in the back of the truck in case we need it."

Jake's eyes narrowed and he tried to push back his irritation. It was only the four of them going on the security mission. Jake suspected the rest of the crew were feigning being too busy. Lately, the complacency of the group when it came to safety made him edgy, especially considering the attack in Texas.

After Tad loaded the rest of the supplies, Jake said, "Okay, let's roll out." He tried to put a little more pep into his voice, not wanting to make the trip miserable for the others. After all, it wasn't their faults, and they'd been gracious enough to volunteer.

Once they left the Estate and were on the road to Lake Piru, talking ceased. Each had their lookout assignment, and they took those responsibilities seriously. Jake drove slowly, while they made their way along the length of the lake. When they arrived at the farthest end, Jake stopped and surveyed the terrain they'd passed.

"Any suggestions where we should check out first?" Jake asked. "Personally, I don't like any area. I see potential danger anywhere I look."

"It's safest if we stay on the highest ground," Tad said. "That way we can see anyone coming our way, hopefully before they see us, so probably back closer to the Estate would be our best bet."

"Don't forget Renee wants to be able to let the girls take a couple boats out," Skylar added.

"There was a boat launch around the first curve that is on the highest ground," Lily said.

"This is fucking nuts." Jake slammed the truck into gear. "We built a tower to watch for danger, so we came out here where we would be sitting ducks. Stupid idea."

Lily patted his shoulder. "No decision has been made yet, honey. Let's look around, so we can give the group an honest assessment. And if our appraisal is that we shouldn't do it, then you need to stand your ground and convince the others. Or you need to use your ingenuity and come up with a plan that will minimize the risk."

Jake nodded but kept his gaze on the road. *Stupid.* After how far they had come, why would they want to take such an unnecessary risk? His jaw tightened. He needed to convince them to make the most of the estate, which was enormous.

When they arrived at their destination, Jake scowled and shook his head. "This launch is completely exposed."

"They all are," Tad said.

"They're going to insist on boating, aren't they?" Jake looked toward Skylar.

"No doubt."

"That's what I figured." He shook his head. "I promised to do our due diligence, so that's what I'm going to do. Let's get to it."

Jake was meticulous. They spent nearly two hours surveying the area and taking measurements. They discovered a secluded area, with a good vantage point, about a half a mile from the boat launch. Although not ideal, it was the best they could do if the women insisted on boating. Although, Jake planned to speak against it.

Skylar calmed him slightly, when she pointed out they could put the boats into the water from the launch, but then the passengers could board much closer to the secure site.

Once they settled on the location, Jake snaked the truck through the trees to ensure they didn't have to get there by foot. A secure location without adequate access to escape vehicles was not acceptable. He still planned on lobbying against the idea, but if he lost, this would be the best possible area. If he were voted against, he'd refuse to come. Who was he kidding? He'd be there on high alert with his weapons. He'd never forgive himself if something happened to the others, while he was in a pout.

Tad had just finished his sketch of the area when Lily said, "Shh, I think I hear something."

Jake was loading the equipment into the truck, but he immediately stopped and came to attention.

Skylar stood next to Lily; her head was cocked to one side as she listened. Without warning, Skylar ran to the truck, nearly colliding with Jake. She grabbed one of the bags he'd just loaded and tore it open.

"Whoa, slow down," Jake said.

"We heard something." She rummaged through the bag and extracted a pair of binoculars. Even though she seemed relatively calm, there was an underlying edge to her that he wasn't used to seeing.

Jake grabbed an assault weapon and followed Skylar, who raced back to where Lily stood.

Lily strained to see and pointed. "I thought I saw a glimmer. It looked almost like metal."

Skylar brought the binoculars to her eyes. "Shit, it looks like we have company."

"What do you see?" Jake asked.

"Looks like a small caravan of motorcycles, followed by two SUVs. They've pulled into one of the small lots adjacent to the water. Looks like they might be thinking of setting up camp."

"Do you think it's the guys from Texas?" Tad asked.

"I hope not," Lily said. "But we need to be careful. From all reports, they don't have a conscience or a soul."

"We're well covered here. I think we need to observe them for a bit," Jake answered.

"Maybe we should call the others," Skylar said.

"Let's not call until we have a little more to go on," Jake said.

Skylar had been watching for nearly ten minutes when she gasped.

Out of instinct, he reached for the binoculars in Skylar's hand but stopped when he noted her white knuckled grip. "What is it?" Jake asked.

"We need to do something." Skylar shoved the binoculars toward him. Her hands shook so badly that she nearly dropped them. Without another word, she raced toward the truck.

After training the binoculars on the camp, he didn't look long before he followed Skylar. She sat in the driver's seat, searching under the floor mat and exploring the visor. "Where's the key?" she yelled.

"Skylar, you need to relax. I'm not giving you the key."

"Why the fuck not? We need to get down there, now."

"No, Skylar." Jake backed away from the truck and unconsciously put his hand in his pocket, making sure he still had the key. "We can't just go roaring in there. We would be slaughtered."

"Did you see what he was doing to her?" Skylar's eyes filled with tears. She jumped out of the truck and stepped up to Jake.

"Yes, Skylar. I saw." He kept his voice level, hoping it would have a calming effect on her.

"Then why in the hell are you just standing there? Give me the fucking key."

Jake put his hands out, palm down, and slowly pushed them toward the ground, gesturing for calm. "You need to lower your voice," he said in a near whisper. "We don't want them to hear us."

When Tad and Lily arrived, Lily put her arm around Skylar. "Skylar, he's right."

"What?" Skylar brushed Lily's arm off and spun around. Her face was full of rage.

While Skylar was occupied with Lily, Jake positioned himself between Skylar and the truck.

"We need to use our heads," Lily said.

"He was raping her. Are you okay with that?"

"Of course not." Lily tried to put her hand on Skylar's shoulder, but Skylar shrugged it off.

"Are you all animals?" Skylar's gray eyes blazed. "What kind of society have we become?"

"If that's one of the teens from Texas, it's not the first time," Jake said, hoping Skylar would see the logic, but his words only inflamed her.

"Seriously? It's not the first and won't be the fucking last, so to hell with her?" Skylar tried to push past Jake.

"Dammit, Skylar, none of us like it, but to help her, we need to stay alive. If we go storming in there now, we all die along with her. We are grossly outnumbered."

"So, everyone stands around and lets him violate her. The way of the world before the Crisis just continues." Skylar slammed into Jake.

Fuck. He hadn't been expecting her reaction and nearly lost his balance. He stumbled against the truck before righting himself. He softened his eyes and spoke in a low voice. He needed to try one final time to reason with her. "Skylar, we need to get back to camp."

Her eyes blazed and she charged him again, but this time he was ready for her and sidestepped her lunge. He made eye contact with Tad and tossed him the keys.

"Sorry," Jake whispered, as he wrapped his arms around Skylar and lifted her off the ground. His heart ached. "Lily, open up the back door. We need to get going."

"No, Jake. Not this way." Lily stared, as Skylar squirmed in his arms. Lily silently opened the door but diverted her eyes from the struggle. Jake fell into the back seat of the truck with Skylar landing on top of him. He immediately wrapped his arms and legs around her as she continued to fight against his arms.

"It's not how I want it either, but we need to get back." Jake's breath came out heavy with exertion, as he tried to calm Skylar. "Call ahead and let them know we're coming. Make sure and talk to Dillon."

Lily nodded. When Lily went to shut the door, she reached out and brushed a strand of hair off Skylar's forehead. Skylar thrashed around harder, a mask of rage on her face. An animalistic sound came from the back of her throat. Lily jerked her hand away and stood immobilized.

"Lily," Jake said. "We need to go, *now!*"

Lily closed her eyes and slammed the truck door, before vaulting into the front passenger seat. Tad fired up the engine.

Skylar continued to scream incoherently, while tears streamed down her cheeks. Jake hugged her tighter, hoping to prevent her from hurting herself or him. Jake's heart broke as he listened to the agonized sounds coming from Skylar.

Lily talked softly into the phone, so Jake couldn't make out what Lily was saying. Dillon would, no doubt, hear Skylar's screams. He prayed Dillon could remain calm and bring Skylar around because he would need them both to protect the group.

Even though the drive took only ten minutes, for Jake it felt like an eternity. Tad skidded around the corner to the back entrance, where the entire group of women were gathered.

Before the truck came to a stop, Dillon raced to the vehicle and yanked the back door open. Her eyes were wild, and she yelled, "Let her go." He was happy to oblige. He fell back against the seat, exhausted, when Skylar sprang from his hold.

Skylar flew into Dillon's arms, rambling hysterically. Jake couldn't make out any of her words, but her message was clear. Dillon held her tightly and whispered into her ear. Everyone else gathered around and stared.

"Please, everyone, I need your attention," Jake yelled. "There's a serious threat. We need to prepare. Now! Come with me."

He stepped away from the truck and turned toward the back entrance. He hoped they'd follow, but he didn't want to look back in case they weren't. When he reached the door, he glanced back. Only Cynthia, Skylar, and Dillon hadn't followed.

༄ ༄ ༄ ༄

Cynthia watched Jake and the others retreat, and then glanced at Dillon and Skylar. Something told her that her presence here would be more valuable than going with the group. She approached Dillon, who stood still holding a distraught Skylar. "Is there anything I can do?" Cynthia asked.

"I don't know what's going on." There was so much pain in Dillon's eyes and Skylar's sobs that Cynthia wanted to wrap them both in a protective hug.

"Skylar, we need to join the rest of the group, so we can be in on the game plan. We need for you to talk to us," Cynthia said, putting her hand on Skylar's shoulder.

"Sky, help us out here." Dillon relaxed her hold on Skylar.

Skylar let go of Dillon, and her arms dropped to her side. She had a blank, distant look in her eyes and didn't speak.

"Come on, Sweetie," Cynthia said and took Skylar's hand. She motioned Dillon with her eyes to the picnic tables near the back entrance. Dillon took Skylar's other hand.

Skylar and Dillon sat on one bench and Cynthia

sat across from them. Dillon put her hand on Skylar's back and lightly rubbed. Skylar had stopped crying but sat expressionless with her shoulders hunched.

"We need you, Skylar, you're one of our best with weapons," Cynthia said.

"If you could tell us what's upsetting you so bad, maybe we could help," Dillon added.

Skylar flinched and turned toward Dillon with anger in her eyes. "What's upsetting me is we're all a bunch of fucking animals. How could we just leave that poor girl?"

"You have every right to be upset." Cynthia hoped her words would be soothing but feared they might inflame Skylar. "Going in outnumbered with guns blazing wouldn't help her."

"How the fuck do you know that?"

"You know it too," Cynthia challenged.

"Sky, she's right," Dillon said. "We all want to help the girl, but we have to be smart about it."

"It'll never change, will it?" Skylar looked down at her hands resting on the table. Tears rolling silently down her face.

"What won't change?" Dillon asked.

"I thought maybe with the Crisis, we were getting another chance. That things would be better, not so ugly. Not so brutal."

"Who hurt you so bad?" Dillon asked. Cynthia cringed, waiting for another reaction out of Skylar, but none came. Instead, Dillon continued. "Sky, it still can be a better world, but there will probably always be evil."

"But you have to believe there is good too," Cynthia said. "We can make it better."

"We're no better. We left her." Skylar's voice

raised again. After her flash of anger, all expression left Skylar's face and tears rolled gently down her face. "I left her again, so he could hurt her. I'm no better. I'm just the same." Skylar's voice was a near whisper.

Cynthia glanced at Dillon, wondering if she'd caught Skylar's choice of words. Dillon looked deflated and stared helplessly at Skylar. Cynthia understood that Dillon was too close to Skylar to do what needed to be done, so Cynthia braced for what she had to do.

"No," Cynthia said forcefully. Both Skylar and Dillon jumped. "Nobody left her. Jake is inside right now working up a plan to help her. So, you can sit out here and feel sorry for yourself, or you can get your ass in there and help."

"Back off, Cynthia," Dillon said bristling. She shot Cynthia an angry look, but Cynthia met her gaze and held it.

"No, I won't back off. Skylar's a fighter. She's a survivor. She'll be angry at herself if she sits out here and gives up. So, I'm not gonna let her, and neither should you."

Dillon's eyes softened. "Cynthia's right, Sky. I don't know what's happened to hurt you so bad, but I know you survived it all." Dillon squeezed Skylar's hand. "You're with people who love you, and you don't have to fight this alone. But we need you, Sky. The girl that you saw earlier needs you too. It's your chance to take back your power and fight back against the evil that you couldn't fight when you were younger. Join us?" Dillon held out her hand.

Cynthia held her breath, hoping Dillon's words would get through to Skylar. Skylar looked blankly at Dillon for several seconds before life began to return to her eyes. When it did, the tears began to flow harder, and she wrapped both arms around Dillon. They held each other as Cynthia looked on, her heart breaking at Skylar's obvious pain. After a while, Skylar's breathing returned to normal, and she relaxed in Dillon's arms.

Skylar startled them both when she leapt from the table. "Let's go. What are you two waiting for?"

Dillon gave Cynthia a startled look before she ran after Skylar.

Chapter Twenty-four

Jake stood in front of the equipment storage area, passing out weapons. Some of the women were eagerly strapping on their guns with a practiced ease, whereas others were tentative and nervous. He missed Skylar's calming influence, especially with those who weren't comfortable with firearms. During training, she put everyone at ease, and soon had even the most tentative handling the weapons as if they'd been shooting for years. Jake didn't have her patience or demeanor, but Skylar's bartending skills served her well working with the women.

Jake started to turn back to the storage area when he noticed the trio crossing the atrium. *Thank God.* His heart beat faster as he watched them, trying to make out Skylar's state of mind. A few of the others noticed their arrival too and were sneaking glances in their direction.

Without saying anything to Jake, Skylar approached Renee, who struggled with her gear and offered her a reassuring smile. Soon, several other women were surrounding Skylar as she assisted them with their equipment.

Jake gave Dillon a questioning look as she passed him going into the storage area. She simply nodded and kept walking. He quietly followed and said, "Is everything okay?"

"I think so."

"What happened to her?"

"I'm not sure, Jake."

"She freaked the shit out of me."

"I know, she scared me too." Dillon turned to look at Jake for the first time; her eyes were watery, but she pushed back the tears. "I think someone hurt her. I think someone hurt her really badly, but she won't talk about it."

"I hope she understands I had to do what I did to get her into the vehicle. I hope you understand, too." He'd grown to think of them as his family and was fearful that he'd damaged it. "I still feel sick about having to use force on her, but I didn't know what else to do."

Dillon put her hand on his arm. "I understand, Jake. And I think she will once this is all over."

"Thanks," Jake said with a weak smile. "Do you think she's gonna be all right for what we have to do?"

"I hope so. We're in for a battle and we need her. All of us need to be at the top of our game."

"No doubt. She'll be okay. She's one tough girl." Jake clapped Dillon on the back with his large hand. "Here, let me help you get your gear together."

"Do you think it's the guys that hit Amarillo?" Dillon asked, while sliding into her vest.

"I'm almost certain. My guess is the women are the ones they took from there."

Dillon secured her helmet and jiggled it a couple times. "Babcock?"

"I doubt it," he answered. "I've never believed it was them."

⚜ ⚜ ⚜ ⚜

It had taken longer than Dillon would have liked to get everyone ready. *Something they'd need to practice.* She pushed the thought from her head. Her palms were sweaty, and she felt adrenaline coursing through her. She wanted to get moving but understood that being properly geared up was essential. The weapons were only part of the equipment that Whitaker had kept in the bunker. Ironically, many of the women hated the military grade helmets almost as much as they hated the weapons. They'd spent several sessions training on how to use the built-in communication system, which finally won the women over.

Dillon cast her eyes to the ground; seeing the entire group ready for battle was too much for her to take in. When they practiced, it had only been with four or five at a time, not the entire community.

Jake gathered everyone in the atrium and reviewed their options when they received a distress call from the tower. Jake pressed his helmet against the side of his head, squinted his eyes, and spoke into his microphone.

"Everyone," Jake called out. "That was the tower. There is an SUV approaching the main entrance. We've secured the gate, so hopefully they won't find a way to drive in. They'll have to climb the fence. Unfortunately, with the tree cover, the tower won't be able to see anything, so we'll be on our own out there."

"Shouldn't we get moving?" someone yelled.

Jake held up his hand. "No, we need to be more strategic than that. There is only one vehicle, so I'm thinking it's a scout team. We'll be better off surprising them. I need a team of four or five of our best marksmen. We need to be small, nimble, and able to communicate effectively."

Dillon's heart clenched. *Skylar was one of the best*. Dillon, on the other hand, was only average when it came to moving targets.

"No, Jake," Dillon said. "I think stealth is more important than gun skills in this situation. We have some great shooters that move around the woods like a herd of wild buffalo. I'd like to volunteer."

"Point taken." He looked around the group. "Skylar, Dillon, Dee, Willa, and I will make up the first team."

Nobody argued. It seemed their training was effective, with everyone accepting Jake's command.

The four joined Jake at the front of the room. Dillon glanced at Willa, who stood tall and at attention. She'd been the biggest surprise, turning out to be nearly as good with a gun as Skylar. She'd been raised in a hunting family, and years later, despite being an animal rights activist, she'd retained many of the skills from her youth. It was her discipline which was more shocking. The rebel with the crazy hair and piercings became an obedient soldier when she put on her uniform. Luckily, they wore helmets so her blue and pink hair wouldn't make her a neon target.

"We'll also need a backup team that will be ready should something go wrong," Jake said. He quickly named the participants for the backup team and returned his focus to the lead group. "We walk parallel to the entrance road through the woods. Starting out, we stay together as a group. We branch out if the situation dictates." Jake pointed at the backup crew that huddled together. "You guys stay back, but if shit goes south, come in hard."

"What about the rest of us?" someone called out.

"Hopefully, you'll never see action, but if you do, remember your training," Jake said. "I want all of you gathered about a quarter of the way down the road. If they get past the first two groups, then we are in an all-out war, and you know what to do."

"We need to get going, Jake." Dillon rocked from foot to foot. "We need to intercept them before they get too close to the mansion."

"Dillon's right." Jake swept his arm around the room. "You guys know who your leaders are. Lead group is heading out; the rest of you get organized and get to your stations. May God bless you and keep you safe."

Jake turned and motioned for his team to follow. They walked quickly across the atrium, went through the lobby, and burst through the mansion doors. They were on the alert as they descended the steep stairs, hoping the enemy was still far away. As soon as they cleared the stairs, they broke into a fast jog.

Until they hit the woods, they would be completely exposed for nearly a quarter of a mile. They debated taking a vehicle but were afraid the intruders might hear the engine and that would give away their advantage.

The beautiful sunny day was a juxtaposition to the intense heavily armed group that ran toward the woods. Making it to the shelter of the trees proved uneventful. They listened intently but did not hear an engine. They hoped it meant the men were on foot and couldn't get the gates opened.

They were nearly halfway to the entrance when Jake put up his hand. Once they stopped, there was no mistaking the boisterous voices in the distance. Jake motioned for them to follow him. They found a spot with heavy ground cover that was only ten feet from the road. They got in position and quietly waited, as the voices drew closer.

Dillon was astonished at the hubris of the men coming up the roadway. Three of them walked in the middle of the road, loudly carrying on about something.

"We'll let them pass our location. Then Dillon and I will confront them from behind. We can hopefully take them peacefully," Jake said.

Watching from her hidden position, Dillon saw they carried automatic weapons, but they carried them loosely.

Jake and Dillon moved silently through the undergrowth, not that they needed to since the men were talking so loudly. Once they were firmly on the road behind the men, Jake and Dillon raised their weapons.

"Freeze," Jake shouted.

The men turned around, stunned to see two guns pointing at them. They looked at one another wide eyed, before setting their guns on the ground in front of them and holding their hands in the air.

"Dee," Jake said. "Get their weapons."

Dee burst out of the trees and moved in to pick up the weapons. That's when things went awry.

As if in slow motion, one of the men made a sudden move and yanked a handgun from his waist-band.

"No," Dillon yelled, but it was too late. Before she could make sense of what was happening, Skylar and Willa opened fire from the woods where they'd remained as backup. The woods reverberated with gunshots, then all was silent except for the screams and moans coming from the four individuals laying on the pavement.

Dillon ran to where the fallen lay and dropped to her knees next to Dee, completely forgetting the three men that lie around her. A crimson stain was slowly spreading down Dee's arm. Dillon examined the wound, which appeared to be on her shoulder missing any major blood vessels. Dee's eyes were closed, but she breathed loudly.

Skylar arrived shortly after and nudged Dillon aside. "Let me have a look."

Dillon moved aside.

"How are you doing, Dee?" Skylar said softly.

"I've been better." Dee opened her eyes. Skylar squeezed her hand. "It's okay, we're going to have Cynthia fix you up." Skylar turned to Dillon. "Contact the others and tell Cynthia to prepare for surgery." Before Dillon could respond, Skylar's full attention was back on Dee, as she gently wiped the sweat from her brow.

Dillon ran to where Jake knelt next to the men. "We have two dead and one seriously wounded," he said. Dillon quickly called in the information and went back to assist Skylar.

Time moved quickly, as Skylar tried to quell Dee's bleeding, while Dillon acted as her assistant. Jake and Willa pulled the surviving man away from where they worked on Dee and began to question him. Dillon could hear the man screaming but preferred not to know what persuasive techniques Jake used to get him to talk.

In no time, two vehicles roared up the road. Tiffany jumped out of the lead vehicle and ran to where Dillon and Skylar were attending Dee. Tiffany went pale when she saw the blood soaking Dee's shirt but did her best to keep her composure. "Cynthia's setting up the surgical room and sent me with a stretcher. Are you going to need it?" Tiffany asked.

"Yes, I don't think we want to jostle her around trying to get her to her feet," Skylar answered.

Dillon jumped up and raced back to the vehicle with Tiffany to retrieve the stretcher. They carefully slid Dee onto the board and lifted her from the ground. When they'd gotten her into the vehicle, Jake yelled for Dillon.

"You guys go ahead with Tiffany and get Dee medical help," Jake said to Dillon. "I'm going to stay here and continue questioning our prisoner. Tell Tasha to hold tight, and we'll ride back with her."

Dillon looked down at the frightened man. He was pale and blood seemed to be seeping out of several wounds. From the looks of him, he wouldn't be much longer in this world. Dillon hesitated for a second, wondering if allowing Jake to continue to question him without medical treatment was the right thing to do. Skylar yelled for her to hurry up, and in that instance, she made a decision that would haunt her for the rest of her life. She turned away from the screaming man and joined Skylar.

⚘⚘⚘⚘

Tiffany sped up the circular driveway and skidded to a stop right outside the hotel lobby doors, which were now ER doors. Cynthia waited outside and ran to the SUV. The four women slid Dee's stretcher from the back of the vehicle and hurried inside.

Dillon glanced off to the right where they'd converted two small offices into examination rooms. They veered to the left, into what used to be the concierge office. Cynthia had converted it into a rudimentary surgical center.

Lily was already gowned up when they brought Dee into the room and set her on the gurney in the center of the room. Dillon glanced around at all the surgical equipment, but quickly looked away.

"Are you sure you don't need me to stick around?" Dillon asked Skylar.

"No, Cynthia and I need to get scrubbed up, so she can get that bullet out."

"But I could do something," Dillon protested.

"Babe, I'm not sure you would be much help. I don't want to be worrying about you passing out and hitting your head on something." Skylar winked. "You need to go and help Jake. It won't be long before the others realize that something happened to their buddies. Once we're done here, I'll get back out there as soon as I can."

"Must be hard being good at so many things," Dillon said with a slight smile.

"Stop." Skylar fidgeted and glanced away. "I'm not sure how to react to people actually needing me."

"I need you always." Dillon wrapped her arms around Skylar. The hug was much too short, but Skylar needed to get on with helping Dee.

"Would you leave my nurse alone?" Cynthia said, when she walked into the room.

"Are you kicking me out too?"

"You know it. But before you leave, come over here and give me a hug. I think we're all gonna need some strength before this day is over."

"I hear ya." Dillon wrapped Cynthia in a bear

hug. Before she left, she hugged Skylar one last time, and without turning back, hastily left the room.

≋≋≋≋

Everyone was crowded around Jake when Dillon arrived back at the atrium. He relayed the information he'd gotten from the wounded prisoner, which Dillon was quick to ascertain was now the deceased prisoner. If Jake's information was correct, there were nineteen men back at the camp, three teenage girls, and two women. Apparently, all the women were there against their will.

"So, were they having a motorcycle gang convention in a cave or what?" Renee asked.

"That's the ironic part. They aren't bikers," Jake answered. "They're a bunch of Wall Street boys who were on a flight back to Las Vegas after a week-long bachelor party when the Crisis happened."

A couple of the women laughed despite themselves. "Why does that not surprise me? Bikers have more class," Renee added.

"No ties to Braxton Babcock?" Katie said, joining the conversation.

"I don't think so," Jake said. "When I mentioned his name, the guy gave me a blank stare. Either he's a good actor, or they are who he said they are."

"So, we're dealing with a bunch of lawless creeps who've watched The Purge too many times?" Renee said, her face reddening.

"That about sums it up. The important thing is these guys are not as skilled with weapons as I'd feared. Nor are they skilled riders either, apparently. They already lost two guys when they crashed their bikes," Jake said.

"We aren't exactly the militia," Katie said and glanced around the room at the women decked out in ammunition belts and fatigues.

"But we've been training, and we've prepared for this moment." Dillon spoke for the first time. Many of the women hadn't seen her walk up, so they turned to her with a hopeful look. Despite her protests, Dillon had become an emotional leader of the group, a calming force when things seemed bleak.

"How's Dee?" Willa asked.

"They were prepping for surgery when I left, or should I say when they kicked me out," Dillon answered. "Cynthia was confident she would be fine."

"Thank God," several women said at once.

"So, did I miss anything?" Dillon asked. "What's our game plan? I'm sure someone will notice the boys are out of contact."

"We've still got two watchers in the tower who will let us know if there is any movement from their camp," Jake said.

"I'm thinking we're gonna want to get in place before they figure it out," Dillon said.

Jake nodded. "Yep, that's what we were about ready to discuss."

Chapter Twenty-five

Dillon fiddled with the strap on her helmet. *Waiting was the worst.* They'd been in position for nearly twenty minutes when the call came from the tower. The entire camp was on the move.

Jake's voice came across Dillon's helmet com. "Dammit. We need Skylar."

Cynthia had run into trouble with Dee's surgery, so Skylar hadn't made it back to the trenches. Dillon knew Skylar would get there as soon as she could, but Dillon was happy she was safe along with Cynthia. *Selfish,* she knew, but she'd be able to concentrate better without them here.

"We've got this," Dillon said with more confidence than she felt.

After a heated debate, they'd decided to open the gate and allow the invaders to drive onto the mansion grounds. The winding driveway to the mansion through the trees offered them the best strategic cover. There wasn't a good vantage point outside the gate to ambush the intruders.

"I'm just glad you remembered that damned scout vehicle," Jake's voice came through her helmet.

"No shit," Dillon said into her mike. In their haste, they'd almost forgot it was parked on the road outside the gate. Luckily, the keys had still been in it, so they were able to drive it deep into the woods to hide it. "Hopefully, they'll think their boys just drove in, so they won't be on the alert. How long do you think we have?"

"Probably ten or fifteen minutes," Jake answered. "I better do one last communication check."

"Go for it." Dillon breathed in deeply, trying to slow her heart rate. Maybe Jake's check-in would have a calming effect.

Jake's voice filled her helmet. "Lookout tower, please respond."

"Check." Leslie said. She was in the tower with one other woman and the children, Jake's youngest daughter and Nancy's two girls. They'd been instructed to run to the bunker should things go wrong. There were enough supplies to hide there for weeks.

"Communication Central, please respond."

"Check." Dillon smiled at CJ's voice. Anne and CJ had set up a makeshift communication hub in the hotel in one of the conference rooms just down the hall from the medical center. Communication was everything, so they'd been tasked with ensuring all the equipment remained functional and all channels continued to work. With the real possibility there could be more wounded, it was important that the medical center and the field had rapid and effective communication.

"Left Rear."

"Check." Tiffany answered.

"Right Rear."

"Check." Katie answered.

"Left Front."

"Check," Dillon responded.

"Right Front is accounted for," Jake said.

They'd divided into four combat groups of five

people, which flanked both sides of the road. Jake and Dillon led the two front groups, which were stationed just inside the gate around the first bend in the road. This is where they intended to ambush the intruders, which would be the most dangerous positions.

The other two groups were further along the road. Dillon hoped they'd see little or no action. If the invaders got to them, it would mean their first line had failed.

Dillon nodded at the four women hunkered nearby, the team she hoped she could lead successfully with no casualties. *Stop!* It was no time for doubts. She'd had no military training, nor had any of the rest, but she knew that thinking about casualties now was not the smartest thing to do.

Her thoughts were interrupted by a call from the tower. Leslie's voice filled her helmet, "To the best of our knowledge, the SUV is bringing up the rear, with the women. The hostages. There is only one man in the vehicle, the driver. The rest are on motorcycles and are leading the pack."

"Great news," Jake said. "We need to separate the SUV from the pack, if possible. I want Maria from my group and Dillon, I want you from yours to move a little closer to the gate. Once the gunfire starts, I want you to approach the SUV from the back in order to rescue the hostages."

"Roger," Dillon and Maria answered.

The communications ended, and Dillon hunkered down, quietly waiting, lost in her own last-minute thoughts. Once the firefight started, everyone would be reacting out of instinct, and there would be no more time left for reflection. Dillon ran her thumb over the pin that said SKY, the one Skylar gave her the first night they met. Dillon had carried it with her ever since, and now she rubbed it between her fingers. She said a silent I love you, knowing she may never see Skylar again. She put the pin back in her pocket when she heard the low rumble of motorcycle engines.

ৠৠৡৡ

Everything unfolded quickly when the motorcycles rounded the corner. The riders rode side by side, one following closely behind the other. To Dillon, the line looked like it went on forever, but she took a deep breath and focused on the eight pairs coming into view.

Their first line of defense opened fire, taking out over half the riders before they knew what was happening. The men still on bikes yelled and gunned their engines, trying to evade their fallen friends.

Dillon tore her eyes away and ran from cover toward the SUV that carried the imprisoned women. Out of the corner of her eye, she registered Maria coming from the other side of the road. They were completely exposed to anyone who noticed them, but in the chaos, no one did.

Dillon yanked open the driver's door and held her handgun to his temple. He raised his hand to knock the gun away, and she saw the face of a young man before she pulled the trigger. Part of his face disappeared, and he slumped onto the steering wheel. Dillon fought down her revulsion and tried not to look at the blood splattered throughout the cab.

She yanked him from the SUV and let his body drop to the ground before she jumped into the driver's seat. Maria was already in the passenger seat, trying to calm the frightened women in the back. Dillon punched the gas and turned the wheel hard, spinning them away from the gunfire. She drove about a hundred yards from the fight and stopped.

"Maria, I'm going back to help the others," Dillon said. "Be ready to get the hell out of here if you need to. I'll let you know what's going on when I know something."

Before Maria could speak, Dillon sprinted to the side of the road. By the time Dillon made her way through the woods back to the action, it was almost over. The men had driven into a massacre, and there were only two still returning gunfire. Dillon hopeful when she heard the heavy gunfire coming from the woods. It meant that the team was still largely intact. Before she could join Tad, who was shooting from behind a large tree, she saw the last man fall off his motorcycle and land face first. The gunfire from the forest stopped, and it was silent for what seemed like an eternity before the quiet was broken.

"I think we've got them all," Jake yelled out. "Let's move in slowly. Be careful; if there is anyone still alive, they might be waiting for a chance to pull the trigger on one of us."

Dillon stood from her crouched position and cautiously walked out of the woods. She saw others moving in her peripheral vision, but her eyes remained fixed on the men and bikes littering the roadway. The group systematically went from body to body and discovered sixteen men all lying dead. Once they were finished, Dillon surveyed their group and noted that there were only seven of them.

"Shit, we're missing three," Jake said.

"No, only two, Maria is in the SUV," Dillon said.

She did a quick mental check and said, "It's Tasha and KC."

"We need to search the woods on both sides. They were on different teams," Jake said. The group naturally split, half going one way the other half going the other. Dillon contacted CJ with an update and told her to send the rest to help find their lost members.

Maria was the first to arrive in the SUV. She slammed on the brakes, came to a skidding stop, and threw open the door. She was near hysterics and screamed Tasha's name as she jumped out of the vehicle. The shell-shocked women also exited the SUV and huddled, staring at the carnage around them. Maria looked around frantically and screamed Tasha's name.

Tad and Dillon were about to enter the woods to search for Tasha and KC when he turned to her and said, "Maybe you should check on Maria. She doesn't sound so good."

"How did you get so wise at your age?" Dillon patted him on the back. "Thanks, Tad." She turned and ran toward Maria.

Dillon went along the side of the road, avoiding the carnage. Tiffany's group had already arrived, and Tiffany had her arm around Maria trying to comfort her. Relief washed over Tiffany's face when she saw Dillon approaching.

"What do you need us to do?" Tiffany asked.

"They're searching for Tasha and KC; they never came out after the shooting was done," Dillon said. She started to say more, but yells coming from the north side of the road interrupted her. "KC was on the north side, so they must have found her," Dillon said to Tiffany. "Send a couple of your team with a stretcher to bring her out. The rest can help look for Tasha on the south side."

Tiffany gave the orders and the group quickly disappeared into the trees. Dillon put her hand on Maria's arm. "Maria, we'll find her. I think it's best if you stay out here and wait for them to bring her out."

"Okay," Maria mumbled. There was a far off look in her eyes that Dillon didn't like. She gently led her to the SUV. "Why don't you sit down?" Dillon opened the back and motioned for Maria to sit.

Dillon turned to the five women huddled against the SUV and introduced herself. The three teens were Austin, Brittany, and Delphia. The short stocky woman was Carol, and her striking companion was Alaina. Dillon quickly sized them up before she spoke.

"Alaina, could you watch over Maria while I go back in to help with the search?" Dillon looked into two clear ice blue eyes. The other four had a glazed look, but Alaina appeared to have some fight left in her.

"Yes, go," Alaina answered. She turned to Maria and put an arm around her shoulder. Maria did not resist and allowed the stranger to comfort her.

Dillon was in the woods for a few minutes when another cry went up about fifty yards from where she was. She broke into a run, only half noticing the branches that whipped against her face. When she arrived, Jake and two other women were bent over a body lying on the ground. She saw the dark-skinned arm splayed out and she immediately knew it was Tasha. Dillon held her breath when she approached, afraid of what she may see.

"She's alive," Jake said. Dillon didn't realize she

was holding her breath until she expelled it loudly. "Her arm is in pretty bad shape, and it looks like she took a glancing shot to the head, but I think the blood is making it look worse than it is. Cynthia will have to decide that, though."

"We need to get a stretcher out here."

"Already on it. Tad should be here with one soon."

The group made quick work of bringing the two women out of the woods on stretchers. With practiced efficiency, they loaded them into the back of the SUV. Tasha had come to briefly but was unconscious again. Her left arm was severely injured, and possibly not salvageable.

They'd been in communication with Cynthia, who instructed them to put a tourniquet on Tasha's arm to stop the blood loss. Upon further inspection, her head wound was superficial and had nearly stopped bleeding. Cynthia stressed that blood loss and shock were the biggest dangers to Tasha.

KC was in much worse shape. She had two bullet wounds in her abdomen that had pierced her vest, and they were unable to stop the bleeding. Her vital signs were weakening by the moment. Cynthia's only advice was to get her to the medical center as quickly as possible.

Tiffany and Dillon volunteered to take the wounded to the medical center; both were anxious to see their partners. Maria insisted on going along with Tasha, so the three climbed into the SUV and left the rest of the group to debrief from the battle.

❧❧❧❧❧

Katie and Renee stood with their arms around each other, unaware of how much they needed to draw strength from the other. Katie had never seen or smelled anything like the carnage around them. Neither had been on the front line, so Katie could only imagine the feelings of those responsible for the death that laid all around them. Several of those gathered were talking about the battle and reliving the moments as if it were a sporting event. Katie was sure this is how people dealt with the stress of something so terrible, but she couldn't stand to listen to a blow-by-blow recap of the kills, so she silently led Renee away from the group.

They approached the smaller group that surrounded the five freed hostages. Katie and Renee joined in the introductions. Soon the women were telling their story as the others listened in silence. The women confirmed that they were captured in Amarillo, over two months ago. They kept the details to the minimum, not wanting to relive their ordeal, knowing they would carry the nightmare with them for the rest of their lives.

"I thought there were six of you?" Renee said.

A hush fell over the five women, and they exchanged glances. In a quiet voice, Alaina told the story of Trisha. She'd been the men's favorite, a gorgeous blonde sixteen-year-old with the body of a twenty-five-year-old. In this case, being the favorite wasn't good, and soon the constant attention wore her down. The women tried to offer her comfort and do what they could for her, but they could only helplessly watch as she slipped away. Then about a week ago, they found her in the back seat of one of the vehicles with her wrists slit. As Alaina told the story, the other four had a vacant, sad look in their eyes, while an angry fire burned in Alaina's.

Katie studied Alaina and couldn't help but think she would have been one of the men's favorites as well. She was tall and slender, with jet-black hair, high exotic cheekbones and ice blue eyes. The experience didn't seem to have broken her, but then again, no one could truly know what went on inside another person.

Chapter Twenty-six

Tiffany hit the brakes outside the hotel medical center, and Dillon leapt from her seat before they came to a stop. She was surprised that someone hadn't been waiting for them at the door. She hoped that didn't mean that Dee had taken a turn for the worse. Dillon threw open the back and started to slide KC's stretcher out. Tiffany was right beside her, helping get KC the rest of the way out. Maria rushed to the door and held it open for them to carry the unconscious woman into the center. It was unusually quiet, and no one greeted them.

"Shit," Dillon said. "I hope they didn't have to go back into surgery on Dee."

"I'll go find them," Maria said.

Tiffany motioned with her head. "Let's put KC on this gurney and go get Tasha."

They carefully set KC's stretcher down and hurried back outside.

Tasha had partially woken and muttered something incoherent when they returned for her. Dillon ran her hand over the uninjured side of her head and offered words of encouragement. Whatever she did, it seemed to calm Tasha, and she stopped talking and appeared to have fallen back to sleep. They lifted her and made their way into the building. Maria still hadn't returned. They gently lowered Tasha to the remaining gurney.

"Where the hell are they?" Tiffany said, her voice betraying her irritation. "I would think either CJ or Anne would come to help since the crisis has passed."

"Do you want to go see what they're up to?" Dillon asked.

"Sure," Tiffany said with a grin. Despite everything, obviously the thought of seeing Anne brought a smile to her face.

Once Tiffany was gone, Dillon looked around the room, not sure what to do. She'd heard about triage but had no idea how it would work in this situation. She feared KC was too far gone, and Cynthia would have to bypass her care to ensure that they didn't lose Tasha as well. She didn't envy the decision Cynthia would have to make.

"Something's wrong." Maria said in a low voice.

"Huh?" Dillon said, finally noticing her return.

"I couldn't find them. Well, I found Dee."

"So, did she tell you where they went?" Dillon was still trying to make sure that Tasha and KC were comfortable, so she'd not looked at Maria yet.

"No, she had a bullet in her head."

Dillon snapped to attention and looked at Maria for the first time. Maria was pale and her eyes were wide. "What did you just say?"

"She's dead. Shot in the head."

"What?" Dillon struggled to understand what Maria told her.

"She was lying on the table with a bullet wound in her head." Maria's voice faltered. "I don't know where the hell the others are."

"What's all the yelling about?" Tiffany said,

coming into the room.

"Where's CJ and Anne?" Dillon said abruptly.

"I figured they were helping out Cynthia since they weren't in the communication center," Tiffany answered. "Where are the others?"

Maria quickly filled Tiffany in on what she'd seen. The gravity of the situation started to register. "Oh shit, we're so fucking stupid." Dillon engaged her helmet com. Jake answered immediately. "Jake, how many dead bikers do you have there?"

"Sixteen, why?" he asked.

"When you talked to the guy from the scout party, didn't he tell you there were nineteen of them?" Dillon asked.

"Fuck! You're right. Dillon, what the hell is going on?"

"I'm not sure, but they're all gone."

"What do you mean gone? I just talked to Lily less than ten minutes ago."

"That's good to know. Hopefully that means they haven't gotten far."

"I'm on my way, wait for me."

"I can't do that, Jake." Dillon clicked off communication. She pushed another button and connected to the tower. "Leslie, did you see anything at the medical center in the last ten minutes?"

"Yeah, I thought the team was going to help you guys out, but they went the opposite way. What's happening?"

"I'm not sure. Which way did they go?"

"They went out the back toward the woods."

"How many were there?"

"I'm not sure. We weren't paying close attention until we realized they were going the wrong way. We

thought there was a vehicle or something out there
but realized there wasn't when they disappeared into
the woods."

"Dammit." Dillon disconnected before Leslie
could respond. "Maria, you need to stay here and take
care of Tasha and KC." Dillon turned to Tiffany. She
was shocked by what she was about to say. "Do you
want to come with me?"

"Of course I do, the two people I love the most
in this world are out there somewhere," Tiffany said.
Her face softened and she put her hand on Dillon's
arm. "You've got three, don't you?"

Dillon nodded and fought back her emotions.
Skylar had insisted that Dillon forgive Tiffany. She'd
pointed out that to repair the fracture in the group, it
all started with Dillon and Tiffany. It had been hard,
but they had gotten to a place where they could work
together. And as the relationship between the two
improved, the group became more cohesive as well.
Now they would need to work as a team to rescue the
people they loved.

"Let's go, then." Dillon grabbed her weapons off
the counter and started for the back door.

They made good time through the woods. The
women had been smart and moved through the terrain, heavily leaving plenty of signs as to their path.
Dillon hoped this was a sign that the captors weren't
intelligent or observant. Hopefully, the Wall Street
boys didn't know much about the outdoors. Her
small-town country upbringing should give her some
advantage.

They'd been tracking for nearly fifteen minutes
when they heard sounds ahead. Dillon put her arm
out and stopped Tiffany from going any further. "I

think I hear something," Dillon whispered.

"Then why are you stopping?"

"I think they may be up ahead. We need to figure out what we're dealing with and come up with a plan."

"Let's just take them by surprise," Tiffany said impatiently.

"No, if we do that, one of them could be hurt... or worse." Dillon grabbed Tiffany's arm to stop her. "Just follow me."

Dillon crouched low and silently moved towards the voices, edging ever closer to the small clearing where they'd apparently stopped. Dillon saw two men, who appeared to be arguing. Unfortunately, one had his gun trained in the direction of their hostages. Dillon's heart clenched when she saw her friends bound together with duct tape. She motioned for Tiffany to crouch beside her.

Dillon surveyed the area. She whispered to Tiffany, "I've got an idea. We need to get their attention away from the girls. I'll sneak around behind the guys, while you get as close to the girls as you can. Then I'm gonna make a bunch of noise and get them to turn toward me. That's when I want you to jump out and start shooting."

"Why don't you just shoot them in the back?" Tiffany asked.

"We can't risk it as long as a gun is pointed at the girls. It could accidentally go off and hit them."

"But if you wait until they turn, then you could get hit. Shit, I could accidentally hit you."

"That's a chance I'm willing to take," Dillon answered.

Tiffany started to protest, but then looked down at the ground. "Okay. Cover me while I get into position. I'll let you know when I'm ready for you to move."

Before Dillon could respond, Tiffany slipped off to the right, crouched low, and moved with catlike quickness through the dense foliage. Dillon glanced at where her friends sat against a tree and realized that Tiffany could get very close to them. The massive size of the tree and undergrowth behind it would serve as cover. She didn't want to study the terrain too long because she needed to keep her eyes on the men, in case they discovered Tiffany. If that were to happen, then things would unfold rapidly.

Dillon watched the men intently, wondering what took Tiffany so long. One of the men's eyebrows rose and a look of confusion registered on his face. Dillon knew what happened an instant before Tiffany yelled out her name. Instincts took over and Dillon opened fire on the two men. The sound of gunfire reverberated through the forest, and the two men laid dead, hit from gunfire from two directions.

"What the fuck were you thinking, Tiffany?" Dillon yelled as she turned toward her friends. Dillon's heart skipped a beat when she saw her blood splattered friends, and Tiffany laying on the ground in front of them.

Anne screamed and tried to break free of her restraints. Dillon leapt over the fallen tree in front of her and headed toward the women in a sprint. Dillon couldn't tell who'd been hit since they were all covered in blood. She breathed deeply, hoping to keep her senses about her.

When she approached, Cynthia yelled, "Dillon, get me untied, so I can help Tiffany."

Dillon slid to a halt and dropped to her knees.

She tugged on the duct tape, but it wasn't budging, so she pulled harder.

Cynthia's voice penetrated the blood that pounded in her ears. "Dillon, are you carrying your pocketknife?"

Dillon looked at her, puzzled for a second before the fog cleared. She thrust her hand into her pocket and found her knife. It only took a few seconds to free Cynthia. Next, she freed the nearly hysterical Anne. As soon as Anne was released, she fell next to Tiffany, sobbing.

Then she freed Skylar, who crawled next to Cynthia and started applying pressure to one of Tiffany's wounds. The blood oozed between Skylar's fingers. Dillon freed Lily next, so she could help the others care for Tiffany. Finally, she freed CJ, who was covered in Tiffany's blood but didn't appear to be injured herself.

While Cynthia worked on Tiffany, Dillon examined the scene. As she did, the reality of what happened began to dawn. Dillon understood why Tiffany had taken so long to get into place. Tiffany must have figured out that she could use her body as a shield to protect the women tied helplessly against the tree, while at the same time her actions would ensure that Dillon would be safe as well.

"Dillon, call Jake. We need to get her to the medical center as soon as possible," Cynthia said, bringing Dillon back to the present.

Dillon reached up to her helmet to make the call, but Tiffany weakly grabbed her arm and looked her in the eyes. "No, Dillon, it's too late. I need to say a few things to you guys."

"What the hell were you thinking?" Dillon said

loudly, fighting back tears. Dillon turned to Cynthia and gazed into her pain-filled eyes. Cynthia shook her head, and Dillon dropped her hand, not making the call.

Anne began to scream, and Dillon tightened the hold she had on her. Tiffany took Anne's hand. "Tiffany wants to talk to you, Anne," Dillon said gently.

The words penetrated and it was as if a switch flipped. Anne stopped screaming, moved closer to Tiffany, and began brushing the hair out of her face. "What is it, my love?" Anne said with tears streaming down her face.

"I've never done anything in my whole life to make you proud. I hope I can in death."

"Oh, baby, no. I've always been proud of you," Anne said.

"You never were a good liar," Tiffany said with a half-smile. "It's okay, this is the first thing I've done right in a long time. I know it won't make up for all the hurt I caused, but I hope it helps." With those words, she turned her head and found Skylar. "I'm sorry, you didn't deserve what I did to you."

"It's okay. I forgave you long ago." Skylar fought back tears.

"I haven't forgiven myself."

Skylar gently touched Tiffany's brow, wiping away the sweat that trickled down her face. "Sweetie, it's okay. Please, forgive yourself."

"Thank you." Tiffany closed her eyes. Everyone looked at Cynthia with fear, but Tiffany's eyes popped open. "Cyn, where are you?"

"I'm right here, Tiff." Cynthia took Tiffany's other hand.

"You were the best friend anyone could ever have, and I never treated you that way. I'm sorry."

"Oh, Tiff, there's no need to apologize. I love you a ton." Cynthia's voice cracked and tears rolled down her cheeks.

"You know I love you too, don't you ever doubt it, even if I didn't show it very well."

Cynthia managed a smile. "I think taking a bullet for me is showing me something."

"I always told you I'd die for you, and here you thought I was lying." Tiffany smirked. She tried to laugh, but it came out more of a choking sound and blood sprayed out of her mouth.

Anne kissed her forehead, and Cynthia applied more pressure to the wound that seemed to be losing the most blood. Blood covered Cynthia's hand, and Dillon wondered how much longer Tiffany had.

"Dillon, I gotta tell you something," Tiffany said after she'd stopped coughing.

"We're fine, Tiffany. I think Anne wants to talk to you."

"I have to tell you something first, then I want to be alone with Anne," Tiffany responded.

Dillon nodded.

"I never really hated you. The money, the power, the looks always softened everyone else, but in your eyes, I saw the contempt for the person I was. The same contempt I felt for myself. You were my mirror."

"Have you seen my eyes lately?" Dillon asked, managing a smile through her tears.

Tiffany returned the smile. "Yeah, my mirror was starting to respect me. And had I stayed around a little longer, you may have even grown to like me."

"I don't know if I'd go that far." Dillon winked.

"I'm proud of you, Tiffany. You were brave and self-less."

"Thank you." Tiffany's eyes filled with tears. "Skylar's amazing, so treat her right. If you don't, I'll come back and haunt your ass."

"No need to haunt me, I'll treat her right."

"Good." Tiffany coughed again. "One last thing. Thanks for being the friend to Cynthia that I wasn't. You were there for her when she needed it the most. When I wasn't. Promise you'll continue looking out for her and be the friend I should have been."

"Of course I will. I love her."

"I love her too, but love's not enough without commitment. Too bad I learned that lesson too late."

"No, it's never too late. Some people go to their grave never having learned it."

"Thanks. Now leave me alone so I can talk with my girl." Tiffany tried to smile.

Everyone but Anne began to stand. Dillon reached out and touched Tiffany's forehead. "Tiffany, you're dying with honor."

"I'll remember you always," Cynthia said as she rose. "I love you, Tiff."

"Love you too, Cyn," Tiffany said, no longer trying to hide her tears.

❧❧❧❧

Dillon, Skylar, and Cynthia made their way over to where Lily and CJ stood off to the side. None could bear to watch Anne lying down next to Tiffany and resting her head on Tiffany's chest, so they unconsciously made a semi-circle facing away from the pair. The conversation was awkward, the reality of the day taking its toll on all of them. Dillon and Skylar didn't speak directly to each other, but Dillon stood with her arm protectively around Skylar. There was so much to say, but now didn't seem like the time.

"We need to call Jake and let him know we're okay. Well, I mean…" Lily said, her voice trailing off.

"It's okay, Lily. We know what you meant," Dillon said. "Do you—"

Dillon's words were cut off by Anne's piercing scream. "*No!*"

Chapter Twenty-seven

Dillon laughed when she walked into the Athens room of the library. "Doing a little research?"

"Stupid, I know," Skylar said and set her book down. "*The Stand* was always one of my favorite books, so who knows? Maybe there's something to learn."

Dillon sat down next to Skylar. It had been nearly three weeks since the battle, and the group was still in shock. They'd buried Tiffany, Dee, and KC in a highly emotional ceremony. They finally allowed themselves to grieve everything they'd lost, with the three deaths representing all the Crisis had taken from them.

"I sometimes feel guilty," Skylar said after they'd been sitting in silence for some time.

"Why?"

Skylar snuggled closer to Dillon. "Because I'm happier than I've ever been in my life. How sick is that?"

Dillon turned and kissed her deeply before she answered. "It's not sick. I know what you mean. We didn't want all this death, but for the first time in both of our lives, we have a true community of people."

Tears silently streamed down Skylar's face. "I'd been on this earth for thirty-three years when this happened, and there wasn't a single person that I ever let in. That ever really mattered. And now, I know what it is to be loved and to love in return. And it's not just you, but Cynthia, CJ and Karen, Anne, Maria and Tasha, and even Katie. There was nothing I would have given my life for, until now."

"You're not alone." Dillon put her hand on Skylar's arm and looked into her eyes. "Tiffany is the ultimate example. Before this, she was one of the most self-centered people I'd ever met. Ironically, she's the one that laid down her life to save the people she loved."

"I think I'm a lot like her. I shut down my heart and kept everyone at bay. I don't think I ever knew what love truly was," Skylar said. "I didn't know how to give it, or receive it, until now. How sad is it that it took something like this for me to figure it out? To be happy."

"I'd like to think I knew the meaning of love before this, but nothing was near as deep as this. Life was so fast, and so easy to take for granted. And even though I loved, it wasn't near as deep or as widespread."

"Hey. What do you mean spreading your love widely?" Skylar playfully slapped Dillon on the arm. "Is there something you aren't telling me?"

Dillon smirked and kissed Skylar again, even more intensely than the first time. After several minutes, Dillon broke the kiss. "No, you're the only one that gets this treatment."

"That's good," Skylar said breathlessly. "Is there any other treatment that you'd like to show me?"

Dillon giggled and rested her hand on Skylar's thigh as she slowly moved it higher. "I'm thinking I have a few more moves you might want to see."

Skylar turned to kiss Dillon again, when a loud voice interrupted them. "There you two are. I've been looking everywhere for you," Karen said.

"What's up?" Dillon asked.

"I'm on a mission for Cynthia. She's called an emergency Commission meeting, and you were the only one we hadn't found."

Dillon smiled. "And here I am only a few doors away. When's the meeting?"

"Now." Karen smiled. "Sorry, Skylar."

Skylar laughed and held up her book. "It's okay, I've got some light reading to do."

"I'll meet you there," Karen said and walked toward the exit.

"Right behind you." Dillon turned back to Skylar. "Duty calls."

"Another example of loving deeper," Skylar said with a smile. "I have a fire burning a hole in a certain part of my body, but the Commission comes first."

"Do you think we should rethink this whole concept of community and love?" Dillon joked.

"Naw," Skylar said with a grin. "The fire can wait."

≈≈≈≈≈

"About time you got here," Cynthia said with a smile. "We were gonna start without you if you were much later."

"Hey now. Can somebody be late to a meeting that wasn't scheduled? Or one they were never informed of?" Dillon plopped into her regular seat. Her gaze went to Tiffany's empty chair, and she quickly looked away.

"Details." Cynthia flicked her hand in Dillon's direction.

"What's this all about?" Renee asked.

"We need to discuss what happened, and how to protect ourselves," Cynthia said.

Renee groaned. "Really, you call a special meeting for this? Our regular meeting is only three days from now."

"This afternoon I've received some new information that I didn't think could wait." Cynthia answered.

Dillon sat up straighter in her chair; it wasn't like Cynthia to be mysterious.

"Spill," Jake said.

"I'd like to revisit our timeline for making a decision on what we do with our Amarillo friends."

"And that's an emergency?" Jake wrinkled his nose when he spoke.

"I have someone I'd like to speak to the Commission, but I'd like us to discuss a few things first."

Dillon stared at Cynthia. "Why are you acting all cloak and dagger? You're starting to freak me out."

Cynthia held her palm out toward Dillon. "Sorry, I'm not trying to. I have Alaina in the other room, and she and I have been talking quite a bit. She has some interesting things to share, but I didn't want to spring her on the Commission without forewarning you."

"Cynthia, would you just tell us what the hell is going on?" Dillon glanced around the table at the tense faces. "The suspense is killing us."

Cynthia's face reddened, and her eyes shimmered. Dillon reached out and put her hand over Cynthia's. "Hey, are you all right?"

Cynthia nodded but didn't speak.

"What's going on?" Dillon asked, becoming more concerned by the minute. "Something's got you shaken up."

Cynthia nodded.

"Just tell us." Dillon put her entire focus on Cynthia, lowered her voice, and squeezed Cynthia's hand.

"I think we could be in more danger than we realize."

"Obviously, something she said has you rattled."

"Yes." Cynthia said in a voice barely louder than a whisper. "But we don't know her. What if she's not who we think she is? Before I brought any of this to you guys, I've interviewed all the others from the Amarillo group."

"You've been busy," Dillon said, trying to lighten Cynthia's mood.

"I had to stay busy, so I wouldn't keep thinking about Tiffany."

Dumbass. Dillon kicked herself for her insensitivity. She knew Cynthia was struggling. "So, what did you find out?"

"Alaina wandered into the Amarillo group a little over a month before they were taken."

"We knew that." Dillon tried to keep her voice even and not show the impatience she was feeling. "What else?"

"None of the others know where she came from, or why she showed up. Carol doesn't like her. She calls her the Ice Queen."

Dillon could see that. After only two weeks of knowing them, Carol was warm and matronly and doted on the three teenagers. Alaina, on the other hand, was standoffish, almost cold. There was no doubt she observed everything and took it all in, but she shared little, so if Cynthia got her to talk, it was a step in the right direction.

"What aren't you saying?" Jake asked.

"Carol's mentioned more than once how strange it is that they were attacked after Alaina showed up." Cynthia looked around the room.

"She thinks Alaina had something to do with it?" Renee asked.

"She hasn't gone that far, but she's planting the seeds." Cynthia's brow furrowed. "But I've been talking with Alaina a lot, and I just can't see it. She's intelligent, articulate, and interesting to talk to."

Dillon's eyes narrowed and she stared at Cynthia. She must have sensed Dillon's gaze because she looked toward Dillon, but as soon as they made eye contact, she shifted her gaze to the others. *What the hell.* How had she missed it? Cynthia had been spending quite a bit of time with Alaina the past couple weeks. *Was Cynthia attracted to Alaina?*

"Are you afraid you can't be objective?" Dillon decided to cut to the chase.

"Well…um…I have been talking to her a lot, and I think highly of her, so I was hoping to get everyone's opinion. In case I'm biased."

Dillon's eyes widened. *Had they slept together?* Dillon's eyes bore into the side of Cynthia's head. Redness crept up Cynthia's neck to her cheeks. *Damn, they had.*

"Has Carol given any concrete reasons why we should be suspicious, or is it just because she wandered in recently?" Jake asked.

"That and she wouldn't tell them where she came from," Cynthia said.

"But you know," Dillon said as a statement, not

a question.

"Yes."

"Care to enlighten us?"

"I'd rather her tell her story for herself, then you guys can be the judge of what you think."

Dillon's eyes shifted between Jake, Renee, and Karen, who all sported the same puzzled look. "I'm all for bringing her in."

The others agreed.

Cynthia stood without looking at Dillon and left the room.

"What the fuck was that about?" Jake said to Dillon.

Dillon shrugged. She wasn't going to voice her suspicions to anyone before she talked to Cynthia, who'd obviously been hiding things from her. "I say we hear her out. It won't hurt anything."

Jake opened his mouth to speak, but Cynthia escorted Alaina into the room.

Alaina strode in, her shoulders back with an almost defiant air. Her jet-black hair appeared windblown, and her ice blue eyes scanned the room. There was an intensity in her gaze that made it difficult to hold it for long, but Dillon locked eyes with her, trying to get a read. Beyond her intelligence, Dillon couldn't make out anything else.

"Welcome," Dillon said, still keeping eye contact. "Please, have a seat."

Alaina followed Cynthia and sat beside her.

Dillon addressed Alaina. "Cynthia tells us that you have information that might be of interest to us?"

"Yes." Alaina paused and made eye contact with everyone around the table before continuing. "I ended up in Amarillo about a month before we were taken.

The fine people of their community took me in as one of their own."

Dillon waited for her to continue. When she didn't, Dillon asked, "Care to tell us where you were before that?"

"Yes." Alaina paused once again and made eye contact with each person before she spoke. "I had been living at Braxton Babcock's Ministry for the past four years."

Dillon felt the energy in the room change, as everyone sat up straighter. "I see," Dillon managed to say. She wanted to ask whether it was voluntary but thought better of it. "Can I ask why you left?"

"That's not important to the story," Alaina said.

Dillon nodded and held Alaina's gaze. "Care to share what is?"

"Yes." Again, she looked at each person before opening her mouth. "You are in grave danger here. Babcock knows where you are."

Dillon heard the inhalation of breaths around the table. She bit her lip before speaking. "And how, may I ask, would he know that?"

"Somebody from the Whitaker Estate has been in contact with him."

"Of course they have." Dillon pointed toward Jake. "He's been talking with Babcock for months."

"Not him or CJ," Alaina said. "Someone else."

About The Author

Rita Potter has spent most of her life trying to figure out what makes people tick. To that end, she holds a Bachelor's degree in Social Work and an MA in Sociology. Being an eternal optimist, she maintains that the human spirit is remarkably resilient. Her writing reflects this belief.

Rita's stories are electic but typically put her characters in challenging circumstances. She feels that when they reach their happily ever after, they will have earned it. Despite the heavier subject matter, Rita's humorous banter and authentic dialogue reflect her hopeful nature.

In her spare time, she enjoys the outdoors. She is especially drawn to the water, which is ironic since she lives in the middle of a cornfield. Her first love has always been reading. It is this passion that spurred her writing career. She rides a Harley Davidson and has an unnatural obsession with fantasy football. More than anything, she detests small talk but can ramble on for hours given a topic that interests her.

She lives in a small town in Illinois with her wife, Terra, and their cat, Chumley, who actually runs the household.

Rita is a member of American Mensa and the Golden

Crown Literary Society. She is currently a graduate of the GCLS Writing Academy 2021. Sign up for Rita's free newsletter at:

www.ritapotter.com

If you liked this book?

Reviews help an author get discovered and if you have enjoyed this book, please do the author the honor of posting a review on Goodreads, Amazon, Barnes & Noble or anywhere you purchased the book. Or perhaps share a posting on your social media sites and help us spread the word.

Check out Rita's other books

Broken not Shattered - ISBN - 978-1-952270-22-2

Even when it seems hopeless, there can always be a better tomorrow.

Jill Bishop has one goal in life – to survive. Jill is trapped in an abusive marriage, while raising two young girls. Her husband has isolated her from the world and filled her days with fear. The last thing on her mind is love, but she sure could use a friend.

Alex McCoy is enjoying a comfortable life, with great friends and a prosperous business. She has given up on love, after picking the wrong woman one too many times. Little does she know, a simple act of kindness might change her life forever.

When Alex lends a helping hand to Jill at the local grocery store, they are surprised by their immediate connection and an unlikely friendship develops. As their friendship deepens, so too do their fears.

In order to protect herself and the girls, Jill can't let her husband know about her friendship with Alex, and Alex can't discover what goes on behind closed doors. What would Alex do if she finds out the truth? At the same time, Alex must fight her attraction and be the friend she suspects Jill needs. Besides, Alex knows what every lesbian knows – don't fall for a straight woman, especially one that's married…but will her heart listen?

Upheaval: Book One - As We Know It - ISBN - 978-1-952270-38-3

It is time for Dillon Mitchell to start living again.

Since the death of her wife three years ago, Dillon had buried herself in her work. When an invitation arrives for Tiffany Daniels' exclusive birthday party, her best friend persuades her to join them for the weekend.

It's not the celebration that draws her but the location. The party is being held at the Whitaker Estate, one of the hottest tickets on the West Coast. The Estate once belonged to an eccentric survivalist, whose family converted it into a trendy destination while preserving some of its original history.

Surrounded by a roomful of successful lesbians, Dillon finds herself drawn to Skylar Lange, the mysterious and elusive bartender. Before the two can finish their first dance, a scream shatters the evening. When the party goers emerge from the underground bunker, they discover something terrible has happened at the Estate.

The group races to try to discover the cause of this upheaval, and whether it's isolated to the Estate. Has the world, as we know it, changed forever?

Other books by Sapphire Authors

Finding Faith - ISBN - 978-1-952270-16-1

Faith Fitzgerald thought that if she got an education and became a high-powered attorney in Manhattan, maybe—just maybe—she'd gain the attention and respect of her absentee father. Considering he was the only parent she had left after her mother's suicide when Faith was just a child, she thought that's what it would take.

She was wrong.

What she dreamed would be glamorous and satisfying turned out to be grueling and thankless. Since she wasn't willing to play the game between the sheets, she was forced to stay in the cubicle jungle doing all the heavy lifting while the men got the credit and the rewards.

Deciding she is done, Faith packs up and, with the flip of the bird to the rearview mirror, leaves New York and heads home to Colorado. She has nothing there: no job, nowhere to live, no relationship with her father. Truth is, she barely has a relationship with herself.

On the drive home, she finds herself in Wynter, a tiny mountain town at the foot of the Rockies. Looking more like it belongs in a made-for-TV Christmas movie than on the map, Faith is utterly enchanted. When she tries her luck and buys a raffle ticket at Pop's, Wynter's charming café, her prize is far more than meets the eye—or the heart.

Enter Wyatt, a feisty, sexy southerner and waitress at Pop's, who just happens to be married to a local sheriff's deputy. All is not as it appears with the All-American boy and his Georgia peach.

A colorful cast of unforgettable and charming characters will teach the jaded attorney that sometimes to find yourself all you have to do is go back to the basics...and have a little Faith.

Survival – ISBN – 978-1-952270-18-5

After surviving a school shooting, Mona Ouellet moves from Montreal to Peterborough, switches her PhD discipline from English Literature to Psychology, and tries to move on with her life. Unfortunately, her nightmares follow her—and so do a host of "bad men" who seem to appear around every corner to make her life difficult. Her only escape is to fall into her research completely, where she soon becomes obsessed with retelling true crime case studies and enamoured by a waitress at a local diner.

Kerri Reznik is a waitress by day and horror writer by night, where she turns elements of her two-month long captivity in the wilderness with her survivalist father into stories to scare others. Though over a decade has passed, Kerri is still haunted by her brother Lee's absence in her life and her inability to reconcile with it. She seeks camaraderie with Absalom Lincoln, a detective on Peterborough police's force, where the two bond over mysteries, both true and imagined.

As Kerri and Mona's connection becomes stronger, their past traumas begin to intertwine and both of their worst nightmares begin to evolve and intensify. Each character must struggle to negotiate how to live in a world where survival is never guaranteed, and even when it is possible, there is always a cost.

Talk to Me – ISBN – 978-1-952270-20-8

Claire takes a turn for the wild side when she chances into a job at San Diego's KZSD radio to work with Marly, the sharp-tongued lesbian shock jock of Gayline. Under Marly's close tutelage, Claire feels the sparks fly as she learns to screen calls and handle board operations. It's enough that her formerly quiet life has been upended after separating from her husband, and at first, she keeps her feelings hidden. Even as bomb threats force the radio station employees to clear out, Claire's attraction to Marly's charisma, wit, and atypical beauty keeps her coming back. Meanwhile, she struggles to maintain a relationship with her teen daughter while her soon-to-be ex makes it clear he wants to try again. Its two steps forward, one step back as Marly and Claire grow closer and admit their feelings.

Will Marly's outrageous "anything goes" attitude be too much? As their on-air shenanigans and romance heat up, Marly's crazed plan to boost ratings threatens their relationship, and ultimately, their lives.

Keeping Secrets – ISBN – 978-1-952270-04-8

What would you do if, after finally finding the woman of your dreams, she suddenly leaves to fight in the Civil War?

It's 1863, and Elizabeth Hepscott has resigned herself to a life of monotonous boredom far from the battlefields as the wife of a Missouri rancher. Her fate changes when she travels with her brother to Kentucky to help him join the Union Army. On a whim, she poses as his little brother and is bullied into enlisting, as well. Reluctantly pulled into a new destiny, a lark decision quickly cascades into mortal danger.

While Elizabeth's life has made a drastic U-turn, Charlie Schweicher, heiress to a glass-making fortune, is still searching for the only thing money can't buy.

A chance encounter drastically changes everything for both of them. Will Charlie find the love she's longed for, or will the war take it all away?

Made in the USA
Coppell, TX
08 June 2022